# DEAD TO RITES

# DEAD TO RITES

## A MICK OBERON JOB

## ARI MARMELL

**TITAN** BOOKS

Dead to Rites
Print edition ISBN: 9781785650970
E-book edition ISBN: 9781785650987

Published by Titan Books
A division of Titan Publishing Group Ltd
144 Southwark Street, London SE1 0UP

First edition: August 2016
1 3 5 7 9 10 8 6 4 2

A CIP catalogue record for this title is available from the British Library.

Printed and bound in the United States.

**Dedication:**
For George, because everything is always in part for George, but it's still sometimes good to remind her.

# A BRIEF WORD ON LANGUAGE

Throughout the Mick Oberon novels, I've done my best to ensure that most of the 30s-era slang can be picked up from context, rather than trying to include what would become a massive (and, no matter how careful I was, likely incomplete) dictionary. So over the course of reading, it shouldn't be difficult to pick up on the fact that "lamps" and "peepers" are eyes, "choppers" and "Chicago typewriters" are Tommy guns, and so forth.

But there are two terms I do want to address, due primarily to how they appear to modern readers.

"Bird," when used as slang in some areas today, almost always refers to a woman. In the 1930s, however, it was just another word for "man" or "guy."

"Gink" sounds like it should be a racial epithet to modern ears (and indeed, though rare, I've been told that it is used as such in a few regions). In the 30s, the term was, again, just a word for "man," though it has a somewhat condescending connotation to it. (That is, you wouldn't use it to refer to anyone you liked or respected.) It's in this fashion that I've used it throughout the novels.

# CHAPTER ONE

Every now'n again, I stop and really listen to the crickets. It's the pixies, see? Some of 'em sing along with the crickets, voices real high and squeaky 'cause their pipes are so tiny. Others got these real little fiddles and... Well, point is, if you bother to listen—which most of you don't—and really know *how* to listen—which even more of you don't—you can hear the pixies in among the crickets. Maybe you can actually make out a few words or tatters of meaning, maybe all you get is their general mood, but it can put you wise to how things are going in the tiny little bastards' corners of Elphame.

Of course, that's what, maybe one night in a thousand? Rest of the time, it's just a whole swarm of bugs makin' whoopee and irritating the spit outta everyone else around 'em. So kinda like all you lugs, then.

Yeah, sorry. I was more'n a little cranky that night. Where was I?

Right. Crickets. There were a lot of 'em, and they were loud.

It was one of those spring nights where you could forget the oven of summer was comin' up before too long and the breath off Lake Michigan was nice and cool enough that you almost didn't mind the stench of fish and the garbage that'd been dumped into the waters. A whole lotta acres of parkland stretch along and away from the lake shore, with winding sidewalks and copses of trees and statues to various folks you all like to think were special or important. Not so far you can't still hear all the lovely sounds of the city, but far enough they ain't too overpowering. Guess that's why the damn crickets hadda pick up the slack.

This particular copse of trees was way on the south side of the greenery, part of a whole slice of park tucked away where nobody hadda lay peepers on it unless they wanted to. Y'know, where they could put the attractions and events meant for the poor saps who didn't have the right income or skin tone. Right now, that slice was playin' host to a traveling carnival, one of about half a million that'd come to the Windy City over the past few months. The Chicago World's Fair was barrelin' down on us like a freight train in heat, and while a handful of circuses and carnies figured they might make a few bucks settin' up shop in town at the same time, most of 'em didn't have much interest in competing. So they came'n went even faster than normal, popping up like weeds and fading again like... well, dead weeds, I guess.

This particular collection of cheap eats and rigged games and rickety rides that shook and shuddered worse'n a palsied Chihuahua didn't strike me as much different than any other. Lights were still on, a few of the machines still ran, a cut-rate band organ still vied with the crickets and the rest of Chicago to see who could be the most obnoxious. I guess the place had a few customers, late as it was. Even from here I could smell the sweat and the grease and the burnt sugar and the drying kids' vomit, and thank God for my *aes sidhe* senses 'cause I sure wouldn't wanna have missed *that* delightful treat, would I?

Point is, I hadn't the first or faintest notion as to what made this traveling carnival at all special. Can't really say I cared much, either. But *something* musta been valuable or hinky about it, since the ginks I was lookin' for wouldn'ta been here if it wasn't.

Half a dozen of 'em, give or take, the usual gorillas in the usual glad rags with the usual bulges in their coats that didn't come from anything friendly. Even if I hadn't already known, I coulda figured what sorta hardware they were packin' by the smell of the steel and gunpowder.

And there he was, right in the middle. The boss, the *capo*, Nolan Shea. Tall, kinda lanky but round-faced. One of those guys whose mug was always flushed, like he was real hot, real lit, or real steamed at someone.

His goons had been jawing for a while now without spouting one useful word, grousing about what they'd rather be doin' or worrying that the Outfit might stumble across 'em. (As if any of the local trouble boys woulda had any reason for being here in the park this time of night. Then again, I still didn't know why Shea's people were here, either.) Now that Shea'd rejoined 'em—they'd all been prowlin' around, trying to get a better slant on the carnival, and he'd been the last to get back—I was hopeful I might actually hear somethin' worth hearing.

At which point I took *one goddamn step* and somehow managed to sidle right on into a protruding tree branch. Gnarled and spindly as a grindylow's finger, it snapped right off, and if it wasn't as loud as a gat, it was sure noisy enough.

Plain, random bad luck. I'd had more'n my fair share of that lately, and if I was the paranoid sort, it might not've been feeling too random anymore.

Well, yeah, I *am* the paranoid sort. So it should be pretty easy to figure on how I felt right about then.

"Evening, fellas."

I didn't exactly have my mitts up as I stepped from the shadows under the trees, but I made a pretty clear show of keeping 'em away from my body. I wasn't lookin' to mix it up with these mugs, let alone get into a shoot-out with 'em.

Judging by the half-dozen roscoes pointed my way, they didn't necessarily share my preferences in that regard.

"Say," I continued, "how about you ask your boys to take it

easy, Mr. Shea? I just wanna jaw a little."

"I know you, pal?" the red-faced thug demanded. He had the kinda almost-Irish lilt you sometimes hear from guys who don't have an Irish lilt anymore. "You're ringin' a bell."

"Vacuum salesman, boss," one of the others whispered to him with that same not-accent. "He broke into your place once."

Shea's lamps widened a bit at that, even as mine narrowed. What were the odds any of 'em woulda recollected me at all from that one night, let alone details like my cover story? More bad luck.

"I remember," Shea growled. "You're one of the Shark's guys!" A few hammers clicked at that.

"You got some sharp people working for you, Mr. Shea. But I'm not your enemy. I ain't a salesman, and I don't work for Mr. Ottati. Well, only the one time."

"You ain't helpin' your case here, boyo."

*Boyo?* "I'm a PI, Mr. Shea. I was helpin' Ottati out on a personal matter, that's all. And I'm only here now to put a question or two to you. After that, I'll be outta your hair and you can get back to whatever the hell you're doing."

I kinda wanted to ask what the hell they *were* doing. I'da just figured they were maybe runnin' a protection racket on the carnival—every one of 'em that came to Chicago wound up lining *somebody*'s pockets—'cept Shea's crew was the Uptown Boys, and *they* answered to Moran's Northside Gang. No way they'd risk the kinda heat it could draw, comin' this far south, this deep into Outfit territory, for something as penny-ante as extorting a cheap traveling show.

Hell, maybe they just had a beef with someone who worked there, or had used the carnival to smuggle something into town. That stuff happens all the time. Didn't make a difference to me—wasn't what I was here for—and I was pretty sure that running my yap about it wasn't gonna make Shea any *less* inclined to fill me so full of holes you could use me to strain soup.

Of course, he'n his torpedoes looked like they were right on the verge of squirting metal anyway.

I decided I didn't feel like getting shot tonight.

"This is how it is, Mr. Shea. I got no intention of ratting you out, either to the bulls or to the Shark. We can have our conversation and go on our merry way. You start with the shooting, though, you think that circus music down there is gonna drown out that much noise? Even assuming you rub me out and make tracks before anyone shows, you're gonna have a *lot* of people askin' questions. You *want* the coppers and the Outfit knowing someone's got an interest in that sideshow down there? Fine, start throwing lead. You wanna keep everything quiet? Let's talk."

I'da climbed into his head if I had to, juggled his thoughts a tad to make sure he did what I wanted, but I was a little nervous about the idea. I was already havin' a run of misfortune, and usin' any kinda mojo under those circumstances is chancy. Fortunately, it didn't come to that. Shea didn't look none too happy about it, but he lowered his piece and waved for the others to do likewise.

Which didn't mean he might not try to have his boys whack me some other, quieter way, but people and creatures a lot nastier'n him had tried, and I remained thoroughly unwhacked.

It also didn't mean he was ready to answer my questions without a few of his own, first.

"How the fuck did you even know to find me here, Mr...?"

"Oberon. Mick Oberon." No sense in *not* telling him. I might look a tiny bit different to every mortal, but still basically like the same guy. Wouldn't take someone with Shea's resources more'n a few minutes to dig up my name once he knew I was a private dick, and I *was* trying to get the gink to trust me some. "And that's what I do. I find people."

"In other words, somebody spilled." His tone of voice didn't leave a lotta doubt as to what'd happen if he found out who the pigeon was. Somehow, I didn't think that me tellin' him the poor sap didn't have a choice, that I'd pushed myself into his head and *made* him sing, would go over real well.

"I'da waited until you weren't in the middle of work," I said instead, "but I'm kinda in a bit of a hurry here. All I need to know, Mr. Shea, is where I can find Phil Peppard."

"Who?" He didn't even *try* to sound genuine.

"C'mon, Mr. Shea. I know he hangs his hat somewhere in Uptown territory. I know you keep tabs on every worker who operates in your kingdom. And I know he's freelance. He ain't one of yours, so you got no cause to wanna protect him."

"Maybe I just don't like nosy bastards askin' questions. Maybe I don't rat on principle. I think it's about time for you to dust, Mr. Oberon, before something ugly—"

"Mr. Shea, you really wanna rethink that."

Wasn't as if we'd been having a calm, friendly chat already, but now the tension got so thick you hadda chew around it to get a word in edgewise.

"You threatening me, pal?"

"No, you got me all wrong. I'm tryin' to do you a favor. The folks I'm workin' for, Mr. Shea? They don't want the coppers involved, see? That's *why* they came to me. But if I can't get 'em their property back, they *will* turn to the cops. And I been keeping 'em in the loop, so right now they know almost everything I know."

That last bit was more fulla horse shit than the back lot at a racetrack, but whatever works, yeah?

"So if *I* don't come up with Peppard, the bulls are gonna go poking around for him next. And whether they find him or not, that's gonna be a lotta uniforms all over your neighborhood. Since my clients are rollin' in dough, the cops are gonna take 'em real serious, which means a *long* search. I don't pretend to know your business, but that can't possibly be good for it.

"We can prevent all that, right now, Mr. Shea. All you gotta do is gimme an address, or at least the alias he's livin' under. Then we can all go home and not worry about career repercussions."

It took some hemming and hawing, some discussion with his boys, a few face-saving threats, but eventually he gave me an address offa Belmont, not too far from Logan Square.

"Oberon!" he called after me as I was just startin' to step back into the trees. "I don't enjoy bein' put in this sorta position. Don't let me see your face again. Ever. Or I might just put a slug through it."

He probably would, too, or try to. I was already pretty well sure it was only the risk of lettin' the cops or the Outfit know about his interests here on the south side that'd kept him from it in the first place.

"Don't worry," I told him. "I've had more'n enough fun dealing with you trouble boys over the last year. I don't mean to get mixed up with you lot any further."

Yeah, yeah, I know. Go ahead and laugh at me.

"...knew where to find him," I was explaining to Mr. and Mrs. Marsters, sitting on a velvet-cushioned sofa in a room that probably cost more to decorate than my office cost to build, "it was duck soup to dig up not just your figurine but a whole heap of other hot goods. Once he knew I had him dead to rights, he sang like a canary. I dunno if your cousin's gonna do any time for hiring him—Peppard ain't exactly a sterling witness, and it basically comes down to who the jury believes—but I figure he'll be too scared to try anything like this again."

My clients, an older couple so pasty and upper-crust they resembled a pair of unbaked pies, and the younger black fellow who worked as their butler, hung on every word of my story. Well, every word I gave 'em, anyway; I left out a lot of the details, things about the underworld or, y'know, magic that they didn't really need to hear. All they hadda know was that, yes, I'd gotten 'em their stupid little crystal wren statuette back—it was sitting on the coffee table in front of me as we spoke—and yes, just as they'd suspected, it'd been their crumb of a cousin who'd had it snatched.

On the square, though, I was barely even payin' attention to my own tale. Whole thing'd been a minor diversion at best, something I'd taken on solely for the fee: a little bit of folding green, just to pay the bills, and an old Swiss pocket watch. No idea why I'd asked for it, but then, that was usually the case with the gewgaws that made up the bulk of my fees. Fae urges and instinct and all.

Point is, run of the mill, everyday case, kinda job you don't ever hear about 'cause there's nothin' about 'em worth telling. Except things'd been goin' just a touch hinky since right about the same time I started in on it. Stuff like that bit with the tree branch, when I was eavesdropping on the Uptown Boys. Or a few days before that, when a hinge stuck and I bashed my nose walking into a door that didn't open. Never anything major, never anything that woulda been at all suspicious by itself. Only the fact it kept happening had made it stand out. I still couldn't tell if it was a "natural" run of bad luck—if that ain't an oxymoron—or if there was some kinda hex or other mystical cause. If it was the latter, it was a damn subtle one, but I didn't wanna take steps until I was sure. Some of the remedies for normal bad luck can make it worse if the source ain't "normal."

And more even than that, it was makin' me paranoid. (All right, fine, *more* paranoid.) I'd been jumpin' at shadows for days by this point, sensing danger where there wasn't any. The Marsters lived on Burton Place, real swanky digs in a real hoity-toity neighborhood. You didn't get random street crime here, but I couldn't shake the notion thatsomeone'd been shadowing me on my walk over. I kept a good slant on my surroundings— eyes, ears, senses you never heard of—and I made a buncha quick turns and detours. Even drew on a bit of extra luck, despite bein' nervous about it. Shoulda been close to no way for anyone to tail me after that, and definitely no way for 'em to do it without me spotting 'em. There'd been nobody I could put my finger on, but dammit if I still hadn't felt peepers on the back of my neck.

So yeah, that's where my noggin was during all this, why I was only halfway there at best when I returned the Marsters' dingus to 'em, and why I only got dragged back to myself in that fancy sitting room when the old lady started getting deep into the "effusive gratitude" part of the visit.

I hate that part.

"...thank you enough, Mr. Oberon! My grandfather had to leave all his glassworking tools behind when he came to this country. This figurine was the first thing he made once he could finally afford a new set."

*Of course it was. And I assume he left it to you on his deathbed?*

"It was the last thing he gave to me before the tuberculosis took..."

We were all damn lucky in that moment that I basically can't vomit.

"You're welcome," I said. Or interrupted? I dunno; I'd stopped listening, mostly in self-defense. "If I could just get the rest of my fee, I'll be outta your hair."

It was Mr. Marsters who answered this time. "Of course, of course! Barry, if you'd be so good as to fetch my checkbook? And a bottle of the Avize Grand Cru, while you're at it."

"Of course, Mr. Marsters." I'm not even sure how, but I'd swear the butler reached the door without actually turning around first. The magic of the domestic servant, I guess.

"Kind of you, Mr. Marsters," I told him, "but really not—"

"It's quite legal, I assure you. Everything in our wine cellar was purchased prior to Prohibition."

"I'm sure it was, but it ain't necessary. I—"

"Nonsense!" You ever hear a guy actually *harumph*? Marsters *harumphed*. I think it actually requires a certain amount of wealth before you're legally permitted to do it. "I insist!"

So how exactly was I gonna tell the man that if it wasn't milk or cream, I not only wasn't interested but actively revolted.

"Look—"

"I insist!" he again, uh, insisted.

He'd also gotten himself good'n riled up in his determination, so that he tried to lean forward and thump a fist on the table in emphasis, all at once. The lunge outta his chair drove his hip into the furniture with a hollow *thump*, an impact that managed to lift the two nearest legs off the carpet and set the whole contraption to rocking.

Not a lot. Just enough.

If he'd hit the table just a few inches to one side or the other, it wouldn't have jolted up that way. If the cushions on the sofa had been a little less deep, or the couch itself a couple feet closer, or I'd been a touch less preoccupied, I mighta reacted fast enough to save it. If the thing itself had been a bit farther from the edge, or landed base-down on the thick carpeting instead of at an angle...

If, if, if. "If" and a dollar are worth about 90 cents.

There was a muted *crack* and then silence as we all stared at the scattering of chunks and slivers and powder that had just been a crystal wren and now made the carpet glitter like a starry night.

Not that it was a *long* silence. Mrs. Marsters began to wail like a deflating zeppelin, her husband gawped and gasped like an asthmatic grouper, and I cursed and mumbled under my breath as it occurred to me that, through no fault of my own, I probably wasn't gonna see the remainder of my fee.

# CHAPTER TWO

Goddamn it, there it was again!

Wasn't too long a walk from my clients'—uh, former clients'—place to the L, but I was in no hurry to get much of anywhere, so I'd been takin' it slow, eyeballing the homes of the well-to-do and mentally cataloging all the wonders I'd seen that were much more impressive than *they* could ever hope to be.

Whaddaya want from me? I was feelin' petty.

The city was just startin' to get dim as we slid on into the evening. Flivvers grumbled by in the street; radios crackled out Ethel Waters (no, thanks) or Handel's Organ Concerto in D Minor (*that's* music, thanks very much) or, mostly in the houses with kids, a new episode of some serial about the twenty-fifth century. All of it was quick enough, or far enough back, that the technology only gave me a mild itch insteada screaming, spike-through-the-conk pain.

It *was* distracting, though, which is partly why it took me a few blocks to realize I mighta picked up a tail. Again.

Wasn't anything obviously hinky about her. Middle-aged dame in a purple skirt-suit and glasses so big'n round you coulda served a cuppa joe on each of the lenses. She'd been a few dozen paces behind me for a while, which didn't prove anything in itself, but... It just *tasted* like I was bein' followed, you know?

Well, no, you don't. Just take my word for it.

Of course, I'd felt that way a lot lately, and I'd managed to prove bupkis, to identify exactly nobody shadowing me. So now that I'd spotted the broad, it was time for a little test.

I kept on goin' my way without a care in the world (though I did decide that whistling would probably be pushin' it a bit). Kept right on, keepin' a slant on her in the reflection of every darkened window and every time crossin' a street gave me an excuse to crane my neck around to watch for oncoming traffic.

Houses gave way to stores as we got closer to the elevated, and I decided I wanted to deal with this one way or the other before I actually reached the station. I'd tried bein' patient, but it was taking too long.

Funny how often that happens.

Anyway, some kinda big delivery truck rumbled on by right after I'd crossed the street, and I used the opportunity to duck into the doorway of a flower shop that'd already closed for the night. Gave me a good slant on the whole block and anyone comin' up the sidewalk while keepin' me outta view. If Glasses *was* followin' me, it should prove real interesting to see what she did now.

Except she didn't do a thing. She wasn't there anymore.

I just stood there like a lump.

What the *hell*? The street wasn't empty or anything—I counted a couple dozen pedestrians just at a quick glance—but she sure wasn't one of 'em. Had she ducked into a shop, same as me? Wasn't impossible, but she must have done it soon as the truck came between us; if she'd waited until she noticed I'd "vanished," she wouldn't have had the time without me seeing it. And I couldn't figure *why* she'd do that before she knew I'd tumbled to her.

All right, then. Loitering in the doorway, bathed in a mixed bouquet of florals from one side and clouds of car exhaust from the other, I tried to think. What I came up with was three possibilities.

One, I'd just gone completely crazy. Totally off the track. But given all the shit I'd seen over more centuries than I'm completely comfortable admitting, it didn't seem *too* probable that Chicago'd finally driven me outta my noggin.

Two, I was barkin' at shadows again. Glasses hadn't been following me, she was just some skirt who'd been walking the same sidewalk. She'd stepped into one of the shops, not because I'd made her, but to do some shopping. It was just coincidence it'd happened right about the same time I'd made my own break for it. Not real likely, no, but possible, especially given how fond random chance is of makin' Fae dance to tunes we can't even hear.

Or three, magic.

You know, one of the reasons I'd been avoiding Elphame for so long was because I'd been lookin' to live a normal life. What's it say about my level of success for the past year or so that "magic" was up there with "some dame went shopping" on the list of probable explanations?

Any number of ways someone—or something—coulda disappeared, even with a whole swarm of mortals on the same street. You people are real good about not noticin' what's happening around you, especially if it don't fit your slim view of the world. Goin' invisible was one possibility. Lotta different sorts of Fae can do that. A rare few might've actually vanished, stepping Sideways or teleporting; not many of us can do it without the proper prep or the right surroundings (like the mildewed refrigerator niche in my office), but it ain't unheard of. And of course any number of Fae and related entities are shapeshifters. I coulda been staring right at the bim who'd been tailing me, and I'd never have known it was...

Was...

Shapeshifting. Aw, shit.

*Goswythe.*

I mean, I had no *proof* this was Goswythe, or even that it was a shapeshifter. It fit, sure, but I hadda lotta enemies from a lotta different time periods. But it was a solid working theory; something to think about, anyway.

It'd been over a year now since I'd last encountered the *phouka* who'd raised Celia, Fino Ottati's daughter, after she'd been stolen away and replaced by the changeling Adalina. He'd up and taken the run-out some time after I'd gotten my keister handed to me by the not-so-dearly departed witch Orsola Maldera, may she rot in pieces. We'd been trying to beat the stuffing outta each other, me'n Goswythe, before Orsola interfered, and I had every reason to figure the gink still held a grudge. I'd poked around some, trying to find him, now and again—partly for my own sake, partly to put the Ottatis' minds at ease. I'd never dug anything up, though, and between my own affairs and tryin' to find some way of waking Adalina from her coma, I hadn't put as much elbow grease into it as maybe I should.

Might be about time that changed.


It was in the stairwell down to the basement level of Mr. Soucek's building, where I keep my office and hang my hat (on those rare occasions I can stand to wear one), that I came real near to killing a buddy of mine.

Well, "buddy" may be too strong a word.

"Jesus *Christ*, Mick!" Mashed up against the wall with my wand pressed tight under his chin, Franky looked paler and just generally more pathetic even than usual. I dunno how he got that nasal whine into his voice when he was hackin' and gaggin' around the pressure on his throat, but he pulled it off. "All I did was say 'Hello!'"

"You shouldn't sneak up on a fella like that." I stuck the L&G—that's the wand, a Luchtaine & Goodfellow 1592— back in the holster under my coat and unwrapped my fist from around his collar. "It ain't healthy."

"I wasn't sneaking! I was just waiting!"

"Yeah, well... Wait louder."

Wasn't his fault, really. I'd been preoccupied and on edge the whole way across town, and I'd make the mistake of relaxing when home came into view. I shoulda known better, really. Wasn't as though I hadn't had more'n a few people waiting for me here now and again who weren't near as harmless as old Four-Leaf Franky.

*Dammit.* "Sorry, Franky. Been a bit outta sorts." Then, since the fact that I'd apologized had him pretty well stunned, I had a breath or two to give him an up-and-down. "Looks like I ain't the only one, either."

His shirt and his coat had more wrinkles between 'em than the firstborn of a basset hound and a raisin, but that was nothing hinky in and of itself. Franky'd never met a suit too cheap, and his apparent allergy to clothes irons went far beyond the usual Fae distaste for the metal. Nah, what was off about him was the gold, or lack of it. Sure, he wore a couple of gleaming rings, and he was using a fifty-dollar tie clip to hold a five-cent tie. But for Franky, who had more'n a little leprechaun blood mixed into his *aes sidhe* ancestry, that was positively understated. In fact, I think the only time I'd ever seen him with *less* gold on him was after he'd been robbed.

Which wasn't uncommon, but that's what happens to guys who wear gold out in the open, ain't it?

Point is, he didn't look banged up at all. Only other reason I could come up with for him goin' out and about without his jewelry was that he was tryin' to be inconspicuous.

I moved back a pace, down a couple steps, and leaned against the banister.

"So who's gunning for you, Franky?"

"Nah, you got it wrong this time, Mick. Or, well, mostly wrong, anyway. Nobody's after me, least not personally. I'm here to do *you* a favor."

"Uh-huh."

Last few times me'n Franky'd crossed paths, things hadn't

been going too well for either of us. I'd seen him on a couple or three occasions since the whole Spear of Lugh fiasco, and we were good—no beefs, so far as I knew—but we hadn't exactly been drinking outta the same bottle since then.

Whatever "favor" he was hoping to do me, he was looking to get something out of it, too. But just bulling through and asking him directly wasn't going to get me anything, and while I could probably beat a song out of him, that *would* be a good way to make him an enemy.

Instead, I asked, "So why the play at goin' incognito, then?"

He didn't pretend not to know what I meant; that was something, anyway.

"Look, Mick, I'm here on behalf of the others. None of 'em really wants to be seen with you given what's going down. I don't really, either, so this seemed a good compromise."

By "the others," I assumed he meant the chunk of Chicago's supernatural community who I sometimes palled around with. Not friends, really, but contacts, informants, people I'd helped and people who helped me—for the right price. Franky himself, of course, but also Lenai; Pink Paddy; the "L King," this strange old entity who lives in one of the tunnel portions of the rail system; Gaullman, when he wasn't committing himself to one asylum or another (for everyone else's protection, he always said); a few others. Colorful characters, and mostly not the bravest sort, so them being too afraid to come to me in person if there was a problem was no big surprise.

Two issues with that, though. First, Franky was no braver'n any one of 'em. And second, given that *what* was going down?

So I asked him about both.

"Hey! I'm no coward!"

I just looked at him.

"I just have a healthy sense of self-preservation," he finished, limp as wet yarn.

I looked at him some more.

Franky sighed. "Okay, so I figured, we all try to ignore this until it goes away and God only knows how long that'll take, or who gets hurt in the process. I get you to suss out what's happening, you solve the problem same way you always do, everything's done with and we can all go back to the everyday."

That... tasted of truth, but it wasn't filling. He wasn't lying to me, but he wasn't spilling everything, either.

So, hey, I *kept* looking at him. Why not? It'd worked out pretty well so far.

"There's people asking around about you," he finally admitted.

*A-ha! Now* we were gettin' somewhere.

And now it made sense he'd come to me. If I sussed out whatever was goin' down, great. If I got involved but *didn't* wrap things up neat'n tidy, well, I woulda found whoever was nosing around. They wouldn't have any cause to keep pestering Franky or Paddy or the others. Either way was good for Franky.

But... "I get that it's maybe worrying for people to come to you about me," I said, "but this ain't exactly the first time *any* of you been grilled about something you didn't want to talk about. And I suspect that if the mugs asking the questions were anyone or anything real dangerous, you'da started off with that, or at least be a lot more frightened than you are. You're worried, not terrified. So what's the skinny?"

Since I know you're wondering, yeah, it woulda been a lot more comfortable and maybe even safer if we'd taken this to my office for a proper sit-down. I'd gotten Franky talking, though, and I didn't wanna risk losing the momentum.

"Well... Part of it, Mick, is still the whole Spear of Lugh thing. After what happened last year, everybody's jumpy thinking about the kinda people we might have wandering around Chicago poking into things. You can't really blame them for that, can you?"

I'd have sighed, then, if I, you know, sighed.

"The spear's gone, Franky. And so's everyone who was here

hunting for it. All we've got now are the usual, run-of-the-mill Fae." As if there were such a thing. "Same sorta people and not-quite-people you been dealin' with your whole life."

"Sure, sure, but nerves is still nerves."

"Whatever."

"Anyway, it might not be too big a deal if it was just a few guys. But Mick, there's been a whole *lot* of folks asking a whole lot of questions about you. Me'n the others, we're getting jittery precisely because there's so many. There shouldn't be this many people that we don't know but who know about us. At all, let alone that we all know *you*."

"Wait, wait, wait. None of you know who these people are? *Any* of 'em?"

"Not a one."

Okay, I hadda give him that one. That *was* reason to start worrying.

"What have they been asking about, exactly?"

"All kindsa stuff. Who you pal around with. Where you go to take a load off. What we know about your cases. Sometimes sorta asking around the edges of what types of magic you can throw, though they've never come out and dug into that directly. Oh! And a lot of questions about that lady you were chumming it up with back during the whole spear affair."

My blood ran cold, and I don't mean I felt a chill. When the *aes sidhe* say our blood "ran cold," we mean it. You coulda wrung out an artery to cool a fifth of Scotch.

"Ramona?"

"Yeah, that's her. Whatever happened with her, anyway?"

Who the hell knew? I hadn't seen her since she'd swished her way outta the Field Museum of Natural History, and I still didn't know if I even wanted to.

No, that ain't true. I definitely wanted to. I just didn't know how much of me wanting to see her was actually *me* wanting to see her. I never had figured out if there was anything more'n her own mojo behind how dizzy I got over her.

But I *was* pretty sure I didn't much like people poking around about her—for her sake or mine.

"And it's been a bunch of different guys asking these questions?"

"Yep. Gals, too."

"And none of you recognized a single one?"

"Nope."

"Fae?"

I'd pretty much given up any of my usual human subterfuge by this point. I wasn't blinking, wasn't fidgeting or shifting my weight, damn near a statue. Not that I had to hide any of that stuff from Franky anyway, but letting all that slide wasn't a good habit to fall into.

He shrugged helplessly. "I really can't say, Mick. They all *seemed* human enough, but you know how hard it can be to tell with some of us."

Yeah. Yeah, I did. *Why'd you have to drop back into my life, Ramona? Things were a lot smoother without you.*

So, who'd I seriously irritated lately? Not a whole lotta people were comin' to mind, surprisingly enough. It was possible Vince Scola—one of Fino's rivals—still held a grudge after our last meeting, but it didn't seem too probable. I'd pretty well convinced his people that my world was something they wanted to steer clear of. Besides, this didn't feel like the Outfit's style.

My only other recent human enemy had been Orsola, and this didn't sound like her, either. Plus the whole pushing-up-daisies thing kinda put the kibosh on that notion.

I had rivals and enemies in both Courts, but the Seelie and Unseelie both had better ways to learn anything they wanted to know about me—and anyway, they already knew a lotta what these people were asking.

Nah, this almost hadda be an independent or an outsider. And hey, who did I know who fit *that* bill?

"Is it possible," I asked Franky, "that this wasn't a group at all? Just one gink wearing a buncha different faces?"

"Uh..." Pretty clear he hadn't thought of that particular notion before. "Sure, I suppose. I mean, I never saw more than one at a time, anyway. Guess one of the others might've, but they never said one way or the other. You got someone in mind?"

"I just might, yeah."

All right, I'll be straight with you. I *wanted* it to be Goswythe. The *phouka* hadn't exactly been haunting my nightmares or anything, but I hadn't much cared for having this lingering threat hanging over my head for a year. Or over the Ottatis' heads, either, for that matter. It'd be not just neat and convenient, but a genuine relief, to have done with the bastard.

So yeah, on the one hand, I mighta been a bit more closed-minded to other possibilities than I ought to have been. But on the other, it *did* all fit. Somebody swapping faces the way most people change underwear woulda explained why I felt like I was bein' shadowed but couldn't catch anyone, *and* the upsurge in the curious masses asking about me. It came together, top to bottom.

Except...

Ramona. Why the hell would Goswythe be asking about Ramona? I'd only spent a few days around her, in the middle of the biggest influx of Fae your half of Chicago'd seen in a good while. At most, she shoulda been lumped in with my other occasional contacts. For Goswythe—yeah, yeah, or whoever— to be asking about her specifically? Meant someone either had a much stronger idea of the connection I'd shared with her, however much bunk it mighta proved to be afterward, than anybody should...

Or that whatever was goin' on wasn't just about me, but was about her, too. She might actually be a target, not just a means to get to yours truly.

Did I care? I shouldn't care. And if I did, was it really me caring? Did the damn broad still have any magic hooks in me? *Goddamn it.*

"Do me a favor, Franky? See if you can find out from any of the others if they've seen more'n one of these ginks at a time?" I didn't figure any of 'em had—and it'd totally sink my Goswythe theory if they had—but better to be certain.

"Sure thing, Mick. Um, okay if I call you, though? Running back and forth across town like this..."

*Makes you look up to your ears in whatever's going on.* But he'd already stuck his neck out, and if it wasn't entirely on my behalf, well, he'd still put me wise to something I really hadda know about. So, much as the skin on my ears crawled just thinkin' of the damn payphone hanging in the hall near my office...

"Yeah, the horn's fine. Just keep tryin' back if I ain't here."

"You got it."

"Hey, Franky?"

He stopped in the middle of turning away, each foot on a different step. "Yeah?"

"Thanks."

Heh. Between that'n the earlier apology, he'd be off-balance for days. I really did mean it, though.

Franky opened the door above and—since the sun had gone and bunked while we were talking—disappeared between the streetlights. I hit the sidewalk just a minute behind him, hands in my coat pockets and leaning into the nighttime breeze. I had more'n a few questions dangling in front of me, some new, some that'd gone unanswered for over a year now. I didn't figure it made any kinda sense to wait until morning to get started.

# CHAPTER THREE

So, which fish did I wanna try'n hook?

Goswythe had managed to duck me for a year, and I had no good cause to think he'd be easier to find now. Although, if he was active again—and all indications suggested "yep" on that one—maybe he would be.

Somewhat easier, but not much. It'd probably be less of a trip for biscuits to hunt up the delightful Ramona Webb instead.

But while that might be simpler, it also meant dealing face-to-face with the aforementioned Miss Webb. And I just wasn't sure how eager I was to do that. If she was mixed up in whatever trouble'd come knocking on my door this time around, it was probably inevitable, but that didn't mean I couldn't put it off as long as inhumanly possible. Frankly, I'd rather have faced down a whole chopper squad or even a few Seelie knights with iron blades. All *they* could do was kill me.

So how to find the *phouka* palooka? No way Franky or the crew knew from nothin'. I hadn't asked around about Goswythe in a while, but I'd poked 'em about him often enough when I first started looking that they knew I was still gunnin' for the guy. If they'd heard something about him, I'da heard it by now.

I'd already run down all the leads I could come up with, all the hunches, and nada. I suppose I coulda gone to Elphame and asked around, but it ain't as though I'd suddenly gotten popular over there in the last few months. Even if anyone there *could* help me, most wouldn't, not without cost, and I already owed more people more'n I wanted. So that was out, too. I just didn't have anything new to try.

'Cept... Huh. There was a thought. Maybe I didn't *need* to try anything new. If Goswythe'd finally surfaced, if he was active or back in town or whatever'd changed, maybe now was a good time to retry something old.

He was gonna need resources if he was up to something. For him, here in the mortal side of Chicago, that probably meant stealing. (Easy enough with his powers, right?) And if *that* was so, well, I had a pretty good idea who might know about it, might even be helping the bastard for a percentage.

Hruotlundt's office was only about a block or so away from where I'd left it. You remember; I told you all about this place. Connects to both worlds, solidly anchored on the Elphame side, little less so on this one. Doesn't move *too* far, and you can find it easy enough if you're already kinda wise to where it is.

And no, I dunno what happens to whatever used to be there when it takes up a new spot, or why most of you mortal saps don't ever seem to notice. It's magic. You want a more detailed explanation than that, you feel free to step into the Otherworld and find an expert to ask. Me, I understand all I need to about it.

So I walked a half mile or so from the L to the door of a rundown building that sorta resembled the last one I'd found him in, tromped on up a few flights of creaking stairs that didn't even remotely resemble the ones I'd climbed last time, and...

Say, you remember those spurts of ugly luck I told you I'd been havin'? Guess I was due again.

I gawked across the landing at them. They gawked across the landing at me. A whole lotta mugs twisted into some real unfriendly expressions, and a few hands slipped under coats, reaching for iron or—in my case—hardwood.

"I thought I made it real plain what was gonna happen if I saw your face again, pally," Nolan Shea barked at me. "You gotta be fuckin' stupid to be following us after that!"

My noggin was spinning so hard I'm flabbergasted it didn't just pop on off. What the *hell* were the Uptown Boys doing here? This was bad news in a dozen different ways, and the strong possibility I was about to come down with some serious lead poisoning wasn't even close to the worst.

"I ain't following you," I insisted, knowing he wasn't gonna buy a word of it. "Hell, I promise I'm more surprised to see you here than you are me. I'm just here to chin-wag with the man for a spell."

"Yeah, right. And you just *happened* to show at the same time, after dark, that we did."

All I could do was shrug. "That's more or less how my luck's been lately, yeah."

"Boys, whack this—"

"*Don't.*" No finesse, no subtlety. I just thrust everything I had through my own peepers and into his. If my usual rummaging around and reorganizing people's thoughts and emotions was somethin' akin to pickpocketing, this was more a solid sock to the brain. Took more outta me than it should, too, but bad luck throws the rest of my mojo off some and I hadn't drawn my wand, since I hadn't wanted to start 'em shooting. Woulda been easier for me to do it the usual way, but not near as swift, and swift was what I'd needed right then.

Shea locked up, frozen like a slab of beef in the freezer. His goons had drawn, but they weren't shootin'. Fact that the boss hadn't finished the order, that it looked to them as though he'd actually listened to me when I told him to stop, put 'em all at a loss.

"We can solve this simply," I said, slowly pulling back from the innards of Shea's head. "And without anyone leavin' here in a wooden kimono. Just go *ask*. Tell him Mick Oberon's here, and *he'll* tell *you* that he knows me. That this ain't remotely the first time I dropped in."

"That..." Shea was shakin' his conk, like he'd just woken up. I coulda done real damage busting in as I had, and while I wouldn't shed too many tears over the Uptown *capo*, I was happier this way. It's an ugly way to destroy a man, crushing his thoughts, and it's not something you ever really get over doing. I'd seen Fae go mad from crumbling too many minds.

"That don't prove you aren't here for us today," he finally finished.

"What kind of a bunny you take me for, Shea? You think if I *were* shadowing you, let alone gunning for you, I'd come barging in here out in the open this way? What was my plan, to come racing upstairs and get-killed you to death?"

"I... Wait, come again?"

"You heard me."

The other thugs were giving me the evil eye—which didn't much impress me, since I've gotten it from genuine witches and King goddamn Balor himself once—and kept sorta twitching Shea's way. Like they wanted to help the boss but didn't really know how, or even what was wrong with him.

Fortunately (for a change), before they could up and decide to try and clip me on general principles, the choice was neatly taken outta their mitts.

"*What in the name of everything living below us is going on out here?*"

"Evening, Hruotlundt," I said. "How you been?"

Hruotlundt was a *dvergr*, which means he was a short lug with skin and beard the color of worn stone—which, in turn, means that even in a good mood he comes across grim as the Reaper with IRS problems. Right now, he wasn't in a good mood.

"Oh, I've been just peachy, Oberon. Right up until my clients started trying *to kill each other in my goddamn hallway*!"

Yeah, that probably woulda steamed him pretty good, at that. As a fence—sorry, "facilitator"—of Chicago's supernatural hot merchandise, Hruotlundt didn't care for his clients even knowing about each other, let alone meeting face-to-face.

Or, of course, shooting at each other.

"You know this fucker, then?" Shea asked, soundin' a little more put-together.

"No, Shea, I called him by name as a sneaky way of hinting that I've never met the man before in my life. You've fallen for my cunning ruse."

All there or not, the Uptown *capo* sure recognized when he was bein' insulted. I told you before his face was always kinda flushed, but it darkened notably now. I decided it wouldn't do anybody any favors to compare it to a flower comin' into bloom.

"I don't like people talkin' to me that way, Mr. Hruotlundt."

"I imagine not. What a shame that I don't remotely care. If that's a problem for you, feel free to take it up with your boss. I'm sure you can suggest someone to him who can do my job better than I can. Who did you have in mind?" Then, "Nobody? Good. Then since our business is done and you were on your way out, can I suggest you *continue* on your way?"

They shuffled past me on down the stairs, Shea glaring fire the whole way.

The last of the Uptown Boys turned out to be either more excitable or more of a bootlicker than the others. He felt the need to stop and poke me hard in the chest with two fingers.

"And don't let us see you around agai*uuuuullk*!"

Whaddaya want from me? I'd gone outta my way to keep things friendly from the first moment I'd stepped outta the trees a couple nights ago, and I wasn't lookin' to escalate things now, but I wasn't gonna be pushed around, either. A quick flash of the hands, a few painful twists, and Shea's toady was facin' his buddies with his back to me, gasping in pain, elbow pressed almost to his spine.

Shea and his boys skinned iron—again—but any shots

they took were gonna perforate their friend well before they reached me.

"You mind terribly asking your goons not to poke me?" I said. "I don't much appreciate it."

"Are you *trying* to make an enemy here, Oberon?" Shea demanded.

"I hadn't realized I still had a choice. But no, Shea. If I were, this arm would never work again."

I released the gink with a rough shove, enough so he stumbled down a couple steps but had no difficulty catching himself. With his *left* hand; he seemed to be having problems with his right.

"As is, he'll be fine in a few hours. Couple days, tops. I'm just making a point, that's all."

Hruotlundt was starting to grumble, which sounded a whole lot like a rock-crusher with a cold.

"If you gentlemen are *quite* finished, then?"

"I don't—"

"You gentlemen *are* quite finished."

I shrugged at Shea. "I'm done. You done?"

Shea shoved his roscoe back under his coat, snarled, and stomped out, his trouble boys right on his heels. Guess he was done.

"So," I said to Hruotlundt, "how's your night going?"


It took some fast talking to convince the *dvergr* to even let me into his office after that, which I guess is only fair. Finally, still sounding as though he was gargling gravel, he pushed open the outer door—still with the Minotaur-head knocker—and through the reception room. His blonde and vacant secretary was perched behind a heavy oak desk, meticulously applying nail polish so bright red she coulda used it to signal aircraft. I couldn't tell without closer examination if she was the real deal or another homunculus crafted to appear human—and

I decided without too much difficulty not to ask Hruotlundt one way or the other, since I'd been responsible for thoroughly wrecking the last one when she (it) didn't wanna let me in.

Huh. You know, it occurs to me that there's maybe a *reason* a lotta folks don't like me.

Office itself hadn't changed, but then, it never did. Everything was old, worn, bland. One lamp, one phone—an old candlestick model—and two doors, one to the storeroom, the other to Elphame. One of these days, I'd have to visit from the Otherworld side of things, see if it was true that the place was a lot swankier if you came from that direction.

"What do you want, Oberon?" He slumped hard into his chair, which woulda been a more significant gesture if he'd had a longer way to go between *stand* and *slump*. "I'm still trying to recover from all the chaos that resulted last time you were here."

I grinned openly at that. "First off, you know damn well that was none of it my fault. I got dragged into the whole mess. And second, I keep my ear to the ground, Hruotlundt. So many Fae in town, digging for the Spear of Lugh? A whole lotta them wound up with other little valuables, and you turned a real nice profit on most of those. So nix the sob story; you ain't had it so good in years."

"What. Do you. Want?"

I jerked a thumb toward the outer door.

"What'd *they* want?" I'd hoped, just tossin' it out that way while he was already agitated, I might surprise some information out of him.

Since the glower he gave me pretty clearly said, "You're *intensely* stupid," it obviously didn't work.

"You know I don't discuss clients, Oberon."

"Yeah, but..."

Dammit. What could I tell him? That Shea bein' here made me nervous? That I'd run into the gink before, even been inside his house specifically searching for it, and hadn't caught even a hint of a whiff of a trace of magic?

I get that I mighta given you cause to think otherwise, since all the events in my life I talk about revolve around magic. But here in your world, it's rare. It ain't something most people are wise to, obviously, and that includes the mob. The old ways Fino learned from his mamma, "Bumpy" Scola's protective charms and private witch? Those are the exceptions, see? They're two of only a handful of the city's crooks who dabble in the supernatural.

And Shea ain't one of that handful. Up until ten minutes ago, I'da signed an oath in blood to that effect. So either I'd missed some signs last year (and a few days ago) that I absolutely shouldn't have missed, or something hinky was up.

But telling Hruotlundt alla that would net me bupkis, and get him even more steamed to boot.

So, something else I hadda dig into. Peachy.

"All right," I said, conceding defeat. Then, like it'd just occurred to me and throwing in a faint grin for good measure. "You let 'em see you as you really are?"

It wasn't a question about them, exactly, and it was the sorta thing we Fae occasionally gab about where mortals are concerned.

"Nah," he said after a minute. "I toss up a glamour when Shea visits. They just see a normal human being."

*Bingo.* "When Shea visits." This hadn't been his first time, then. That was *something* to work with, anyway.

And all I was gonna get on that score. Figured I'd better get to the point of my own visit, before he tumbled to what I'd just done—or he just got impatient enough to give me the bum's rush for wastin' his time.

"Right, then. I'm lookin' for a *phouka...*"

I didn't give him the whole skinny, of course. Just the basics, that Goswythe'n me had butted heads a while back, that he'd vanished, and that I had reason to believe he was back and pokin' his schnozz into my business.

And that he was quite probably supporting himself by stealing and cons.

"Now don't blow your wig," I said quickly as the *dvergr* started to inflate like he was literally gonna bust and take everything in the room with him. "I know you just got done tellin' me you don't talk about clients."

Hruotlundt didn't sigh, exactly, so much as exhale what'd been buildin' up into a shout at the very least.

"But..."

Inflating again.

"It ain't just me he's gunnin' for, see? If it was, I wouldn't be here at all. But Goswythe, he's threatening some folks who're important to me. If I don't find him before he does whatever he's plannin', they're gonna suffer for it."

I *was* just talkin' about Celia and maybe Adalina Ottati, right? Not Ramona. I wasn't talkin' about Ramona.

Definitely not Ramona.

Definitely.

"You know me, Hruotlundt," I finished. "You know I ain't gonna stand for that. And you know the lengths I'll go to if my hand's forced."

It's hard to read a *dvergr*'s emotions—their expressions are literally stony, and even their peepers are more rock than anything else—but I could see he was dithering, even torn. Nah, he wasn't feelin' sorry for me or my friends. Hruotlundt didn't much care about anything beyond his professional rep and his profit margins. Rather, he was decidin' just how much of a pain in the ass I was gonna make myself tryin' to protect my people, how much it'd impact his business, how much ground he could afford to give while protecting that reputation (not to mention his mountain-sized pride).

"As we both just said," he finally answered, "I won't give you any personal details about my clients. What I *will* tell you is that, so far as I know, none of my current clients are *phouka*. Most of my regulars, I know well enough to say for sure. The newer clients? I can't be positive, obviously, but I've no reason to suspect they are. Furthermore, if this Goswythe is newly active, he's either definitely not one of my new customers or he's being *damn* subtle about it. I had a few strangers with high-end merchandise in the weeks following the Spear of Lugh affair, but since then the newcomers have only provided smaller, less valuable goods. Nothing remotely suspicious about any of them.

"No, Oberon. You are, as they say, barking up the wrong tree with me. And I do trust you'll remember that when deciding whose life to make miserable while you're engaged in your wild *phouka* chase."

Well, that was plain enough. And frankly, about as clear'n complete an answer as I had any right to expect from him. Since no good woulda come from pushing any further, I offered up a few of the usual pleasantries, threw in a thanks for good measure, and dusted outta there.

Hadn't been a complete trip for biscuits, since at least it ruled out a few options—to say nothin' of putting me wise that Nolan Shea might be a bigger part of my world than I'd thought. I was gonna have to dig into that, maybe pump Fino the Shark for some information. (I also hadda be real careful leaving Hruotlundt's place, in case the Uptown Boys had decided to wait around and tune me up or put some slugs into me. They hadn't.)

But what the trip *didn't* do was put me any closer to finding Goswythe, or whoever else was out there askin' about me. I decided to head back home for the rest of the night; I hadda lot of pondering to do, and some uncomfortable choices to make, and I needed some peace and privacy in order to make 'em.


Turned out my office wasn't gonna prove as peaceful and private as I'd expected.

She was waitin' inside, perched on the edge of the desk like she owned the place, knees crossed in that weird way that *should* be demure but really says, "Get a load of these getaway sticks." Her dress and hat were robin's-egg blue, her hair brown as good coffee and wavy as a calm tide, and I knew right away somethin' was seriously hinky because my brain just don't get that poetic over a dame anymore. Hadn't since well before I'd left the Courts behind.

Well, no, that ain't true. It'd happened once, a few months back.

*Fuck me.*

"Mr. Oberon?" Her pipes sounded just like they should have, soft and throaty, sultry, as if they were made for singing insteada speaking. Singing or... Let's go with "other sounds." "My name is Carmen. Carmen McCall. I need to talk to you about—"

"No. Get out."

Clearly *not* what she'd expected to hear. Her lips actually kept movin' for a few seconds after sound stopped comin' out. When she spoke again, all she seemed able to manage was, "What?"

"Oh, you're good, sister. Outrage *and* that little emotional little hitch in your voice. Not many people can manage both at once."

"I don't... I don't understand. Why are you treating me this—?"

"Oh, knock it off."

I felt it, crashin' over me, an avalanche of emotions and longing. Some of the most potent feelings I'd ever had, even if they were comin' from outside, enough to drive most people— Fae or otherwise—to their knees. To make 'em a willing slave, a puppet dancing on heartstrings.

Hell with *that*.

I ain't gonna pretend it was *easy*, but it also wasn't ever in doubt. Partly cause, if I say so myself, you ain't gonna find many with a stronger stubborn streak'n me. In my time, I been on both sides of a *lot* of different magics, thrown by a lot of different creatures. Even when I'm not at my best—like, say, when I'm riding a crest of random bad luck—it ain't easy to get too deep into my noggin.

But part of it—a whole lot of it, maybe—was Ramona. I'd *been* through this already, see? What this Carmen McCall was doin' now? Exact same mojo Ramona'd hooked me with months ago. She'd been more subtle, taken her time, and I've already been square with you, so you know she had me for a couple days. Now, though, I knew how it felt. I knew how to work through it. I was on guard.

And just maybe there was still enough of Ramona's influence hidden somewhere in my deepest thoughts that this new twist couldn't get her mitts around 'em.

"I said *knock it off*!" Wasn't just a shout, either. I threw a heap of my own mojo into it; not exactly muckin' around with her luck or the magic in her aura, or even gettin' into her head, just a wave of magic to metaphorically knock her on her keister. Her peepers went wide and the emotional pressure building up against me popped like a soap bubble.

"I dunno what you are, lady." I probably sounded meaner'n I meant to, but I was angry. Angry at people tryin' to manipulate me; angry at Ramona for refusin' to admit to me that she wasn't human months ago—which was pretty clear now, in light of there bein' someone else whose power was *exactly* the same as hers; angry at myself for still carin' enough to be angry at Ramona at all. "But I don't want any part of it."

"Fine." Her whole demeanor shifted as quick as if someone'd just flipped a switch. The puppy eyes, the waterworks, the whole "seductively helpless" spiel, gone, leaving nothin' but all business. "Clearly I approached this wrong. My apologies."

"I don't want you to apologize. I want you to leave."

Even as I said it, though, somethin' occurred to me.

"And don't think I haven't tumbled to your people watching and asking around about me, either. They're good, but they ain't *that* good."

You should know me well enough by now to recognize one of my test questions when you hear it. I was still more'n half convinced it'd been Goswythe all this time—shadowing me, talking up my friends, all that. (Hell, if I hadn't felt the empathic whammy Miss McCall had tried to put on me, I mighta believed she *was* Goswythe.) But it still wasn't a sure bet, and her showin' up now probably was no coincidence. I wanted to see what kinda reaction I got.

And what I got was a twitch around the peepers and a quick frown, a brief return to the worry and fretting of a minute ago. I didn't know her well enough, and she was way too skilled, for me to tell in that moment if the fear was genuine or a real solid act. It *tasted* real, but with another Fae or one of our relatives? Unreliable evidence at best.

"I hadn't realized you already knew they were out there," she said, sliding off the desk and beginning to pace a neat track in the age- and foot-packed carpet. "They're not my people, Mr. Oberon. In fact, they're why I came to you. If they find my sister before I do..."

She let it hang there, almost daring me to make the obvious connection.

I made the obvious connection.

*Damn it to hell, Ramona, what'd you get yourself into now? And for that matter, what've you gotten* me *into?*

"Yeah," I told her, "I can see how that might be a worry."

She brightened, flashing blindingly pearly whites.

"So you'll help me?"

"To find the door, yeah. Otherwise, no."

Oh, but she went icy at that. Either she didn't have the same fine control over her mojo that Ramona did or she wasn't botherin' to exercise it, because I felt a tangible wave of cold fury shoot across the office.

"What is wrong with you, Oberon?"

"To start with, I don't know you from Eve, toots."

"You don't know *most* of your clients before you take them on!"

"Most of 'em don't show up and try to dope me with a mystical Mickey, either."

She stamped her foot, and I knew *that* was an act. Her anger, her *real* anger, was far too intense for dippy gestures like that.

"I need you to find Ramona and bring her to me, Oberon. It's the only way she'll be safe. The only way *either* of you will be safe!"

"Sorry, not buying it. I don't trust you. I don't trust you *so much* that it's actually makin' me trust *other* people less."

Funny thing was, I wasn't entirely exaggerating with that. I was goin' back in my head and questioning even what little I'd thought I'd known about Ramona.

"I'm *sure* as hell not handing anybody over to you without a lot more than your reassurances to go on. Now I'm gonna ask politely one more time, and then I'm gonna *help* you leave."

And just that quick, her anger vanished. It was so sudden, I almost staggered. She smiled, and it was the most worrying thing she'd done since I stepped through the door.

"Maybe you'd reconsider," she murmured, tapping a fingernail to her lip as if she'd only just come up with the idea, "if I offered you a way to wake the little changeling girl."

I lost it.

The lights dimmed, in the office, in the hall, the filaments fading to an evil, sickly orange. I even heard one of the bulbs in the bathroom shatter. The fan, which wasn't on and I'm not even certain was plugged in, slowly began to rotate backwards. Out in the hallway, the phone rang once, a sharp, shrill sound that faded and staggered to silence as if choked. I gripped the L&G in a fist clenched tight enough to make the hardwood beg for mercy, and I didn't remember drawing it. Through unblinking eyes I stared at her, pummeled her, laying siege to her thoughts.

"*What do you know about Adalina? Tell me how to help her! Tell me! TELL ME!*"

I couldn't begin to say if I'd actually shouted it aloud or if it was all in my head. Didn't matter either way.

She fought me. Walls of willpower like stone and iron, way

stronger than anything mortal, rose to blunt the edges of my attack. Whatever she was, McCall was strong, powerful, but if that'd been her only defense she never could've kept me out.

It wasn't, though.

Again emotions buffeted me from across the office, a storm front of fury and hatred and unadulterated pain. It held just a part of me at bay, forced me to devote some of my magics to protecting my own mind instead of hammering at hers.

For long minutes we stood, probably looking like a pair of angry mimes to anyone who couldn't sense what was happening. My anger built, heated to boiling, and I knew— suddenly, without ever quite recognizing *how* I knew—that I hadn't reached my limits. That I had unplumbed depths of power I could delve into, enough to overwhelm anything McCall might throw into my path. Power I'd deliberately put aside long ago, power I'd somehow forgotten.

And I knew, too, that if I dipped so much as a toe into that black maelstrom, I wasn't coming back out unscathed. That I'd *made* myself forget, because I couldn't be me—the "me" I was now, that I'd chosen to be, the "me" I'd named Mick Oberon— with it roiling inside me.

My anger cooled; not a lot, but enough. I stepped back from the abyss. The lights flickered one last time, then brightened back to normal, and the fan slowed to a halt. Grudgingly, I lowered my wand, letting my arm hang at my side, and studied her.

She was studying me back, staring. I figure she'd expected some kinda mental duel, but nothin' close to what she got. Her peepers were wide, her chin hanging. Still, she was in better shape than most woulda been after a clash like we just had. Broad was hardboiled, hadda give her that.

Guess I shouldn't have been surprised, not if she really was related to Ramona.

Gave some serious consideration to makin' a dive for the Murphy bed. My rapier lived in the niche, next to where the frame folded up into the wall; if I couldn't whammy the story outta her, maybe a bit of physical intimidation'd do the trick.

Honestly, though, probably not. As I said, she was a tough one. Plus, I still had no notion of how dangerous she mighta been in turn—to say nothin' of the fact that she could easily reach the door and make tracks well before I could retrieve the blade and get back to her.

No way to know if she'd sussed out what I was thinking, but either way she smiled again and shook her head.

"Wow. You're even stronger than I'd heard, Oberon. I believe I could come to like you."

She was layin' on the false charm again; just a trickle this time, not the earlier flood. I completely ignored it.

"That so? Don't figure you'd wanna make me an enemy, then."

"Oh, but I don't. I'm still trying to hire you, you foolish *sidhe*. And I'm offering you a higher fee than you could possibly have asked for."

She was, too, damn her.

"How do you know about it?"

"Really, Mick. You don't mind if I call you Mick, right?"

"I—"

"You weren't exactly shy about searching for a changeling, were you? All your asking around? Challenging a Court clerk to a duel in the middle of City Hall to force Judge Ylleuwyn to see you? The whole Chicago Seelie Court heard about it, and you know how aristocrats are. People *will* gossip so. It's not terribly difficult to trace the rest of it, if you're so inclined. I found Adalina rather easily, and I doubt I'm the only one."

Well... Fuck. I mean, it ain't as though I'd had any reason to keep my investigation quiet at the time. Hadn't learned why that woulda been wise until a lot later. Still, hearin' it just laid out this way made me feel kinda goofy.

Of course, it *also* meant that she'd been workin' this angle for a while, getting herself ready to hold it over my head. That didn't seem to jibe too smooth with the idea that she'd only come to me because someone was gunning for Ramona. Not proof she was lyin', but definitely hinky.

"Yeah, okay, but why were you diggin' in the first—?"

"Oh, Mick, none of that matters, and it's not what you want to know. You want to know how I can do it."

Well, yes, there was that, too.

"Quite simply, I have the means of brewing an elixir," she said. "It's tricky, a great deal of work, and the ingredients are... tough to come by, to say the least. But when mixed properly, there's not much shy of death itself that it cannot cure. It'll awaken your little Sleeping Ugly, guaranteed."

I decided to ignore the dig and focus on the big picture.

"That's mighty convenient, Ms. McCall, and a pretty ambitious claim. I don't suppose you'd be willing to provide this elixir in advance?"

"You don't suppose correctly. And please, call me Carmen, since we're such good friends now."

"So how do I know you're being square with me—Ms. McCall? Why should I believe you can do what you say, or that you'll come through even if you can?"

"Because as I just said, I'm not looking to make you an enemy." Guess *she* decided to ignore the dig, too. "You're a detective, and you've made it very clear just how dangerous you can be. It'd be more trouble than it would be worth to double-cross you over this and try to get away with it, don't you think?"

Made sense. Sounded good. I didn't trust a word of it, since I actually do *have* a brain, but it ain't as if I had much choice. It'd been more'n a year now, and I still hadn't been able to help Adalina one iota. If McCall was bein' even halfway straight with me, I hadda go for it.

Long enough to learn more, if nothing else. And I'd already known I was gonna have to go find Ramona at some point, even if I'd rather have done it *without* a new leggy Sword of

Damocles hangin' over me.

"All right, lady, you got yourself a deal. I find Ramona for you, and then—"

"Then you contact me. Without letting her know I'm the one who hired you. We've had, let's say, a bit of a spat lately. I'm afraid she's not going to let us help if she knows I'm involved. We'll talk about what I need you to do then, how we'll set up the meeting."

Oh, yeah. That didn't sound hinky at all.

"My card," she said, handing over a torn strip of paper with a number scribbled on it. "Call me when everything's ready. And chin up, Mick. You're *this* close to Adalina's cure. See you around, you big lug."

And then there was nothin' for it but to watch her go swayin' and swishin' on her merry way, wondering again what the hell Ramona'd gotten me into—or maybe what I'd gotten her into, or what we'd both stumbled into—and also wondering why, as always, I seemed so damned determined to dig myself in even deeper.

# CHAPTER FOUR

"Hey, Bianca. Mick Oberon."

"Mick!" Even over the blower, through the cracklin' and poppin' of the line, she sounded all in. Sure, it coulda been the wee hours, but she *usually* sounded like that these days. Guess havin' one daughter pullin' a Rip Van Winkle while you're still tryin' to figure out what species she is, at the same time you're tryin' to get to know the other daughter after sixteen years apart, will do that to a person. Still, she was clearly thrilled to hear from me. Nice lady, Bianca Ottati. "How are you?"

"Oh, can't complain."

I mean, sure, I *coulda* complained. I coulda complained until I was blue in the cows and my face came home, or however that goes. Not least because my ear was near on fire and my whole head buzzed like I had bees makin' whoopee in my sinus cavities. Damn, I hate using the phone. But I wasn't willin' to trundle across town to speak with her right now. Not this late at night, when there were fewer trains and the trip woulda taken hours, and not with Carmen McCall out there. She already knew too much about Adalina, but I couldn't be sure *how* much. Yeah, she almost certainly knew where the Ottatis lived, or at least enough to look 'em up—but just in case she somehow didn't, I wasn't gonna lead her right to their doorstep.

Guess, with the way my luck'd been running, I oughta have been thankful the phone was even working after my little display earlier.

"Listen, Bianca, I won't keep you long. I'm just givin' you a ring to see how Adalina's doin'."

Nice, but no bunny. I heard her mood change, her whole body tense and the hair on her neck stand up, even before she said another word.

"She's fine. I mean, as fine as... as usual. Why? What's wrong?"

"And Celia? She's home? Everyone's good?"

"Tucked in bed. Mick, what is it?"

Hadda pick my words carefully here. I wanted 'em on their guard, but not panicked. Enough to do what little good they could, not enough to make 'em worry over the fact that if one of the Fae really *did* have a beef with 'em, nothin' they could do *would* prove much good. I hated to upset the Ottatis even that much—especially since I'd done pretty much the same, a few months back—but if I were them, I'da wanted the warning.

And no, I sure as fuck was *not* gonna tell her about McCall's supposed cure-all elixir. No way I was gonna get *those* hopes up until I had it in my paws and *knew* it was more'n snake oil.

"It's probably nothin'," I hedged, knowing it wouldn't do any good. "Really. But just in case, you and Fino may wanna have a few of his boys keep close to Celia for the next few days. Maybe put an extra man on Adalina's room, too.

"Um, and they probably oughta be carryin' iron pipes or knives in addition to their gats."

"Oh, God. Why do these things keep targeting us?"

I decided to assume it was "present company excepted" where *things* were concerned.

"I meant it when I said it's probably nothin', Bianca. But, if it *ain't* nothin', no, you don't have anyone new after you. It's possible—just *possible*—that Goswythe's back in town."

She spat somethin' in Italian then that I knew, one, she'd

picked up from her husband, not her mother, and, two, she wouldn'ta wanted translated.

"I want that bastard out of our lives, Mick."

"Trust me, we got similar goals here."

"Do you think I should tell Celia?"

Hmm.

"Probably," I conceded. "I don't wanna panic the girl. But she lived with Goswythe for most of her life. If anyone'll know what to watch for, or see him comin' no matter what shape he's taken, it's her. Probably fairer and safer to let her know."

"You know best."

Ha! Good one.

"Just make sure she knows this is a precaution. Better safe, 'n all that."

"All right."

"And that I'm lookin' into it."

I never have figured out how some people manage to smile so that you can hear 'em over the blower.

"That'll make her feel better."

*Makes one of us.*

"Listen, while we're jawing..." Much as I wanted to just hang up already and get as far from the damn payphone as the building's architecture would allow, I wasn't gonna waste a resource. "I could use your help on somethin' I'm investigating. May or may not be related to the Goswythe thing."

"Whatever I can do."

"This is really more a question for Fino, but... Nolan Shea." I knew she'd know who he was, if nothin' more; the Uptown Boys'd been some of her husband's biggest enemies, back before the Outfit and the Northsiders stopped openly warring on the streets.

The name elicited another quick bit of Italian I ain't gonna bother translatin' for you.

"What about him?"

"I know the Uptown Boys answer to the Northside Gang,

but I don't figure Shea reports to Bugs Moran directly, does he? So who's *his* boss?"

"No, not to Moran. I think Shea answers to..." She paused, pondering. I let her ponder.

It finally came to her. "Fleischer! Saul Fleischer!"

I seemed to remember hearing the name a time or two, but I didn't know the first thing about the guy. Well, except— judging by the name—his religion, but I guess that didn't help me a whole lot.

"Anything you can tell me about him?" I asked.

"I'm afraid I don't know a great deal about the man. I've only heard the name on occasion when Fino's been... uh, 'talking' about Shea and the Uptown Boys."

Heh. I've heard Fino when he goes off on somethin' or someone he hates.

"I'm surprised you could make out a name in all the profanity."

Bianca laughed softly. "I've been with him long enough to speak his language." Then, more seriously, "He's out right now, but when he comes back—or if Archie stops by—I'll have one of them give you a ring if they think there's anything you ought to know about Fleischer."

"Appreciate it, Bianca."

I let her keep me on the horn long enough for a couple more reassurances, another minute of pleasantries, and then I slammed the receiver down like I was drivin' a railroad spike. *Fuck*, I hate that thing!

Spent the rest of the night in my office, starin' at the walls and goin' through a whole quart of milk trying to drink away the lingering pain of the phone. I wasn't tired enough to need to sleep tonight, but there also wasn't a whole lot more I could do until the sun came up, not with so few leads. Plus, it was nice to be able to put off trackin' down You-Know-Who for a few extra hours.

When dawn *did* show her rosy cheeks, though, I'd spent

enough time mulling things over that I had myself a plan, and some idea of where to start.

As often as I've visited the station, at so many different times of day, it's always got the same sorta crowds hangin' around the entrance, sitting on uncomfortable wooden chairs, keisters slowly going numb, as they wait to make whatever report or demand whatever answers brought 'em here. Always the same volume, too, as bulls and detectives and secretaries holler back and forth, raisin' their voices high as they'll go to be heard over everyone *else* shoutin' because God forbid they get up and walk a dozen steps to ask for a file or tell someone they got a dil-ya-ble on the front desk telephone.

Sometimes I wonder if most of it's the *same* crowd every day. If some poor saps got stuck in some kinda Purgatorial loop, or the intense emotion of the throng's just generating its own faceless members. I think Poe wrote something like that, once.

Couple of times on the way there, I got that same hinky feeling of someone watching me. I took a few turns, made a few stops, doubled back now and again, and either I managed to ditch 'em or they got a lot better at hiding.

I'd gotten to the drab block of a building later'n I'd hoped, thanks to a delay on the L—somethin' about one of the trains breaking down a ways down the line—but still by mid-morning. Cops were used to seein' me and some of Chicago's other private shamuses around, so nobody objected to me just pushin' through the swinging door and heading back to the "here's where we actually do our work" part of the clubhouse. Well, nobody but the desk sergeant, who always wanted me to sign in even though he really hadda know by now that it wasn't gonna happen.

Wending my way between rows of desks, dodging legs both human and chair, I traded a wave here or a nod there. Polite, if not exactly friendly; not that these coppers had anything against me, but to most of 'em I was just another PI, see? An amateur who might occasionally be useful, but who'd probably get in their way more often than not. A few of 'em knew me better, sure, but only a few.

Pete, who was the only guy on the force I'd call a real pal, was usually an afternoon- or night-shift guy, and even if he *had* been workin' the morning, odds were he'da been out on the beat, not parked on his keister here at the clubhouse. So I wasn't even lookin' for him. I'd been hoping to run into Lieutenant Keenan, though. We might not be exactly friends, but we'd worked together and got along well enough, and he *was* a good buddy of Pete's. I could usually count on the guy to gimme a hand if it wasn't interfering with one of his own cases to do it.

He wasn't around either, though. Dunno if he was off work or out on a case, and I don't guess it matters. Point is, no dice.

I'll tell you who *was* there, though, who saw me wanderin' the paperwork-and-cheap-desks labyrinth and took it on himself to say somethin' before I could figure out how to duck him. He marched right on up to me, all doughy and florid, mustache you coulda used as a whisk broom carvin' out a path for him.

"Oberon."

"Galway."

"Havin' a good morning?"

"Not bad so far."

"Great. The fuck are you doing here?"

And that, ladies and gentleman, is a picture-perfect example of why—even though his job in Robbery made him better suited to the questions I wanted to ask than Keenan, who's Homicide—I really hadn't wanted to talk to Donald fucking Galway.

He hadn't seemed to care for me much when we first met, a few months ago, but I didn't guess he cared for much of anybody. And yeah, I'd skipped out on a meeting with him, but the department had rescinded the job offer we were supposed to discuss anyway, so he *shouldn't* have any particular beef with me.

I wasn't gonna put too many nickels down on that "shouldn't," though.

"Was kinda hoping to look at some recent robbery and theft reports," I told him.

"Why?"

"I'm tired of the pulps and lookin' for some light reading. Why do you *think*? It's for a case I'm working."

See, one of the few details I *had* managed to learn about Ramona—which you'll remember if you been payin' attention—is that she worked for a collector, someone among the ranks of the Windy City's high and mighty who gathered mystical and mysterious objects for fun and profit. So if I was gonna dig her up, I'd decided that lookin' into the disappearance of items that might fit that bill—and that *hadn't* been fenced by Hruotlundt or his ilk—might lead me somewhere.

"I meant," Galway half-sighed, half-shouted (and no, I can't explain how he managed that), "why would I waste my time helping you?"

"Goodness of your heart?"

"I'm a Chicago cop. They confiscated that when I got the job."

"Okay, how about 'cause it'll take some of the workload off your shoulders if I close a case or three?"

"And it'll add to my workload if I take the time to walk you through a whole fucking pile of files and you *don't* close anything."

"What can I say? You coppers get paid to take risks."

"But not enough to deal with certain kinds of nuisances. How about you go climb your thumb and I go back to work?"

Yeah, so this wasn't getting me much of anywhere. I looked around at the rest of the clubhouse, watchin' cops pounding away on typewriters or gabbin' away between desks, creating enough of a hubbub that I doubt anyone even really noticed me'n Galway talking, let alone paid us much attention. Swell: meant I should be able to stick my fingers in his head— metaphorically speaking—without anybody noticing.

I turned back to him, gathering my focus, and—

"Officer, that's him! That's him, right here!"

The both of us—and everyone else around—turned at that shout, saw a uniformed bull escorting a scrawny, mustached fellow with a black eye and swollen lip. He'd raised a spindly finger when he shouted, and that digit was pointed at me like the rifle on a firing squad.

"That's the man who mugged me!"

I been in an interrogation room before. All drab walls and cheap furniture and a bright lamp. They don't get any prettier with repeat viewings.

Galway was there, and a couple uniforms, and the guy who'd accused me. His name was Phelps; I'd picked up on that, on account of that's what the cops were calling him. That's my keen detective skills at their sharpest, see?

Wasn't exactly normal, us all being packed into one room this way, but this wasn't exactly a normal situation. We'd all come in here mostly to get out of the public eye, not so much for an actual grilling. Though it could still have gone that way.

"...understand you're upset, Mr. Phelps," Galway was saying. "And I know you think you've got the right guy. But Mr. Oberon here, he's a private dick. He's worked with us before, a lot."

I'll give the man his due. He may not be all that fond of me, but he still stepped up.

Not that Phelps was buyin' a word of it.

"I don't care if he's the son of the Pope!"

"Uh..."

"I know what he did! It wasn't even dark; the sun hadn't gone down yet! He got in my face and laughed at me before he beat me!"

"Wasn't me," I said, not for the first time. I was leaning back in the chair, arms crossed, lookin' more at the ceiling than anyone in the room. "I've never seen you before in my life, bo."

"You're a damn liar!"

Yeah, we'd been here before a couple times already. This conversation was chasing its tail something fierce.

Galway leaned in, which gave me a nice snootful of sweat and what I think was some combo of eggs, coffee, and liverwurst.

"Listen, Oberon, the guy's pretty firm. I don't think you did it, but I dunno if we're gonna have any choice but to book you until we can get this straightened out."

Hmm. No, we didn't want that, did we?

"What time did I supposedly attack you?" I asked Phelps.

"Huh?"

Since I was surrounded by mortals, I went ahead and sighed.

"You said the sun hadn't gone down. What time was it?" Then, when he just glared at me, "You *were* gonna actually included minor details like that in your police report, yeah?"

"About six-thirty or so," he grumbled.

I did some quick subtraction in my head.

"There's a couple lives on Burton Place, name of Marsters. Give 'em a ring. Ask 'em how their evening went yesterday."

Took a bit of persuading—though not too much, and nothing mystical—and a lot of suspicious glares from Phelps, but one of the bulls finally went and got on the horn. Came back a few minutes later shaking his head.

"They ain't too happy with you, Oberon."

"Yeah, I figured. Wasn't me who broke their crystal dingus, but whatever. I ain't looking to be pals with 'em. I just need to know if they told you I was with 'em."

"That they did."

"And when did they say I left?"

"They weren't *exactly* sure, but..."

"But?"

"Definitely after six."

I raised an eyebrow at Phelps. "You wanna tell me how I got from Barton Place to the west side in time to put the broderick on you?"

"They're lying! Or mistaken! Or—!"

"Look, Mr. Phelps. I'm real sorry you got beaten and robbed. But it *wasn't me*."

"I *saw*—!"

"Come on, Mr. Phelps." Galway stepped around him and opened the door. "Officer Nichols will take your statement, and we'll be on the lookout for someone who *resembles* Mr. Oberon here."

"But—!"

"I'm sorry, he's got an alibi. You heard it. Let's go."

Phelps glared at me the entire way out the door, nearly walking into the doorframe in the process.

As for me, this whole affair had me pondering a whole new heap of questions.

What'd been the purpose behind this? I sure as hell didn't believe for one second it was a coincidence, that someone who just *happened* to look like me had mugged this poor sap. I may not look exactly the same to any given mortal, but I'm still me; still pretty close, between one soul and the next. This all but *had* to be deliberate. Disguise at least, and more likely magic. All kinda ways someone coulda done it—hell, give me a minute in someone's head, muckin' with their perceptions and memories, and I could make 'em believe something this way— but the most obvious answer? Shapeshifting. Again.

Goswythe (or whoever) clearly wasn't too worried about me suspecting him. But why pull a stunt like this?

If he'd actually meant to get me pinched and thrown in the cooler for any real time, it was a clumsy setup. Way *too* clumsy. This frame wouldn't have held a Monet, let alone me.

Sending me a message? "I'm watching you and I can get to you," that sorta thing? Maybe, but I'd already known that, and he shoulda known I'd already known. It was dippy to expend that much effort, and confirm for me there was shapeshifting or other magic involved, just for that.

Hell, maybe the whole point was to be inconvenient and irritating, in which case he'd succeeded. *Phouka* can be that way. Didn't really seem Goswythe's speed, but you never know; we all gotta act according to our nature. Not probable—he was too much the consummate schemer—but possible.

Goddamn it. Way too many "maybes" and "could bes" and "possibles." Welcome to my life.

"Mick! Hey, Mick! Where are you?"

Couldn't help but grin. Even in *my* life, I got certain things I *can* count on, see?

I stood up and stepped outta the box.

"Heya, Pete. Over here."

My buddy'd clearly taken just enough time to force himself awake and make himself vaguely presentable. He'd brushed his hair neat enough, but his thick mustache was lookin' a bit wild and prickly, and it was weird seein' him in the clubhouse while outta uniform. He elbowed his way toward me, drawing growls and grunts and glowers from the various elbowees.

"What's this bullshit about you bein' accused of mugging someone?" he demanded as he neared.

"Eh, nothing much." I'd explain it in detail when we had some quiet—and no other ears around—but not now. "Just a misunderstanding."

I felt Phelps's peepers boring into me from across the station. But someone else was gettin' real steamed at *Pete*, though.

"*Officer Staten!*"

Pete went rigid as a two-by-four in an icebox.

"Sir?"

Galway stomped back over, face red, chest heaving, his own mustache raised to attack and bristling in a show of dominance over Pete's.

"How the fuck did you hear about this?"

"Well, sir, Mick's a friend of mine, and I—"

"I didn't ask why the fuck you were here! I know why you're here! I asked how you knew!" Then he didn't narrow his eyes so much as scrunch his whole face up around his nose. "Someone called you. Who was it?"

"I'm not at liberty to say, sir."

"I asked you a question, Staten!"

"Yes, sir, you did. But I'm not breaking any rules by coming in early, and I'm declining to answer."

"I could bring you up for disciplinary action!"

"That's an awful lotta paperwork when I didn't actually do anything, sir."

Galway spluttered and cursed and threatened some more, but he was runnin' outta steam quick. I was relieved, to tell you square, and not just for Pete's sake. I was glad he hadn't ratted out Officer Nichols, too. The poor mug hadn't really had a choice about gettin' Pete on the horn and telling him what was what. I'd put the thought in his noggin with a quick stare and a whispered suggestion, while they were hauling me into the box to be grilled for a bit, so I'da felt guilty if he'd gotten in Dutch for it. Not a lot, savvy? But some.

Especially since it woulda been for nothing, what with me having smoothed it all over, more or less, before Pete even showed.

"Well, shit, fine then," the detective said when he'd finally wound down. "Since you're here anyway, Staten, *you* can spend your afternoon digging through files with your buddy here. Me, I got better things to do with my time."

Pete'n me watched him stomp away, glaring other cops out of his path.

"So," I said, smiling, "really appreciate you coming in before your shift. How well do you know Robbery's files?"

Pete's own expression wasn't near so much of a smile as mine.

Since we didn't have Galway's assistance—or anyone else's in the Robbery Division, for that matter—the detective seemed to have something else for every last damn one of 'em to work on, and it all hadda be done *right now*—it took us a couple hours to go through enough of the recent reports to convince me I wasn't gonna find what I was hoping for.

Well, not here, anyway. But this had always only been step one. Many of the kindsa goods I suspected mighta been snatched belonged to people who wouldn't call the police at all. Didn't mean I couldn't dig 'em up elsewhere.

I thanked Pete, politely, for his time. He groused something, a lot less politely, in reply. And then I made tracks.

# CHAPTER FIVE

I couldn't go back to Hruotlundt. As I said, if Ramona'd been glomming magic goods, it wouldn't be to sell 'em, and even if the *dvergr had* heard something—rumors, whispers, whatever—spillin' it to me wasn't exactly good for business. Same reasoning ruled out all the other Chicago fences who dealt with the supernatural. But that didn't mean *nobody* was talking.

Track down Franky? He'd be the easiest of the bunch to find, since everyone else was lying dormy, waiting for the latest trouble to blow over. But we'd just talked; I didn't wanna get him any deeper into whatever was goin' down, not since he'd been the only one with the guts to come tell me about the guys—or guy—askin' questions. I'd only look him up again if I absolutely couldn't unearth any of the others.

Which meant it was time to find one of the others. Fact that they were lyin' low would make it harder, but not impossible.

I ain't gonna bore you with the details. Let's just say that after hours and hours and hours—far longer than it shoulda taken—of askin' people who knew people who'd heard of people who knew people I could ask, I finally got myself an address.

The next dawn found me standin' in front of a filthy, rundown redbrick building in Canaryville, a rough neighborhood down south near the Union Stock Yards. The whole place had a weight to it: the weight of dust and sweat and poverty on the building itself, the weight of hostile peepers on my shoulders as folks glared at me from between twitching yellowed drapes.

Never been fond of outsiders, the people of Canaryville.

The door to the old tenement was locked, but that didn't prove too tough to deal with. My luck may not've been at its best—there's a reason it took me so damn long to track anybody down, and it wasn't 'cause they'd done such a swell job of hiding—but I'd have to be dead before I couldn't handle a chintzy pin-and-tumbler. I sucked the luck outta the dingus, bits and pieces fell into or outta place, and it clicked open with an ugly grinding sound.

Now, I don't wanna queer your impression of Canaryville. Place is poor as a beggar's dog and rough as tree bark, but most of the people here got their own dignity. They ain't animals, and they keep their homes neat as circumstances allow.

Most.

But every neighborhood's got its bad seeds, and this particular place? Not even the thick miasma of the stock yards could cover the stench of unwashed misery and calcifying piss. That was actually how I knew when I'd finally come to the right door, down a dusty hallway on the second story: The ambient stench abruptly vanished beneath the scent of soap suds.

I didn't really expect a response to my knock, what with the whole "in hiding" thing. I knocked anyway. No response.

I knocked again.

Then I said, quiet as I could while still figuring I'd be heard through the door, "It's gonna attract a lot more attention if you make me bust this thing down to jaw with you."

The door opened just as far as the security chain permitted. The woman staring up at me—I ain't exactly a beanstalk, but if she ever managed to top four feet tall it'd only be thanks to some towering footwear or extra thick carpeting—was the spittin' image of an Old Country washerwoman. Her hair was the gray of a cloud's underside, dress was undyed wool, and her face and hands had enough deep wrinkles to hide about three bucks and seventy cents-worth of dimes.

"Mornin', Lenai. You shoulda told me you were movin'. I carry a mean sofa."

"You wouldn't have had to kick the door down, you jackass!" Rough and shaky, her voice actually sounded a lot like she herself was bein' rubbed across one of those corrugated washboards. "You got much quieter ways than that!"

"Yeah, but they wouldn't have gotten you to open up, would they?"

"Go away."

"Can't do it, Lenai. We gotta talk. Lemme in and I'll get this done with quick as I can."

"You're a jackass!"

"So you said." I pulled a handful of folding green out of a pocket and slipped it through the door. "More of that when we're done."

Grumbling, she yanked the lettuce outta my fingers and shut the door to move the chain. She was still grumbling when she opened back up.

"Get in here before somebody sees you."

I slipped past her, staring at a one-room apartment that looked... well, exactly the way you'd expect. Mattress, cheap table, cheaper icebox, toilet and sink. You don't move out of this sorta place; you escape it.

The door thumped shut behind me, I turned back around, and Lenai was about twenty years younger. Face was just lined, not wrinkled, 'cept around the eyes and lips, and her hair had come over blonde. The frumpy ensemble had fit perfectly a moment ago; now it looked real outta place.

I felt bad, actually. She only gets younger when she's real stressed or frightened.

"Why are you bugging me, Oberon?" Still not exactly musical, but at least her pipes didn't sound like she was begin' throttled by an epileptic python anymore.

"I'm diggin' into whoever's been nosing around about me."

"You don't say. Hey, you know what I would've done if I wanted any part of that? *Not* gone into goddamn hiding!" She paused, sucking on her lower lip and scowling. "Franky told you, didn't he? I'm gonna kill that gold-sucking clover-cock."

"Don't. I appreciate he was the only one of you had the balls to warn me."

"You appreciate his balls? I'll mail them to you in a box."

"There's almost gotta be a law against that sorta thing, don't you figure?"

She leaned back against the door, crossing her arms.

"You were telling me why we're having this conversation."

So I did. Not in any real detail, just that I was lookin' for anything about mystical relics having been snatched lately, or occultists being burgled. Anything that might lead me to one of the city's collectors.

Lenai bitched at me that she'd been lying dormy for days, so how'd I expect her to know anything? I explained that I was lookin' for information that went further back than that. She told me to go do rude things to myself. I waited.

Once she got tired of cursing at me and actually took some to think about it, yeah, she'd heard some talk about some mugs being "relieved" of certain goods, gewgaws of the sort you really didn't want falling into the wrong hands, but that the bulls couldn't do a damn thing about. Never anything big, nothing like, oh, just for example, the Spear of Lugh, but still significant. A talisman here, a tattered fragment of ritual there.

"Names, Lenai. I need specific names."

She called me plenty of 'em. Not exactly the ones I was lookin' for, though.

"The hell makes you think I'd even remember?" she finally demanded. "We're talking rumors here. And not about anything I thought was important."

"Because you remember everything."

"When I'm old and wise!" she crowed, spitefully triumphant. "I'm younger right now! I don't remember. You'll have to leave."

"Nah, I can wait."

In mythology, the glare of Medusa turned men to stone. Lenai's glare woulda turned statues to flesh—mostly so they could get up and scram.

"You said you'd make this quick," she accused.

"Yeah, quick as I can. So soon as you calm down and get to aging, I can call it a day."

"You being here agitates me!"

"You'd be surprised how often I been told that. I suggest a stiff shot of whiskey."

All right, I've subjected you to enough of this. Today was a bit worse'n normal, since Lenai was worried about whoever knew enough to look her up to ask about me, but on the square, she's pretty much like this all the time. I did eventually coax a few names outta her, tossed another few bucks her way, and blew the place quick.

It's *tiring* bein' around her.

Anyway, names. None of 'em were anybody I knew well, and most I hadn't heard of at all. That bugged me some. Much as I wished otherwise, the last year-and-change had made it clear I wasn't gonna be able to restrict myself to "mundane" cases; that what you call the supernatural was gonna keep intruding itself into my life. This bein' the case, I really hadda do a better job of keeping track of who in Chicago knew something about something, savvy?

All that said, one of the names did jump out at me, but at first I couldn't figure why. "Georgina Kessler." I knew I'd come across it, but I'd left Lenai's dump and ankled a good couple of blocks before it dawned on me.

I hadn't *known* the dame as "Georgina." I'd only learned that was her full name when I poked into her background a little after the fact. Now that I'd sussed out who she was, though, it oughta be duck soup to actually find her.

And it was. Place was in her boss's name, not hers, but that wasn't much of a hurdle.

How many apartment tenements you want me to describe to you, anyway? It was a lot nicer'n the one I'd just visited, not quite as swanky as some. Comfortable without being ostentatious. That enough for you? Good.

Spotted a couple goons keeping a slant on the place, too. Oh, they were makin' a stab at inconspicuous, but their aim was off. One guy had his keister planted on a bench and was peeping over the top of a folded newspaper, but you only hadda watch him for a few minutes to figure that either he wasn't reading at all, or he had the reading comprehension and speed of a particularly uneducated marmoset. Down by the corner, another one sat behind the wheel of a cherry-red Packard 840, smoking what—to judge by what looked like a fog bank struggling desperately to escape the car—hadda be his forty-ninth or fiftieth gasper.

I didn't figure them for the mugs—or mug—who'd been following me. Didn't seem to be their style, and anyway they'd already been here when I showed. Whatever else Goswythe or whoever might be, I hadn't seen any sign yet that they were prophetic.

Which still left any number of options. Coulda been coppers. Coulda been some of her boss's rivals, or even his own guys keeping tabs. Hell, coulda been a couple of jilted suitors for all I knew.

Or for all I cared, really. I reached into my coat, put a finger on the butt of the L&G, and threw a couple quick thoughts their way. The palooka in the car dropped his cigarette butt and scrambled to grab it before it singed the leather, and the guy with the paper got real interested in a tomato in a tight skirt strutting past him on the sidewalk. I was across the street, up the steps, and through the front door before either of 'em turned blinkers back to the tenement.

I probably hadn't even hadda do that much, since I had no reason to suspect they'd have the first notion who I was. I'd probably have been just another fella heading on home or visiting a pal. But why take the chance?

Plus, it'd given me an opportunity to stretch the old magical muscles. I was still leery, what with the bad luck I'd been having, and...

Say... Could this be her? Had she put some sorta hex on me? It wouldn't be the first time, though the last witch who'd tried it was a damn sight more powerful than the lady about to get an *aes sidhe* house call.

I mostly dismissed the notion soon as it occurred to me. I didn't think she had that kinda power, and given how we'd parted ways last time, I'm pretty sure she was too scared to try.

Mostly. I kept it in the back of my mind, even as I knocked on the door.

Her "Yes? Who is it?" was only slightly muffled by the wood.

"Bumpy sent me."

The door swung open—real trusting for a gangster's moll, even one who dabbled in the "dark arts"—and there she stood, staring at me, peepers gone wide and skin turning whiter than a polar bear eating rice.

"Hiya, Gina."

"Oh, God..."

"Nah. 'Mr. Oberon' is fine. Appreciate the thought, though. Mind if I come in?"

Not that she coulda stopped me. She'd actually staggered back three or four steps, and woulda fallen if she hadn't thumped hard into the edge of a coffee table. It'd probably leave a bruise. I don't think she even noticed.

She hadn't changed since I'd seen her last, 'cept she was dressed a lot more casually. Blonde, thin little thing with a bright smile—when she was smiling, anyway.

Right now, she wasn't smiling so much as gasping in terror.

I revised my estimation from "Probably didn't hex me" to "No way in hell."

"Breathe," I told her, shuttin' the door behind me. "You're about six heartbeats from fainting."

"I didn't do anything I swear I didn't. You told me to stay out of your world and I have, I been telling Bumpy to stay out too I promise I—"

"Whoa! Slow down, doll. I ain't here to hurt you."

Then I noticed that she wasn't randomly edging and clutching her way around the table. Panicked as she was, she was clear-headed enough to keep a goal in mind.

"Though if you take one more step toward the blower," I said, glancing meaningfully at the phone, "that could change real quick."

She froze.

"Better." I took off my flogger and draped it over one of the coat hooks by the entrance. "Gina, grab a seat before you fall over. I promise, I'm just here to talk."

She sat.

And I couldn't help but smile.

"You ain't really cut out for this business, are you?"

"I was when it was just a few protective charms, or reading the cards to tell Mr. Scola if a job was a good idea or not."

"Before me, you mean?"

Gina nodded once, then shrank back as if worried I might take offense.

"Trust me, babe, it was never just me. If you knew the sorta mojo Fino Ottati had access to... Well, that ain't here nor there." I pulled out a chair and sat down across from her, trying to decide the best way to tackle this.

All right, quick refresher. Gina was a witch, though not exactly a potent one, in the employ of one "Bumpy" Vince Scola. Scola was the *capo* of his own crew, and one of Fino Ottati's biggest rivals in the Outfit.

Fino has a *lot* of rivals, come to think of it, Outfit and

otherwise. Cost of doin' business in his, uh, business, I suppose.

Anyway, last time we'd met, Gina and some of Scola's boys had come real near to getting in so far over their heads they were getting shoe prints in their hair. I'd made it clear in the nicest way possible—by which I mean I hadn't croaked any of 'em or used their minds as bongos—that they didn't want any further part of Chicago's supernatural community.

Judging by her reaction to seeing my puss in her doorway, Gina'd taken me seriously. Smart girl.

Probably wisest to just get right to the point, then. Get in, get out, not drag her any deeper in when she'd tried to keep out.

"I'm lookin' for someone who makes a habit of snatching some pretty select merchandise. Talismans, relics, anything with a legit occult pedigree. Rap on the streets is that you lost something that answers to that description."

Then, when she hesitated and her expression started goin' a bit wild again, "Gina, I appreciate the instinct as much as the next guy. Right now, though? You wanna protect yourself, you do it by singing, not clamming up on me. For a whole number of reasons."

"I... take your point. Yes. I'd recently gotten my hands on an old grimoire. Nothing of any *real* power, nothing you'd have heard of, but enough to enhance some of my spells, maybe make me a little more of a player.

"Not—not to challenge you or your people," she clarified quickly. "Just, I thought I maybe ought to get better at protecting me and mine, you know?"

If she felt the need to tell me at every step of the way that she wasn't my enemy and wasn't trying to be, this was gonna take all day.

"Yeah, makes sense. I take it you didn't get to keep your new book for long?"

"I still don't know how they did it," the witch confessed. "It took me *weeks* of constant searching to find anyone who had one and was willing to sell, and then it was gone ten days later. Bump—that is, Mr. Scola's always got a guy watching my place, and he swears he never saw anyone suspicious. Though I guess he wouldn't really know what 'suspicious' looked like in this situation."

*A guy, huh? Interesting.* That could mean at least one of the two ginks outside was here on someone else's say-so. Not my circus for the moment, though.

"Any idea who mighta wanted it?" I asked. "Maybe the seller decided to take it back and keep the dough?"

Gina rested her hands on the table and stared off into nothing—specifically the nothing over my left shoulder.

"I shouldn't think so. The man I bought from is... reputable, in my circles. And I can't think of anyone else who'd particularly want this grimoire, or even could've known I had it!"

I figure anyone who knew anyone who knew anyone she asked during her search coulda learned she had it, but I kept my head closed on that one. No sense making her feel any more of a bunny about it unless I couldn't stir up any other leads.

"The police *were* in here briefly," she admitted after thinking on it. "Several of Mr. Scola's places got raided or searched a few days after I got the book. Just one of those things you gotta put up with now and again. But they only took a quick look around, since most people think I'm just some crook's skirt, you know? Far as I could tell, none of them found it, and I don't figure they'd have known what it was even if they had."

"You're probably right." And she was, too; a police raid wasn't a probable source of the leak. I'd keep it in the back of my noggin, though, since it wasn't impossible, either. "What about a rival? Sounds as though a skilled practitioner probably wouldn't go outta his way to get hold of your grimoire, but what about an up-and-comer? Any new witches or warlocks in town you know of?"

I could see—and even taste—her indecision as to whether or

not she oughta take offense at that, before she decided, nah, it was a pretty accurate assessment.

"I haven't heard of any. But," she admitted, "that doesn't mean a whole lot. We don't necessarily go around announcing ourselves, and I don't have the power to just 'sense' someone unless they're real careless, making a whole lot of noise."

So, this was all real fascinating, except the parts that weren't, but it didn't seem to be gettin' me any nearer to an answer. Time to change tacks.

"You're a witch."

Gina blinked at me. "Good of you to notice."

"What I mean is, if you dunno who took your spellbook, why not do some magics to locate it?"

She smiled—a sad, limp expression with nothin' pleasant behind it.

"Don't you think that was the first thing I tried, Mr. Oberon? I even tore part of a page out of the grimoire—blank, I assure you—when I acquired the damn thing, so I'd have a focus if I ever had to ward it or scry for it. Whoever's got it hid it, though, and they're a better practitioner than I am. Not that that's real difficult, I guess. I've tried three different times, but I just don't have what it takes."

Yeah, in case you're wondering, I *did* feel sorry for her. Poor girl'd found a talent that made her stand out, made her important, and then learned the hard way—multiple times—that she was a teeny fish in a deep and *very* dark pond, and was never gonna be anything more'n that.

I didn't guess she'd appreciate hearing that from me, though, and she sure didn't need her confidence shook any more'n it already was.

"I think I got us a way around that," I said instead.

*That* got her attention.

"Oh?"

"Sounds to me as if you need some extra mojo and a lot of extra luck."

"Uh, well, yeah."

I slowly—no need to spook her again—drew my wand from under my coat.

"Guess what I'm real good at providing?"

For the first time since I'd showed up at her place, her smile felt genuine.

# CHAPTER SIX

"So why're you searching for this 'talisman thief,' anyway?" Gina asked me a while later.

"'Cause I dunno where he is."

"Ah. Right."

I'll say this for the baby witch. She'd been working with the trouble boys long enough to know when a wise-ass comment meant "Stop askin' questions."

We were sittin' at her table again after forty minutes of gathering gewgaws and whatsises from around Gina's place. A bowl, a tiny mortar and pestle, some rose petals, a silver chain, chunk of quartz, buncha other ingredients and components and whatnot. Centered in the middle of it all was a scrap of old paper with nothin' written on it, nothin' to make it stand out, except it had sort of picked up a tang that didn't belong to it. You ever keep a couple fruits too close together and one adopts the other's flavor? (No, I don't eat fruit—not in your world, anyway—but I do talk to people, and guess what? Most people eat.) Like that, but with magic instead of flavor.

So, I ain't gonna bother talkin' through the whole rigmarole, see? There was chanting in three different languages, there was burning of this and stirring of that, dripping oils into water, and more or less a bunch of rituals that may or may not actually've been necessary. Through it all I had the L&G out and aimed, carefully drawing currents of luck and magic from our surroundings—never enough from any one spot to cause problems—and carefully feeding it to Gina, layering it on top of her aura so she could draw on it as if it were her own.

Then a china cup-and-saucer toppled from an open cabinet where it shoulda been secure, shattering into a psychotic jigsaw puzzle, startlin' the hell outta both of us and queering the whole effort so we hadda start over from scratch.

More of that free-floating bad luck I told you about. That was starting to get aggravating, I don't mind saying.

Once I'd explained it to Gina—I wasn't real comfortable doing that, but I didn't have much choice if it was gonna be interfering with us working magic together—she tossed a couple quick charms at me. They mighta been helpful if I'd been a human having a normal run of misfortune, but since I wasn't, they weren't. Nice of her to try, though. And then we started all over.

When all was finally said and done, I'd stripped enough luck from her apartment that she'd need to walk on eggshells for the next day or two, since the tiniest bump or trip would probably cause something or other to collapse. But it'd worked; I'd fed her enough mojo to punch through whatever protections Ramona—or whoever, but c'mon—had raised to keep herself hidden. Gina, forehead glinting with sweat, handed over the quartz, which was now wrapped up in one end of the silver chain.

"Whenever you need to get your bearings," she told me, "hold the chain in your left hand and spin the crystal widdershins. Uh, that's counterclockwise."

I'm pretty sure my face was so still I didn't actually *have* an expression when I looked back at her.

"I'm a goddamn *aes sidhe*, doll. I know what the fuck widdershins means. We invented the concept."

"Um. Okay." Then, with reluctance thick enough to lie

down and nap on, "So, what do we...? I mean, should I bring...? Where...?"

"Forget it, sister. No way are you comin' with me. I appreciate your help, but you did your job. You're out."

She argued with me a minute, mostly because she felt like she should. Her relief when I refused to take her along was intense.

"I'd lie dormy a few days if I were you," I said as I got up to dust out. "Ain't any reason the people I'm gunning for should know to look you up, but better safe. Oh, speakin' of..." I didn't want to spook her any more'n she already was, but it'd be pretty low not to give her a head's up. "You said Bumpy had a guy watching your place?"

"All the time, at least when I'm home. Why?"

"'Cause you got *two* of them out there right now." Then, when she started to pale again, "I don't guess it's got anything to do with me or your occult practices. Didn't get any sense of that from 'em. I figure it's either the law or one of your boss's rivals. Have him look into it, maybe."

I didn't really care to answer any more questions about it, especially since I didn't *know* anything more about it. I'd collected my coat and was almost out the door when I remembered one last thing that *I* really oughta ask *her*. Dammit.

"Say, I don't suppose you got a spell available to you that'd let you pick out a shapeshifter hiding behind somebody else's mug, do you?"

"Pick out a... You mean those are *real*? Some of you can actually do that?"

Right. So much for that, then. I told her to keep herself safe, stuck the crystal dingus in a flogger pocket, and blew the joint.


Hey, whaddaya know? More hoofin' it block after block. More planting my keister on the L and letting it trundle me across town, tryin' to ignore the buzz of technology scratching like a starving cat in the back of my melon. More apartment buildings. I felt like a tourist without a guidebook.

But yeah, Gina's dingus worked. Every time I spun it, it'd stop short, pointing the same way. I hadda circle back around a few times, since the trains sometimes didn't run in precisely the right direction and I didn't figure folks'd appreciate me traipsing through their houses, but eventually it did lead me on to yet another tenement.

And for a spell, no pun intended, I wondered if maybe the pendant hadn't worked as well as it seemed. I didn't know Ramona as well as it felt like I did, but I'da wagered a pretty thick wad of kale that she'd never bunk in a place as rundown and dingy as this one. It was only about two steps up from the slum Lenai'd gone to ground in. If this building'd been in any more of a shambles, the rat droppings would've been load-bearing.

Then again, it *was* the last place anyone'd look for her— whether they knew her as Ramona Webb, or just as "that person what snatches magic trinkets."

The next spin ended with the quartz not just pointing forward but slightly up, so I pointed my Oxfords toward the stairs. A gaunt, pasty-faced gink was smokin' a butt in the stairwell, turning the whole thing into a stinky chimney. He glared at me. I glared back, lettin' enough of the real me show in my peepers until he dropped his cigarette and bolted, whimpering.

What can I say? I've had more'n enough years to perfect the art of being petty. I stomped out the cherry-glow of the ember on my way; that counts for something, don't it?

Fourth floor: men's shoes, polish brushes, the stench of poverty, and *femmes fatales*. Everybody out.

I was fairly sure from the minute I left the stairwell that she wasn't home; I think I'd have sensed her if she were that close. When I got to her door, or at least what my spinning crystal guide told me was her door, I was damn near positive.

I dropped to one knee to get a good slant on the lock and, oh, yeah, this was the right place. She'd made a pretty good effort to stain and score the brass, so it looked a lot rougher'n it was, but the quality of the lock was way too high for a garbage dump like this place.

The teeny Aramaic, Latin, and even Enochian glyphs etched into the brass were something of a clue, too.

Under normal circumstances, the lock woulda been eggs in the coffee. I ain't come across one yet I couldn't get through with the right juggling of luck inside the tumblers. Those wards made it tougher, by a lot. I'd have to slowly draw the magic out of 'em, layer by layer, peepers peeled the whole time in case some of 'em were designed to react to exactly that sorta tampering. Plus I hadda figure out what kinds of energies were involved, whether it was safe to just pump 'em back out into the air and let 'em dissipate or if they needed more ornate methods. In a perfect world, I'd scribe some counter-runes over 'em, maybe surround the whole thing in protective circles of salt or whatnot. Even without those precautions, though, it'd be doable, just painstaking, nervous work.

Notice that real important key phrase, though? "Under normal circumstances." Even for me, nothin' about today qualified as normal, not with that haze of bad luck that'd been clinging to and sucking on me like a leech. A leech made of... haze... Okay, that one got away from me. You get what I mean, though.

At this point, some of you are wonderin' why I hadn't taken any steps to shake it off. Truth was, I *had* made a couple gestures in that direction. Handful of salt over my shoulder after the first couple days, wanderin' clockwise around Mr. Soucek's building one morning with my shirt inside-out—and lemme tell you, that ain't a comfortable thing for the Fae to do, either—stuff like that. And if this'd just been a typical run of misfortune, that woulda fixed it right up. We may get stronger "streaks" than you do, good or bad, but it's still chance; just a tad less random.

But that *hadn't* fixed it, which was more evidence—still

not *proof*, but gettin' there—that I was laboring under some sorta hex. And if *that* were the case, no way did I wanna try countering it with magic until I had a better idea what it was. There's about a zillion different traditions of magic out there, human and Fae both, and every one of 'em has multiple ways of giving someone a rough time. Use the wrong sorta mojo tryin' to fix it, you risk makin' it worse. And I simply hadn't had the time to investigate it, not with everything else goin' on.

But with the interruption of Gina's scrying spell, and the necessity of dealing with these friggin' wards, it had now become less an irritation than a genuine threat. Maybe I couldn't shrug it off, but it was time to devote some real effort to mitigating it.

And hey, what'd I have right in front of my mug but a whole damn reservoir of mystic energies that I hadda put *somewhere*. Two birds, one stone.

I drew the L&G, jabbed it against the lock like I was tryin' to stab it into opening, and started—real slow and real careful— to siphon the magic.

Can't say how long it took, but I know it hadda be at least fifteen minutes. Slow, gradual, like removing the rind from an entire watermelon with a potato peeler. Tiny slivers of magic, sliced right off the top, fed through the wand and into my own essence where I transformed 'em into tiny puffs of good fortune to smother the stains of bad luck infusing my aura... Yeah. Tough to explain in terms that have any meaning to you, but you get the gist.

On the square, I don't even know for sure what the wards woulda done if I'd triggered 'em. Cursed me? Alerted Ramona from wherever she was? Blown up the apartment in a burst of profane fire? I was too focused on suckin' 'em dry without settin' 'em off to really sniff out their nature. I was curious, sure, but not so curious it was worth interrupting what I was doing.

I *thought* I got lucky, that the fortune I was manufacturing from the shreds of magic in the lock kept me from bein' spotted by anyone on the floor, despite how long the damn process took. Turned out not to quite be the case, but I'll come back around to that.

Finally, after however long, the glyphs gave up the last of their mojo with a sorta protesting hiccup and the lock just smelled of brass and old oil and steel springs. I took a sec to unknot some mental muscles, zapped the lock with the wand so the tumblers broke down, and walked in like I owned the place.

And then took a few just to stare, try to take in what I was seein', as the apartment reminded me real firmly that I did *not*, in fact, own the place.

I'd fully expected the inside to be a lot nicer'n than the outside, see? I knew Ramona wasn't gonna live in the kinda squalor implied by the rest of the building. This, though? This went beyond "nicer" and plunged straight into the heart of "you gotta be kidding me!"

The lingering scent of fine incense and perfumes was one thing; I wouldn't have wanted to smell the rest of the building, or the corpses of a few hundred dead cigarettes, either. But beyond that? Mink carpeting. Silk curtains. Crystal chandelier. Fine china and polished silver settings on antique furniture. Quick glimpse through one door revealed a massive full-canopy bed with honest-to-Dagda gold caps on the posts.

Beyond luxurious, this was. Opulent, excessively so. Frankly, it disturbed me more'n a little; this was a side of Ramona I hadn't seen and didn't much care for.

Because of that, it took me a minute to recognize some other important signs. That chandelier in the main room? Only electric light in the place; the bedroom and bathroom had candles, just waitin' to be lit. No radio, just a hand-cranked phonograph. The apartment *did* have a phone, but it was off in a corner in the kitchen, far from the bedroom as you could get and still be inside the apartment.

Well, okay, I'd already supposed Ramona wasn't human, especially after discovering Carmen McCall had the same magics, but corroborating evidence never hurt any. Neither that, nor critiquing her interior decorating—however much it wanted critiquing—was why I'd come, though.

There was no real point in tryin' to hide that someone had been here; she'd be able to tell that much soon as she discovered the broken wards on the door. But I didn't see any sense in wreckin' the place, either. Might as well try to minimize how steamed she was gonna get when she discovered the B-and-E. So I started my search real careful, rifling through the wardrobe without pulling anything out, digging through drawers with everything in place rather than emptying 'em, that sorta thing.

I shouldn't have bothered. She hadn't even gotten around to puttin' the damn thing away yet.

I found Gina's missing grimoire buried in a heap of papers on the end table beside the bed. Seemed kinda careless to me at first, but I guess Ramona'd figured that her wards were security enough. Guess in most cases they woulda been.

It wasn't much as magic tomes go, pretty beginner-level stuff, but that made sense. I stuck the grimoire in a pocket, to decide later if I was actually gonna return it or not. Nah, it wasn't that potent, but I wasn't entirely sure I wanted Gina learning *anything* more'n she already knew. Right now, she was smart enough to keep outta mystical goings-on that didn't concern her; gaining even a little new power might change that.

But as I said, I'd decide later. Right now I hadda find the lady of the house herself.

The rest of the papers didn't tell me much. Few days' worth of newsrags, some bills addressed to a couple different names I'd never heard. (Figured 'em for Ramona's aliases.) A few scraps and envelopes with notes penciled on 'em. Those had some potential, but I couldn't make head nor tail of 'em. Some were names, or times, or addresses, but none matched up. Without context, there was no real way to know what any of 'em meant, or how significant they were. Certainly not enough to tell me who she was working for, or what she was working on, or where she was, or, well, much of anything at all useful.

I stopped and went back to a couple of 'em more than once, though. Something about the handwriting... It wasn't Ramona's, but I had this nagging in the back of my noggin that I'd seen it before.

Gah! This was more frustrating than if I'd found nothin'. What little I had wouldn't have been enough to recognize even if I'd known the writer real well. If it was just somebody's scribbling I'd seen in passing? I could sit here noodling over these broken scrawls from now until doomsday and never come up with a name.

Goddamn it.

I was just deciding that I had no options but to settle in and wait for her to come home—however long that might take— when the front door drifted open with a low, furtive creak.

And yes, a furtive creak sounds different than a normal creak. Just trust me on this.

Even if it hadn't, though, I'da known it wasn't Ramona. The emotions pourin' off the guy like a fever sweat were clearly masculine. The gink was absolutely furious, terrified, obsessed to a scary degree, and lusty as an adolescent satyr.

"I know you're in here, you fucking bastard!" Something *whooshed* through the air, followed by a loud and teeth-jarring crash.

Terrific.

I dropped the papers back on the nightstand and stepped out into the main room—a room that was now decorated with the shards of what used to be a fairly nice picture frame.

"What'd that glass ever do to you?" I asked him.

He was unshaven, unshowered, and smelled like a laundry hamper. His current wardrobe was an undershirt and slacks, shoes without socks, and a baseball bat with some brand-new shards of glass stickin' out of it.

"You can't have her! You can't fucking have her! She's mine! *Mine!*"

"Well, long as we're gonna be reasonable about this..."

He charged me, shrieking, glass crunching underfoot, bat raised overhead.

*Aw, Ramona, what'd you do to this poor dumb sap?*

I stepped into his lunge, grabbin' the bat in one fist just above his grip. Swept one foot out and back, stomping on the inside of his knee. He went down; the bat stayed up. Then, since I had it anyway, I swept it back toward him, smacking the back of his conk with the butt. Not all that hard, but enough to put him on his face on the carpet, rather than on his knees.

I turned, tossed the bat over one shoulder, reached down and flipped him over like a pancake so he was starin' up at me. Then it was just a matter of divin' in through his peepers like they were a swimming pool. Wasn't quite the duck soup it shoulda been—in addition to being royally scrambled by Ramona's magic, the guy was so sloshed on cheap hooch you coulda gotten lit off a fifth of his sweat; so his thoughts were a bit harder to sort than normal. Try to imagine shufflin' a deck with cards made outta onion skin. Still, it only took a moment or two.

Look, I ain't gonna repeat the conversation verbatim, okay? Even with me in his head, he spent way too much breath rantin' and ravin' about Ramona, how much he loved her, how it was only a matter of time before she gave herself to him, how me'n all the other guys who wanted her were flat-out goofy for even thinkin' we hadda chance but he was still gonna beat us bloody, etcetera and so on. I ain't got the stomach for quoting all that. So you get the summary.

Thank me later.

Obviously, Ramona can't have this effect on anyone and everyone nearby; if she did, it'd be impossible to hide. So I wasn't surprised when Mr. Smitten admitted to me that she stopped to jaw with him regularly—never for very long, just a quick "Hi, how ya doin'?" but that was more'n enough for her to do her thing. Long as she touched it up every now'n again, she had the guy wrapped so tight around her finger she coulda had him set with a diamond.

Odds are he wasn't the only one, either. I wasn't gonna take the time to confirm it, but she probably had half the hallway swept off their feet. Made sense, really. If you're gonna be in and out at all hours, movin' stolen goods, meeting with God knows who, you can try to hide all that from the neighbors— probably without much success in a tenement where the walls are fingernail-thin and the rats can be bribed—or, if you happen to have the ability, you can bind 'em to you with mystical fishhooks through their hormones, and not *have* to hide.

And no, before you even stoop to askin', I wasn't jealous of the attention (however twisted) she was payin' these mugs. Not remotely jealous.

Not jealous.

(And if I *had* been, it wouldn'ta been my fault, anyway. Just so's we're clear.)

So of course, I grilled him about the last time they'd booshwashed, if she'd said anything about where she might be goin'. He hadn't wanted to spill—which was less about protectin' her, I suspect, than about not wanting to tell one of his "rivals" how to find her—but I was already in his head, so it didn't take long to pry it outta him.

She'd been on her way out, just that mornin'. And in exchanging the usual pleasantries, she'd told him she was off to a day at the fair.

Well. Well, well, well now.

Chicago had more'n a few, of course, little festivals and traveling carnivals and all that, but usually not *too* many at any one time—especially these days, as I think I mentioned earlier. I told my reluctant stoolie to take a long nap, wandered back into the bedroom, and checked the newspapers again. Sure enough, an older one—from a few weeks back—had been opened to a page that included an ad for one of those traveling carnies, listing its dates of operation, hours, all that good stuff.

She hadn't left it open on that page, but it ain't just my peepers, ears, and scnozz that're keener than yours. I could feel in the folds where the paper'd been left open a lot or flipped back to a lot. Sure, that wasn't proof that she was goin' to *this* particular fair, but it was a pretty solid sign.

But none of that mattered. I'd hadda pretty solid guess which carnival she was goin' to from the instant I'd heard the word, see? All this diggin' through papers and all was just me confirming what I already knew.

I knew, because I'd been there a few days before. Because I never had sussed out why Shea's Uptown Boys had had the slightest interest in a cheap amusement park, never had figured what connection they had with Hruotlundt or the rest of Chicago's nonhuman community.

But if Ramona was lookin' into a carnival, too? Nope, I wasn't about to buy *that* as a coincidence. There was somethin' hinky about that carnie, and I wanted to know what—and I particularly wanted to know if it had anything to do with whoever was lookin' into me'n Ramona both.

I coulda just settled in and waited for her to come home, of course, but that wouldn'ta gotten me a look at whatever was goin' down out there. So, pleased as punch that I might finally be on the verge of some answers, I headed back for the parklands off the shores of Lake Michigan.

# CHAPTER SEVEN

Had me some time to ruminate on the L, during my ride over, but I was still comin' up empty. I just couldn't figure why Shea—or his boss, Fleischer—would have much interest in a podunk carnival, leastaways not one so far south in enemy territory. And any ideas that seemed even vaguely possible didn't explain Ramona's interest. Nah, it hadda be something more occult than criminal, but what?

Yeah, I was about to find out, but I hate goin' into a situation blind.

Was comin' up on late afternoon by the time I finally made my way to the front gate, idly wondering if any of the Uptown Boys were back up on that hilltop, keepin' a slant on the place. All the greasepaint and sweat and manure, helium and oil, sweets and slow rot, spun and twisted around each other like partners on the dance floor, mixing to create an atmosphere you just don't find anywhere else. Balloons bobbed above the heads of the listless crowds, occasionally escapin' to go drifting off to wherever they were destined to end up. (A small portion of 'em wouldn't come back down to earth anywhere in *your* world.)

Kids skittered all around me, dressed for a day out, parents chasin' after 'em with a lot less enthusiasm. Thankfully, whenever I almost got used to the shouting and screeching, the carnie's pipe organ burst out with the shrieks of the damned cleverly disguised as music, just to make sure I couldn't get too comfortable. My dogs stuck to the ground every fifth or sixth step, and I decided I was happier just assuming it was due to spilled soft drinks and lost tufts of cotton candy. The other possibilities didn't bear much thinking on.

You know what, though? I'll give the place this much: set up here, near some of Chicago's less hoity-toity neighborhoods, the carnival was a lot more mixed than a lotta the city's other entertainments. Children black, white, and various shades in between ran and played together without much care, and if some of the adults occasionally cast a few suspicious glances when they thought nobody'd notice, at least they were all civil about it.

Yeah. Welcome to "Rounser's Remarkable Fun Fair and Excellent Exhibition." I had no notion who Rounser was, but I gotta say he had a more generous definition of "remarkable" and "excellent" than I did.

I wandered through the gates, poured my handful of change into the waiting palm of a barker who was either too young for his beard or too old for the rest of his face, and just set my Oxfords to wandering. I didn't really have anywhere specific to look, so I waded through a shallow ford in the stream of kids, dodged one kiosk where a perky brunette sold candy at a markup that woulda made Capone cry robbery, slipped beside another where they were takin' song requests for the band organ, nearly socked a horrific and phantasmal face leering at me outta the shadows until I realized it was a clown (and then nearly socked him again because I'd realized it was a clown), and finally found myself in a tiny pocket of peace and relative quiet, beneath a heavy banner swayin' gently in the lake-blown breeze.

At which point I looked up and actually *read* the banner.

"Aw, fuck."

See, I'd never gotten anywhere near enough to see the signs on my first visit. I was too busy chattin' with Nolan Shea, and also not having the slightest inkling the carnival mattered. And on my way in today? I'm sure they *had* banners up out front, since this was obviously their main attraction, but I'd missed 'em. Just chance, I guess. I'd wandered in at the wrong angle, or I'd been distracted by the crowd. Now, though? Now it was emblazoned overhead like the word of God Him-, Her-, or Themselves.

"*THE DUSTY TOMBS OF FORGOTTEN DYNASTIES OFFER UP THEIR SECRETS!!*" it said. "*COMMUNE WITH A GOD-KING FROM THE DAYS OF ANCIENT EGYPT!! WITNESS ONE WHO WATCHED THE BIRTH OF CIVILIZATION WITH HIS OWN 2 EYES!!*"

Then, in much smaller print, "Bring the family! Educational and fun for kids, all for less than you'd pay for a day at the museum! Only at Rounser's Remarkable Fun Fair and Excellent Exhibition's Funhouse of Mystery!"

They had a mummy. This rundown, flea speck of a sideshow carnie had a goddamn mummy.

Didn't know they did that? Yep. Respect for the dead's nifty and all, but it don't pay. Some of Egypt's preserved dead got lucky; once their burial treasures'd been raided, they at least got sold to this museum or that private collector. Sure, they'd be displayed like something from a tourist gift shop, but they were reasonably well preserved and often stored alongside some of the riches that'd been theirs in life and afterlife.

Others, though? Well, if they weren't sold as kindling—yes, really; kindling—a few ended up as attractions in traveling fairs and funhouses. Offered a nice touch of spooky atmosphere, something to chill the onlookers just enough to tell their friends and maybe sell another fucking ticket.

Some carnivals pretended to have 'em and didn't, of course; just more fakery and sleight-of-hand, another con in a long line. But Rounser's? Had too many peepers on it—some of which belonged to people who knew their stuff—for it to be a sham. There was a genuine mummy here, and both Ramona's and Shea's bosses clearly believed it still had some power or value to it.

And hey... That might explain somethin' else, too. This wasn't the only mummy in town; the Field had a new Egyptology display that included a couple. But those didn't have any lingering mojo, or at least not enough to reach beyond the walls of the museum.

If this one did, though? Well, some of that power might be in the form of a curse. Yeah, mummy's curses are real, though not exactly common. And if most but not all of that curse had faded over the centuries, there might not be enough left to pester you lugs—but some of us Fae, with our sensitivity to luck and magic? Yeah, the last fading echoes of a curse might, just might, explain the run of misfortune I'd been having lately.

Seemed as though this desiccated corpse might hold the answers to a whole variety of questions. If nothing else, I needed the chance to give it the up-and-down before Ramona or Shea or whoever else tried to make off with the damn thing. It mighta still held traces of genuine Egyptian magics; *heka* they called it. Or it coulda had old spells or occult knowledge written in the wrappings; that was a pretty common part of the ritual. Or, or, or. Without knowing *why* they wanted it, or what sorta power or secrets it held, I wasn't real inclined to let it fall into *anyone's* hands, and this place sure didn't have even the mundane security of the Field, let alone defenses against more magically inclined thieves.

Casually, tryin' to make it look like I was just idly wandering and taking in the sights, I started making my way toward a funhouse I didn't honestly figure was gonna be much fun at all.

As far as what happened next, I'm gonna make some excuses for myself. I was focused so hard my thoughts were aching and my brow was furrowed so deep my skull almost folded. I was casting out in all directions for the slightest feel or mystical "scent" of Ramona, or anyone else who mighta been packing magic heat, while also keepin' on guard, ready to push back against the first hint that she was plucking at my emotions. I knew what kinda power she held, what kinda effect she had on me, and no way was I gonna let myself get empathically bushwhacked. *And* I was working at staying inconspicuous in the process, which don't exactly come easy when you're a lone grown man in a greatcoat at a carnival fulla kids and families.

In other words, I was a touch preoccupied.

If it'd been an attack of some sort, it woulda caught me square on. Since it *wasn't* an attack, I only almost jumped outta my skin when the call rang out, "Come, stranger! Vould you gaze into your future and see vhat destiny has in store for you?"

She was addressing me, specifically. I dunno how barkers and showmen do it, somehow "aiming" their voice through a milling crowd, but the experienced ones somehow pull it off. Guess I coulda ignored it, but I'd already turned to look despite myself.

Short. I dunno why that was my first impression of her, especially since she was behind a kiosk, and sittin' on a stool to boot, but it was. Dusky skin, Mediterranean if I wasn't totally daffy, dark eyes, black hair tied up in something between a normal scarf and a babushka. She also wore heavy kohl around her eyes, lipstick so bright it looked like she'd smooched a wet stop sign, and enough gaudy rings I was amazed she could bend her fingers.

She was also a lot younger'n she was tryin' to look, and pretty behind that mask of showmanship; surprisingly so, the sorta pretty that sneaks up on you, takes a second look to notice but then won't let you forget it.

"Come!" she called, once she'd seen her pitch'd snagged my attention. "Come and let Madame Tsura impart her visdom. You... you..."

Her lips kept movin' but the only sound was a tiny squeak. Cheap brass clattered and gouged furrows into the wood of the kiosk as she clutched at it to keep from toppling over.

Me, my shoulders went tight as a snare drum. Oh, yeah, I knew that expression. I'd seen it before, most recently on Gina's face a few months back. And I was startin' to get downright irritable about how many people in this friggin' town knew I was more'n just some average Joe.

Muttering under my breath, I made my way over.

The kiosk was even gaudier than she was, painted in bright colors and designs meant to look exotic without actually meaning anything about anything. It was only just starting to peel, too. The curtains were velveteen, a sorta pinkish-purple, I guess intended to enhance the idea that "Madame Tsura" could see into the fuchsia.

I'm so sorry I even said that. Too much time hangin' around with Pete.

"All right, toots." I leaned in, elbows on the counter where the cards or crystal ball would normally go. "Spin me a tale."

"I don't... I've never seen anything like..."

"Is this part of the act? Does it cost extra for punctuation or somethin'?"

"Who *are* you? *What* are you?"

"Careful, doll. Your accent's slipping."

Somehow, despite her shock and behind her stage makeup, she blushed.

"I'm not actually a gypsy," she admitted.

"No kidding. The Roma would laugh at you."

"Yeah. It's embarrassing, really, but..." She shrugged.

"But it's what the rubes expect."

"Something like that."

I studied her, lookin' past the makeup, not that I had to. I could taste the tang of history around her, the weight of civilization.

"Greek?"

She didn't seem surprised.

"Guessin' your real name ain't 'Tsura,' then. Madame or otherwise."

No doubt about it now. She blushed redder than the rouge on her cheeks.

"I just go by Tsura these days."

"Uh-uh. You're the one who—"

"Hey! You! Yeah, you, pal!"

I sighed, pretty much for her benefit.

"Speaking of rubes... Excuse me a minute."

Then I turned to face the gink who'd shouted at me. He was a burly fellow, round-faced and red-haired, with two equally round-faced and red-haired brats. Each of 'em clung to one of his hands with one of their own, stuffing wads of cotton candy into their traps with the other.

"Speed it up, would ya?" he demanded. "My kids wanna get their fortunes told already!"

I stared at him. Down at the kids. Back up at him. Finally back down at the boy, pushing a sliver of power through his blinkers and into his thoughts, just enough to give an extra nudge of motivation to what would probably've gotten him all riled up anyway.

And then I said, "Isn't your sister's cotton candy bigger than yours?"

When they finally faded from sight in the crowd, dad—his coat now well-smeared with sugary strands—was still strugglin' to drag both of them along while also straight-arming 'em enough that neither could reach the other, and going hoarse trying to shout over the boy's banshee-esque screeching, the girl's wails, and the roar of the throng around 'em. Poor sap didn't even have the effort to spare to glare back at me.

"Right. Where were we?"

Tsura, or whatever her name was, was doin' the "jaw-gaping" thing again, so she probably wasn't gonna be much help answering that question.

It was weird. She obviously knew I'd done something more'n just talked to the kid, but she just as obviously didn't have a good grasp of what. Awareness, maybe even power, but not a lotta knowledge. The hell was I dealin' with here?

And why'd it have to crop up *now*, when I had seven-hundred-and-four other things to worry about?

"Oh, yeah. You're the one called me over here," I reminded her. "Why'd you pick me?"

"It wasn't... I just call to people in the crowd."

"Nope. Ain't that simple. Never is, with me. Why?"

"I just... felt I should. That's usually how it wor— I mean, how I do it. Something about you called to me."

"Great. Calling all around, then. Point is, I'm here 'cause you wanted me here. So your name ain't too much to ask, is it?"

"Fedora," she mumbled, apparently to her feet more'n to me.

"Okay."

Oh, *now* she was lookin' at me again.

"No jokes? No wise-ass comments?"

"It's a perfectly good Greek name. Pretty traditional, ain't it?"

"I could kiss you! *Nobody* here knows that! My parents named me soon after they passed through Ellis Island, long before they actually assimilated. They had no idea—"

"That it was a hat?"

"Well, yeah."

This was takin' too long. I kept smiling, but it felt stiff.

"So, look, Fedora—"

"I still prefer Tsura, though."

*Oh, for...* "Fine. Tsura. You need to spill. Why'd you pick me? How'd you know there's somethin' different about me?"

"I told you, though!" She waved her arms, catching the curtains with a dull *flump*. "I just get hunches. Almost whims."

Well, I sure couldn't cast the first stone where *that* sin was concerned.

"And I just... know things," she continued. "That's gonna have to do you. It's a long story you wouldn't believe anyway."

Yeah, I wouldn't be too sure of that, sister. She wasn't wrong, though. It *was* gonna have to do me; I'd already spent way too much time, gotten off-track. I was gonna have to dig into this dame, no question, but I couldn't afford to burn any more daylight on it *now*.

"Well, I appreciate the chin-wagging, Tsura. I don't think my future's any clearer'n it was when we started, but it's certainly five minutes closer. You have a good afternoon, now."

"Wait!"

I stopped but didn't turn back. "Yeah?"

"What's *your* name?" She sounded more intense, more intent, than I'd yet heard her.

And I gotta say, for a minute I wasn't real inclined to tell her. I had no good reason for it, didn't suddenly mistrust her or suspect her of anything. But I didn't know who, what, she was, what she knew or how she knew it. And it felt... heavy. Like the question was way more important than it sounded, and once it was answered, there was no goin' back, for good or ill.

But in the end, I couldn't come up with a solid answer to "Why not?" And it ain't as though my identity's some big secret.

"Oberon. Mick Oberon."

Then I *did* look back, my attention snagged by a sudden clatter. Soon as she'd gotten my name outta me, she'd ducked back inside, closing off the kiosk with a wooden shutter that had "Back Soon" scrawled across it in cheap paint.

That sorta reaction didn't exactly make me feel any better about having answered her question.

Much as I wanted to know where she was dusting off to in such a rush, though, Tsura still wasn't my priority. So, muttering to myself again and maybe not so worried anymore about seeming all casual and inconspicuous, I resumed my interrupted trudge toward the funhouse.

Wasn't difficult to find the place, and it wouldn't have been even without the half-dozen signs and a couple of bandage-wrapped dummies or scarecrows pointing the way. It was the biggest structure on the fairground that wasn't either a tent or obviously a ride of some sort. They'd put up cheap wooden siding to make the thing appear to be an actual building, rather'n a collection of large tractor trailers pushed together. Then of course they'd tried to make it look Egyptian, with a few haphazard obelisks, a pyramidal top that didn't remotely match the lower floors, and an even cheaper fake stone facing over that cheap wooden siding. The "hieroglyphics" were random scribbles and sketches, and the sphinx was a plaster lion with a crooked headdress and his snout sanded off.

On the square, I was tempted to turn around and walk away. If someone'd dug me up from my eternal rest to stick my carcass in a decrepit embarrassment of a joke like this, I'd *want* someone to come and steal me, and I don't figure I'd much care who.

And yet, there was a whole line of people waiting to get in, snaking along the path, around and between some of the other kiosks. Kids whined over how long they'd been standin' there; some of the supposed adults did, too. None of them cared how chintzy the place looked, or how goofy its attempts to even evoke, much less resemble, the real thing were. Nope. All they knew was that, inside, there were rides, and displays to spook 'em, and somewhere in the midst of it all a guy who'd been dead longer'n their religion had been alive.

You know you're all insane, right? Scrambled noggins, the lot of you. Dead body's a dead body. You got a million of 'em within spitting distance, and if someone dug one of *them* up and put it on display, you'd be screaming your guts out and callin' the cops. Let someone else unearth it, though, from far enough away, and as long as it don't stink anymore, it's a friggin' ornament.

Freaks.

But since I still didn't know why certain people wanted this particular ornament, or what power it held...

I wasn't about to stand around for an hour waitin' to get in, of course. Made a beeline for the door, figuring I'd play the

"PI on a case" card—and if that didn't work, assuming the looming bad luck didn't kick too hard, I could always head-whammy whoever was workin' the door.

"Hello, Mick."

Assuming, of course, I'd *reached* the door.

"Hey, Ramona."

"You're looking good."

"You're lookin' better." Least that got a smile outta her.

I wasn't sure where she'd come from, not that it mattered much. She'd put herself between me'n the funhouse, loitering on the edge of the path—far enough to the side for passersby to, uh, pass by, but still clearly in my way. She wore a deep green number that set off her crimson hair and really, let's say, emphasized what she wore it over. Even if she'd just been a normal broad, she'd have gotten more'n her share of appreciative looks.

Not that Ramona was a normal anything. And it was 'cause I already knew that, and was braced for it, that I wasn't totally steamrollered by what came next.

Everything I'd ever felt for her, every sappy thought and dizzy moment, flooded back over me at once. The fiery passion of a first love; the old comfort of a romance longer'n any human lifetime; the need to possess and the urge to protect, the pounding heart and the rising... pulse. Trust. Affection. Yearning. Lust. The primal core of the ultimate connection between two souls and two bodies, distilled into a wave of emotion.

I dunno if Ramona was just better at it, or if it was because of our past connection, but nothin' McCall had thrown at me could possibly compare. And I ain't just puffing myself up when I say that there aren't a lotta folks, human or Fae, who coulda stared into the face of it and not been swept away.

But I been here before, see? I knew what this was, knew what she could do. I knew how it felt, 'cause I *had* felt it—maybe not all at once like this, but heavy enough. And this was what I'd been bracin' myself for since the minute I knew Ramona was mixed up in whatever was going on, to say nothin' of how on guard I'd been since arriving here at the carnival.

So I let it wash over me, let myself feel it just around the edges so that I wasn't pushing back against the *entire* weight of that tide. And then I walked right through it.

"Not this time, dollface. Not anymore."

Maybe she coulda thrown more into it. I dunno; I got no notion of exactly how far she can push it. Then again, I still had my wand. If she wanted to escalate this, well, I could escalate right along with her.

Whether she chose not to or ran outta gas, though, she didn't. She actually smiled, and it looked genuine enough; the emotion *tasted* genuine enough. The smile, and the touch of sorrow underlying it.

"Is that all we are now, Mick? Rivals?"

"You're the one who tried to Mickey Finn me in the brain, Ramona."

"Not everything you just felt was artificial, you know."

I hadda smile back at that point.

"Been living with it for months, so yeah, I know. But if I can't quite tell how *much*, ain't sure I can trust it, whose fault is that?"

"Yeah. Sorry."

"Makes two of us."

Felt weird having this chat in public, but nobody was hearin' us too well over the noise of the carnival, or makin' much sense out of any of it if they did.

After a few long seconds of silence, she said, "I wouldn't have tried to make you do anything you wouldn't have approved of."

"Uh-huh. That's why you just asked nicely first, before you tried to—"

"I know. I *said* I was sorry."

"Yeah, you did."

It's funny, I don't think most of you woulda even noticed the change. Wasn't in her expression, wasn't in her posture, wasn't really in anything. But even before her tone changed, I knew the moment she went all business, clear as if she'd run up a flag that said so.

"What are you doing here, Mick?"

"Lookin' for you, kitten."

I hadn't yet decided if I wanted to tell her straight out about her "sister" hiring me, holding Adalina over me, or if I wanted to deal with this ostensible mummy caper first, but either way I figured I could be square with her about that much.

Now she *did* tense, a real fight-or-flight hunch of the shoulders and raising of her mitts.

"I can't let you stop me, Mick."

"Uh..."

"Christ, why do you even *want* to stop me? What's your stake in *any* of this?"

Now we *were* startin' to draw some interested peepers. People are always so damn eager for a show, even if it's two people they don't know arguin' about something they don't understand.

Keepin' my voice down as much as I could while staying sure she could hear me, I said, "Ramona, there's power in there. I got no clue what kind, or how much, but it looks like it's enough to make things tough for me all the way across town. You bet your keister I'm gonna be *real* careful who I let get their paws on somethin' like that, and I still got no idea who you work for."

"I told you, he's a collector. That's all."

"To what end? With what goals? Sorry, babe. Ain't good enough, not by a long shot."

And with that, she smiled that sad smile again. Gotta admit, I didn't expect that.

"Is it always gonna be this way with us? Hunting for the same thing but on opposite sides?"

"Well, this ain't exactly like the Spear of Lugh thing, but... I dunno, Ramona. I hope not. Long as you're playing fetch for whoever it is got you running errands, I don't see it changing—but I hope not."

"Yeah. Me, too." Her sigh was the sound of that smile, weak as it was, sliding completely off her lips. "I'm sorry, Mick. I really am. I just... I want you to know I wouldn't do this if I wasn't sure they couldn't *truly* hurt you."

Well, shit. *That* didn't sound good. I lunged for her, not knowing what stunt she was about to pull, just knowing I'd better stop her before she did it. Problem was, not only was I not fast enough—I got plenty of swift, but not *that* much—but jumpin' at her that way played right into her hands.

She retreated back onto the grass; for some reason I clearly remember the sound of it folding and crunching under her heels. Her step had a hitch in it, a sudden stagger—an act for the cheap seats. She pointed at me, screaming for help.

And I felt it again, a goddamn explosion of emotion: lust, desire, the need to possess, to protect. Oh, especially to protect.

I felt it, but only as it flowed by me, 'cause it wasn't *aimed* at me.

Wasn't the *entire* crowd crashed down on me like a flesh-and-bone avalanche. Didn't include the younger kids, and a handful of adults who, for whatever reason, just didn't respond to the sorta signals Ramona was broadcastin', even with the extra magical *oomph*. They sure were the minority, though.

Parents dropped their children's hands, lovers took their arms off each other's shoulders, everyone forgot about everythin' other'n beating every last bit of stuffing outta yours truly. Nearly all the men and not a few of the women came at me, jostling and shoving over who'd get their paws on me first.

Wasn't anywhere to run; I was surrounded before I could make tracks. Nothin' mystical I could do; I'd be pounded into hamburger before I could get into more'n a couple of minds or draw more'n a few shreds of fortune outta the air.

Damn, but this was gonna hurt.

First few weren't too tough to handle. I caught the first punch on a forearm easy enough, grabbed and twisted, launching the guy into one of the others comin' up behind me. The third went down when I swept his ankles; the fourth caught my knee in her stomach and then, as she was doubling over, got neatly shoved into an oncoming pack of three. If they'd kept comin' at me that way—or if I'd been more willing to actually hurt 'em, break bones, dislocate joints, risk rupturing organs—I might even have come out ahead, despite being outnumbered dozens and dozens to one.

I *didn't* wanna do 'em any real injury, though, and damn Ramona for knowing that. And yeah, I may be faster, stronger, and a hell of a lot better trained than these mooks, but I still gotta have room to *move*.

The rain of fists and feet wasn't too awful, least at first. I felt every poke, was definitely gonna be sore, but none of 'em were doing me too much damage. The clubs, though—random branches people picked up off the ground or pulled off nearby trees, or brooms wielded by carnie staff—those were adding up. I actually felt blood vessels pop, the bruises spreading through skin. None of 'em had the strength to fully break bone, not *my* bones, anyway, but a few cracks and fractures crawled their way through an arm here, a leg there. I don't remember droppin' to my hands'n knees, but that's where I ended up. Wasn't even a flurry of individual blows, now, just a constant force of impacts, one blurring into the next.

*Still* it wouldn't have been *too* awful. I'd need a day or three, but nothing more'n—

"Mick!" I heard her over the constant barrage and the mindless screams of animal fury. "Mick, watch out!"

I actually laughed, which did me no good but got me a shoe in the teeth. She'd set this mob on me, and now she was tryin' to warn me? And even if something'd gotten outta hand, gone further than she meant, what exactly was I supposed to do about it now?

And that's when I learned, one, what Ramona was shoutin'

about; two, that my run of bad luck was still truckin' right along nicely, thanks; and three, that some bastard in the crowd had come to a friggin' carnival packin' something a lot hotter'n a tree branch.

I only heard the first half of the first shot.

# CHAPTER EIGHT

My head hurt.

Which, y'know, is maybe to be expected after some stupid hormone-addled gink's put a slug through it. Any human woulda been deader'n driftwood at this point, so a migraine was gettin' off easy. Didn't much feel that way, though.

But it wasn't just that. There was another pain, felt wrong, not part of the headache at all. Took me a good spell of half-awake pondering over it before I realized I was feelin' a length of bandage wrapped tight enough around my noggin to slowly change its shape. And 'cause whoever'd giftwrapped me was mortal, and thus hadn't seen the extra pointy shape of my ears, the bandage was pinching 'em something fierce.

What else? Strong smell of alcohol—rubbing, not drinking—and some nostril-stinging store-bought salves that weren't half as effective as the herbs we'd used a few hundred years ago. Cleanser and mothballs, carpeting and some kinda fabric or bedding that somebody'd tried hard to keep neat and clean long past the point where anybody with money woulda replaced 'em. Nice warm blankets, swaddling me up to my chin—probably the source of that scent. The cushions under me were small, squarish; sofa, not bed.

Ticking clock. Faint musty tang of some old books. Oh,

right, and the inexpensive perfume and deep worry radiating from the middle-aged woman sitting over me.

Huh. Come to think of it, her emotions had a familiar taste to 'em. I knew this dame, though with all the various other distractions, I couldn't immediately suss out from where.

Guess it was time to take a look. I ain't sure which of us was more surprised when my peepers popped open.

"Martha?"

Her gasp was almost a choke, and her eyes teared up as I watched.

"You're awake! Oh, praise Jesus!"

Mrs. Martha Ross, a middle-aged black woman, sat beside the sofa dressed in what I'm pretty sure was literally her Sunday best. Sorta blue-green dress and hat, and a string of old, yellowing pearls around her neck. Although come to think, I'd never seen her wearing anything too much sloppier. Not a lotta money to her name, but she had her pride, Martha did.

She was also a client I'd worked for exactly once, a couple years back, and other'n a few random run-ins that hadn't lasted more'n a minute or so each, I hadn't dealt with her much since. So what the hell?

"What the h—What on earth're you doin' here, Martha?"

Her laugh was, for lack of a better word, boisterous.

"You don't even know where 'here' is, Mr. Oberon."

All right, that was fair. But...

Let's get a good slant on the place. I was right about bein' on a sofa; what I could see of it beneath the threadbare blankets was a neutral brownish shade. Bookcase behind me, couldn't really see much of what was on it. (If I'd hadda guess, I'da said "books." I'm sharp that way.) But on the desk across the room was an old, worn Bible, and the wall behind it boasted a simple wooden cross and a framed painting of what you skin color-obsessed bunnies today imagine Jesus looked like.

"I'm gonna go out on a limb," I said to her, "and guess I'm in a back office in a church somewhere."

"Can't ever turn off the detective in you, can you?" she asked with a smile.

"Well, *somebody* sure tried to." Then, when her whole face fell, "Sorry, Martha. Gallows humor."

"You know you oughta be dead now, right?"

*Yeah, I hear that a lot.* But I didn't say it; figured I'd traumatized the poor woman enough with my first shot at bein' funny.

Instead, I said, "Yeah, I sorta got that impression. Who do I thank for stitchin' me up? You?"

No mistakin' her intention as she looked over at the portrait on the wall.

"Him."

"Um..."

"No other answer, Mr. Oberon. It's a miracle. You *really* shoulda been dead."

"Well, I'll... certainly think about that."

"You do that." She stood, paused a moment to squeeze my hand. "You rest up. I'll go get the others."

Alone for a while with nothin' to do but think, I'd just reached the point of contemplating goin' back to sleep when the door opened up again. Martha was first through the door, followed by "the others." One of whom I knew, if only just. I dunno who I was expecting, if anyone, but if I'd hadda make a list, she wouldn't even have been on it.

"Tsura?"

The Greek faux-gypsy—who I almost hadn't recognized in normal clothes and a more human amount of makeup—seemed almost embarrassed. Or maybe just seriously uncertain.

The other fellow I didn't know from Adam. Tall, well over six feet, and though he was pretty scrawny now, broad shoulders suggested he'd been a mountain when he was younger. Had skin darker even than Martha's, and his beard and receding hair were somewhere between "snow" and "iron." He wore an ash-gray suit, and while he didn't have any sorta collar or anything, I recognized a priest when I saw one.

Sorry, guess "pastor" is the right word here. You guys got way too many denominations to keep track of.

"Glad to see you up and around, Mr. Oberon," he boomed. Yeah, guy born with *that* voice? Pretty much *had* to become a preacher. Or else maybe a politician, but who'd wish *that* on anyone?

"Makes two of us," I said.

He smiled, more outta politeness than amusement, and pulled up the chair Martha'd been sitting in.

"My name is Calvin Hewlett."

"Good to meetcha. This is your church, I take it?"

"I prefer to think it belongs to God and the neighborhood, but I run it."

"Well, long as I'm talkin' to *someone* in the chain of command." And hey, there was that non-smile again.

I'd actually hearda Hewlett, even though I hadn't recognized him. Guy was bein' modest. He spoke for a wide neighborhood, not just one house of worship, and he'd made himself heard. Oh, not the sorta changes that were gonna get him into the history books, but a few blocks of the Windy City were better off now than before he got started. He'd even run for alderman once, though he lost bad. Mostly because he wouldn't take money or backing from the sorta scary people you don't win without in Chicago.

"So," I said, "don't for one second think I ain't grateful, but... Someone wanna explain to me what I'm doin' here?"

"This young lady phoned me for help."

If I'd been any more puzzled, I'da been made of about five hundred pieces with scalloped edges.

"I appreciate the assist, Tsura," I said, hopin' she heard the unspoken *We're gonna discuss this later* I tacked on there, "but if you were lookin' for someone to perform last rites, you shoulda called up a Catholic."

"I thought almost the same thing," the old man said while

Tsura stammered. "When she first shoved you into the back of the car, I was flabbergasted you were still breathing. I argued for taking you to a hospital, but Ms. Sava insisted that you wouldn't want the attention—and that the people who'd hurt you would be able to find you too easily.

"To be frank, Mr. Oberon, if I'd thought there was one chance in a million you'd live, I'd have insisted. But I was quite sure she, and you, were just waiting on the inevitable. It wasn't until we'd gotten back here and Mrs. Ross insisted on redoing your bandages that I saw your injuries had already begun to improve."

"A miracle!" Martha asserted again. And to be fair, it ain't like she had a better explanation available to her.

Hewlett didn't seem so sure.

"Might be. It's hard to come up with any other explanation. We haven't been able to feed you. Your wound shouldn't have healed at all, let alone with the rudimentary care we can provide. But either way, you were here and clearly improving, so they convinced me to give it more time.

"You really ought to eat something, though," he added.

"You in the habit of takin' in random stiffs, preacher? Or almost-stiffs?"

"I very nearly didn't. Don't misunderstand me, Mr. Oberon, I believe our role on this earth is to help others where we can. But this city is brimming with elements I would prefer that I— and certainly my parishioners—avoid where possible. And to put it plainly, without meaning offense, I find that most sorts of people who find themselves shot and then *don't* want to seek the help of the proper authorities to fall into those categories."

"No offense taken. It's smart thinkin'."

"Indeed. And while Ms. Sava has been quite friendly to the parish children when we've visited her carnival, she and I aren't especially well acquainted. Frankly, the only reason you're here is that I'd been speaking with a few of my people when Ms. Sava called, and Mrs. Ross overheard your name. She convinced me you were worth helping, that if you were mixed up in something shady, it was as victim, not perpetrator—and I've seen enough of my own congregants in that position. For that, of course I would help, *if* it were accurate.

"She said you're a good man. Are you a good man, Mr. Oberon?"

I scooted my shoulders against the sofa arm until I was sitting upright. Neither Martha nor Tsura seemed real happy with me movin' around that much, but nobody said anything.

"That's a more complicated question than it sounds, uh... Preacher? Reverend? Pastor?"

"Preacher Hewlett will do fine. Or just 'Preacher.' And yes. Yes, it is."

"Heh. All right, Preacher. I dunno if I'm a good man. Frankly, I dunno if I trust anyone who can easily answer that question. Let's say I been trying my hardest to do what seems the right thing at the time."

For eleven seconds—I can say that exactly, 'cause of the clock tickin'—he chewed that one over.

Then, "I believe you." He rose, the chair scraping softly over old carpet. "I don't know precisely what you *are* caught up in, Mr. Oberon. And I don't know how you're recovering so quickly, or at all. Perhaps it *is* a miracle, at that, or maybe it's something else. I wouldn't presume to say. But you're welcome to the sofa, and I won't tell anyone that you've been here.

"Come, Mrs. Ross. I believe Mr. Oberon and Ms. Sava have their own conversation ahead of them."

Martha smiled, turned to follow him, and they'd both reached the door when I said, "Preacher, thanks. I owe you one."

This time his smile felt a lot more genuine.

"You didn't ask for my help, so I'm going to let you take that back if you want."

"Why would I do that?"

"Because I have a lot of people who depend on me, Mr. Oberon. If you insist that you owe me, I *will* take you up on it someday."

"I'll consider myself warned. But I pay my debts."

*Oh, if you only knew how important that was, and why...*

He watched me a few more seconds (five, if you care), nodded and left. Martha pulled the door to behind her on her way out, but I noticed she left a gap of a couple inches.

Well, they *were* good church-goin' folk, and Tsura was a young unmarried dame... I hadda swallow the laugh, hard. They meant well, and I had more important topics to talk about. Besides, hysterics'd probably hurt right now, anyway.

"All right, sister. Spill."

Tsura took the chair with a sight and a tight smile.

"Where am I starting?"

"How long I been snoozing?"

"Um..." She glanced at the clock. "Day and a half? A little longer."

*Fuck.* Then again, considerin' the slug'd passed through my skull, I was damn lucky it'd only been *that* long. If it'd gone through the center, rather than just clippin' the side the way it did, it probably woulda been three or four times that before I woke up. Guess even my current luck couldn't be awful *all* the time.

I know nobody makes bullets outta iron, but I still couldn't help shuddering just thinkin' about it. I'da been dead, pure and simple. And for good. I ain't come that close in a while.

To say nothin' of the people in the crowd I coulda hurt, bad, if I'd had time to get desperate enough.

Ramona. Damn, but that broad had a few things to answer for.

"I'm sorry if this is awkward for you." I guess Tsura decided not to wait for me to prod her with another startin' point. "I've met Preacher Hewlett a few times. He's brought some of the church kids to the carnival the last two or three times we've been in Chicago. He knows my fortune-telling's all in good fun, and the children seem to enjoy it..."

Yeah, he'd basically just told me alla that. In fewer words. But I swallowed my impatient interruption to go keep that laugh company, and let her finish.

"Anyway, I... It's not exactly the basis for a deep friendship or anything, but I don't actually know a lot of people in the city, and most of the others I *do* know aren't in any kinda position to help, so..." She shrugged, scuffed her feet in the carpet, and seemed real nervous about meetin' my gaze.

A lot younger, I realized, than she'd looked in her performance getup. Figure maybe mid-twenties. Somethin' about her, though... Somethin' inside of her was a lot older than her flesh and blood.

"That why you took the run-out soon as I told you my name? To go call Hewlett?"

"Well, and gather some bandages. And some of the staff to help get you out to the parking lot."

I snorted. "Carryin' stiffs just part of the job for most of you, then?"

"Winston—that is, Mr. Rounser, the owner? He doesn't exactly want a lot of police attention. Traveling outfit like ours, we're not always too careful about who we hire or making sure all the permits are in order, you get me? I hid the worst of your injuries, told him you were only hurt—which wasn't even really a lie, when you get down to it—and he was just happy to have you off his hands. And property."

"Thanks. Funny thing about your story, though? You got the chapters outta order."

"What do you mean?" she asked, while her tone, her lowered expression, the faint flush in her cheeks all screamed at me that she knew damn well what I meant.

"Well, let's see. You knew I wouldn't want any kinda official noses poking into my business, even though I never told you any such thing. But all right, I'll give you that one free; it ain't too hard to guess, in this town.

"You knew I wasn't normal, though, and that's a lot harder to just suss out. Ain't any reason you shoulda called to me in the first place, or known a shot to the conk like the one I took wasn't gonna kill me.

"But here's the rub, doll. You ran to call for help *before* I got hurt. Before anybody had reason to *expect* me to get hurt."

Tsura was fidgeting again, enough to make the chair squeak beneath her.

"The 'gypsy' part of 'gypsy fortune-teller' is the only part that's bunk, ain't it?"

Chair stopped squeaking. "You're ready to believe that? So easily?"

"You sound incredulous."

Not sure if the sound she made was a laugh or more of a bark, but it was bitter.

"I haven't had much luck telling people the truth in the past. I haven't bothered in years."

"Yeah, well, how many of the mugs you told just got done healing overnight from being plugged in the noggin?"

"There's that," Tsura conceded. Then, "I don't... tell fortunes, exactly. I get, well, flashes. Feelings. Sometimes actual images, but they're always short or vague. Broken. Premonitions but not what you'd call full-on visions. It's sort of like remembering pieces of a dream. I don't always know what I'm seeing, or even why I'm doing what I'm doing, but it's never wrong."

Huh. Sounded like the sorta Fae hunches I get, but taken up about ten notches.

"You got any kinda control over it?"

"A little. If I really focus on something, I can sometimes bring on a premonition about it. But it's not what I'd call reliable."

So where'd this come from? She was human, not Fae; I'da sworn to that. If she was being square with me, and her words tasted of truth, this wasn't comin' from any sorta witchcraft or occult practice. I...

Wait a minute. She was Greek. That couldn't... What where the odds of...?

"You're an oracle?"

"Momma told me over'n over, while I was growing up, that we were descended directly from the very last Pythia. Uh, that is, Apollo's priestess at Delphi."

I knew what "Pythia" meant, but I let her talk.

"I was all proud of that, as a child," she continued, "until I got old enough to read the myths and realize what a heap of horsefeathers the whole idea was. I was a bit of a brat to her about it for a while after that, honestly."

"Lemme guess. And then you had your first premonition."

"And then I had my first premonition, yes."

"So that's not just *how* you helped me," I guessed, "but why. Just had the feeling you oughta?"

"Yes."

"Well, that's the kinda feeling I can get behind."

After a quick courtesy chuckle, she said, "All right, your turn to sing. What *are* you?"

Y'know what? I told her. Didn't go into a lot of depth or detail, but the basics? *Aes sidhe*, former noble of the Seelie Court, alla that? Gave it to her straight. Didn't seem to be a whole lotta point in doing otherwise, given what she already knew.

Explained Ramona, too, so far as I could. That I didn't know what she was, exactly, but that I knew what kinda power she could throw around, and how she'd used it to put us in our current circumstances.

I did *not* mention Adalina, or why I was involved in this steamin' heap as deep as I was. I wasn't anywhere close to trustin' her *that* much. Hell, I only barely trusted *Pete* that much!

By the time I was through... Well, my mouth tasted like sandpaper and I wanted milk, but that ain't the relevant part. Tsura's blinkers were right on the verge of poppin' out and bouncin' around the room like billiard balls. I figure she musta wondered in her life, *If I got these weird abilities, what* else *is out there?* But whatever she'd imagined, obviously it hadn't gone far enough.

And in the midst of all that, she'd still had it in her, when I talked about Ramona, to look at me with... Not pity, no; that woulda steamed me but good. Sympathy, though. Genuine sympathy. Guess she read more of my history with the woman in what I said than I'd meant to reveal.

I tried to give her a few minutes to take it all in, but I'd already lost a couple days. Patience wasn't really my strong suit at the moment.

"Hey." I snapped my fingers at her. "Hey! Fedora!"

I knew that'd do it.

"Please don't call me that!"

"Sorry. Tsura. We can discuss the finer points of possible and impossible later on, if you want. Right now, I gotta know what I missed."

"How do you mean?"

"The carnival, sister. I'm sure you been checking in, even if you've spent most of your time here. Tell me what's happened since my, uh, sudden headache."

"How did—? Were you expecting something to happen at the fair?"

"Wasn't there to ride the Ferris wheel, doll."

"I suppose I should have guessed. Well, the... Mr. Rounser's trying to keep it out of the papers, but the mummy's been stolen from the funhouse."

Can I just tell you how utterly not shocking that was? 'Cause it was *so* unsurprising I think it could actually have cured a heart attack.

"Nobody's entirely sure when or how," she continued. "I mean, everyone was running around like their trousers were on fire after you got... Um..."

"Beat to a pulp and shot? It's okay to say it."

"Yeah. It was weird, Mick."

"Heh. You shoulda tried it from my end."

"I believe I'll pass," she said, chuckling softly. "I think it'd look even worse on me than it does on you. But no, I mean, nobody seemed to know exactly why they'd attacked you. Once you went down, everyone just sort of... woke up. They're all convinced you were hurting somebody and they were trying to stop you, but none of 'em could say what you were actually doing! I'm guessing that was the work of this... Webb person?"

"Ramona Webb. Yep."

"Well, of course, some of the people who weren't involved called the police, especially once you'd been shot. And everyone was dealing with that, and trying to figure out what'd sparked the mob, and where the victim was, and—"

"Wait. Nobody reported that you carried me outta there?"

"I'm not really that distinctive out of my 'Madame Tsura' makeup. And you looked bad, but not as bad as somebody who'd just been shot in the head, so I don't think some of the witnesses even realized you were the guy they'd been attacking.

"Plus, most of the people who'd actually been pounding on you skedaddled as soon as they heard the cops coming, *and* Rounser had the staff giving contradictory reports because he didn't want anyone looking too hard at his people. Bottom line, Mick, is it's a damn mess, but I don't think anyone knows who you were, or who yanked you out of there."

That sounded a little *too* convenient to me, honestly, but I wasn't gonna push it.

"And you know all this 'cause of...?" I tapped the side of my head.

"Huh? Oh, my visions? No. Just from talking on the horn with my friends back at the carnival." That surprised me to hear, at first, but then I vaguely recalled seein' a payphone near the premises. "This, uh, this isn't the first crime we've had on premises that Mr. Rounser made go away. Though I think it's the first near-murder."

I'd slid into a sorta slouch while we'd gabbed. Now I shifted my back a little, trying to get the arm of the sofa out from between my shoulder blades, and squeezed a finger up inside the bandages to scratch. I tried not to shudder or change my expression any when I felt a small bit of skull move under the pressure.

"Well," I said, "it's always nice to be first."

"Uh-huh. Anyway, everybody was so wrapped up in all that, it was a few hours before they noticed the robbery. Police asked Mr. Rounser if anything else was out of order, messed up, or missing, so then he hadda do a whole walkthrough of the park—insurance and paperwork and all that—and it was only then that he discovered the missing mummy."

I spent a while after that pressin' for details—any damage to the surroundings; obvious points of entry to the funhouse other'n the usual; suspicious activity beyond what'd happened to me—but Tsura wasn't a whole lotta help in that regard. Even if she'd known what questions to ask, it ain't as if that woulda been easy to work into conversation over the blower. Nah, there was no help for it. I was gonna have to give the crime scene an up-and-down myself, and hope that neither the bulls nor Rounser's people had trampled too hard over the evidence by the time I could get there.

Not that "hoping" seemed a real effective step to take right now. What about the curse, assumin' there was one? If the mummy *was* the source of the sour luck that'd been haunting me, I obviously didn't have to be too near it—just bein' in the same city seemed to be enough—but would it have left any sorta aura or residue behind? If I walked into its former resting place, in all its sideshow glory, would it be just another patch of floor? Or would I wind up even more behind the metaphysical eight ball than I already was?

I'll tell you what, though. If nothin' else, I oughta have an easier time deflectin' Ramona's mind-whammy next time we crossed paths. Right now, between the broderick, the shooting, and the missing mummy, I was angry enough to spit nails. *Iron* nails. It'd take a lot more'n even she had to push through that shield of fury, savvy?

Just thinkin' that way set my conk spinning something fierce, though. Obviously I still needed another day or two before I was anywhere near a hundred percent.

I suppose a slug in the brain'll do that to even the best of us.

Dunno what Tsura saw, but she leaned in and stood at the same time, comin' uncomfortably close to toppling over on me. That also probably wouldn'ta done my somewhat mushed skull any favors.

"Are you okay? Do you need anything?"

"Just... glass of warm milk and a while longer to snooze, I think."

"I understand."

She helped me slide back down so I was lyin' flat, which was nice of her.

"I don't know if I'd recommend going home, but I'm sure Preacher Hewlett can spare the room another night or two. Or I could take you to those friends of yours, you could stay with them a while..."

"Friends?"

She was half-lost in thought, gazing at the wall like she was regretting her choice in paint.

"The couple with the strange-looking girl, the sick one. They—"

I don't remember the words that followed. I don't remember deciding to sit up, or how I did it without intense pain or my head spinnin' hard enough to unscrew itself and fall off. I don't remember anything but findin' myself half off the sofa, fist wrapped right in Tsura's collar, and her startled yelp as I hauled her down until our noses damn near bumped.

"What do you know about them?" I demanded.

"*Wha*—Jesus, Mick! Simmer down, and—"

"What do you *know*?"

"Nothing, you creep! Get your mitts off me!"

Not that she was gonna wait to see if I listened to her. She smacked my hand away with the back of her own, and I wasn't in any shape to hold on, so I wound up not only lettin' her go but yet again slumping back down onto the ugly brown sofa.

"It was just an image!" she snapped at me, switching back and forth between rubbing her wrist and straightening her collar. "Something I saw while I was helping nurse your crummy carcass back from the brink of death!"

"Sorry." I probably meant it, but no way she was gonna buy that, not when I didn't have it in me to even try to sound as though I *did* mean it.

It was too much. I was tired, I hurt, and now this? Somethin' *else* for Adalina to get dragged into? No. Uh-uh. I hadn't mentioned her earlier, with good cause, and I hadn't suddenly changed my mind about that in the last few minutes. I had every reason in the world to trust that Tsura wasn't a threat, but I didn't *know* her, not really. And more to the point, I didn't know who else knew *about* her.

Yeah, I was behaving the fool. I coulda handled it a hundred better ways. Played it off as nothin', unimportant. Or explained that it was somethin' I couldn't have her digging into. Made up any number of lies.

But I hadn't. I'd blown my wig at her, and I didn't see any way of fixin' it that wasn't too exhausting to fathom right now.

"Sorry," I muttered again, then rolled over with my back to the room, burying my face against the back of the couch. "I need to sleep."

"Yeah. Yeah, you do that."

Pretty sure it was respect for Hewlett, and not concern about letting me nod off in peace, that kept her from slammin' the door on her way out.

# CHAPTER NINE

Took me another thirty-some hours before I was shipshape enough to dust out. I heal swift, but there's only so quick even the best of us can recover from *that* kinda hurt. Tsura didn't show again during that time, and Preacher Hewlett was far too proper to stick his beezer in and ask why. We shook hands, I passed him a card for if and when he needed to call in his marker. He insisted I take a handful of change for the L— along with a clean shirt from his wardrobe, which hung loose on me but had the advantage of not bein' blood-encrusted— and we parted ways.

It was raining when I left the church, a light shower as much flyin' in the breeze as falling. More a wet wind than anything else, just enough to make everything glisten and squelch. Streetlights and passing flivvers reflected off wet walls and wetter streets, and the folks still out and about after sunset quickened their paces to that silly, useless run people do when they get weather on 'em. Some held newspapers or umbrellas overhead, equally useless since the water wasn't comin' straight down.

Me, I ain't gonna say I didn't notice it; I'm way too sensitive for that at the best of times, even more so when I'm still— pardon the expression—under the weather. The rain was a nuisance, gettin' into everything, makin' the wound itch where it'd healed over. And the train was worse. Dry, sure, but the usual buzz in my head from sittin' inside a moving box of technology turned that itch into a dull pounding. Guess I looked none too happy about the whole thing, 'cause the other passengers gave me a wide berth.

That was good by me. Helped me focus past the discomfort and do some noodling.

I never much care to put my pals in danger if I can help it, but sometimes I ain't got a lot of choice. I had too many opponents on the board, and I still wasn't even sure quite what game we were playing. How were Ramona and McCall tied together? What kinda mojo or secrets did the stolen mummy hold? Was Ramona's boss the only one who wanted it? What about the Uptown Boys? What was their interest? Was Goswythe tied up in that, too, or just after me personally? Or even involved at all?

Goddamn it. At least when I'd been chasin' the Spear of Lugh, I'd known what the fuck everybody wanted. Or, well, I'd *thought* I had, which had been enough for me to keep it all straight in my head. This? Still way too much I didn't know.

Until I did, and while I was still less than my full self—health-and luck-wise, both—I needed help. That meant Pete. Soon as I made it back to the office, I'd get on the blower to the station (and lemme tell you, I was lookin' forward to *that* like it was a lemon-juice enema), and leave a message for him to gimme a ring.

Maybe I should phone Rounser's carnival while I was at it. Me'n Tsura weren't exactly best buds, but she'd done right by me. No, I didn't want her involved any further in what was goin' down, but I didn't much wanna leave things off where they were, either.

Or maybe I could...

Hmm.

I was on foot again, tracin' the old familiar steps from the L to my office. The drizzle was even lighter on this side of town, to where it was somewhere between real rain and just patches of excess humidity. It wasn't even enough to wash the smell of industry and meat processing outta the air.

And someone was tailing me again.

I couldn't tell who, not this time. Couldn't even be positive I wasn't jumpin' at shadows, imagining the whole thing. It ain't as if I didn't have good reason to be paranoid at this point. But I had that hunch, that feeling, of unfriendly peepers locked onto me from the darkness, probably from behind a mug I wouldn't even recognize. Maybe even one that wasn't the *same* mug from one blink to the next.

So... what? I was on my guard, one mitt in my coat and wrapped around the L&G. (And I only now thought to wonder what Hewlett or Martha had made of it, when he found a hardwood stick in my shoulder holster instead of a roscoe.) But what else could I do? Location of my office was no secret, and I had nowhere else to go right now anyway. All I could was keep alert, try to get a slant on whoever was dogging my steps, and hope I spotted something before they *started* something.

And I did, though it wasn't what I expected.

What I spotted was a sleek black Cadillac Fleetwood Imperial limo idling at the curb in front of Mr. Soucek's place, and a handful of mugs in fairly spiffy glad rags loitering around the stoop, huddling under the overhang to avoid the worst of the not-quite-rain. The bright cherry glow of gaspers were a constellation in the shadows, reflecting off teeth and castin' just enough light for me to make out some features I'd seen a few days ago.

"I ain't an expert," I said as I approached, "but it seems to me that when you tell a guy you don't ever wanna see his face again, it's maybe counterproductive to show up at his place afterward."

Nolan Shea spat the almost-burnt-out butt of his cigarette onto the steps.

"Was up to me, boyo, I *wouldn't* be seeing you again. Or maybe one last time, over a gat. Ain't my call to make, though."

"Lemme guess. You're about to invite me to take a ride with you."

"Ain't with me. And it ain't an invitation."

Shea and a handful of Uptown Boys? Pretty sure I coulda handled 'em, even in my current state. Probably not without makin' a lotta noise, though, and maybe not without takin' a few more injuries I could really do without. And hey, a sitdown with Fleischer—to whom I figured the flivver'd take me, since I couldn't off the top of my noggin come up with anyone else Shea'd be playin' messenger for—might just get me some answers.

It meant time in one of those motorized hell-boxes, which was enough to make me sick as a dog on a good day, but I'd live.

"All right," I told him. "You think we can pick up my dry cleaning while we're out?"

"Get in the damn car, Oberon."

I moved toward the flivver, slow and sauntering. I'm sure Shea took that as me bein' a wise-ass, tryin' to make like I wasn't scared of him. Fine; let him think that. What I was *actually* doin' was suckin' up some of the ambient luck, not too much from any one thing or any one guy—'cept Shea himself, who cursed somethin' fierce when he tried to light up another butt and burned the hell outta his thumb in the process—and feedin' it into my own aura. Wouldn't provide *much* of a buffer against the chafing of the motor on the raw edges of my soul, but some was better'n nothin', right?

The interior of the Caddy was customized, stretched some— not quite to the point of bein' what you'd call a genuine limousine, but near enough—with a bench seat installed back-to-back with the driver. Perfect setup for a private little gab session. Since that backward-facin' seat was the only one available, what with the two mugs already planted in the others, I took it.

Reminded me some of my trip inside Eudeagh's horse-drawn carriage, 'cept the leather seats here were more comfortable. Also, silky smooth as it was, presumably not made outta tanned baby skin. I may have a serious hate-on for the Mob, but it ain't anything compared to how much I despise the Unseelie Court.

Right. Two guys in the back with me. I focused on 'em, piecin' together what I could, partly since it was the only wise thing to do, and partly so I could concentrate on somethin' other than the fingernails dragging across my brain as the driver put the damn contraption in gear and took us rumbling off down the street.

Gink on the right—well, my right—was your typical suited gorilla. Big square jaw, soulless blinkers, reeking of cheap aftershave, shoulders wider'n a *buggane*'s appetite, and carryin' a heater under his coat so damn big and heavy I wasn't sure *it* wasn't wearin' *him*. I could safely ignore him until and unless things went south.

Well, souther. Gotta figure my whole situation had already gone far enough south I was straddlin' the Mason–Dixon.

The other guy, though...

He looked like a grammar-school teacher. Couldn't say for sure with him sittin' down, but I figured him for average height, certainly not tall. Sorta roundish face, and even with his hat on, his hair was obviously goin'. He clasped his hands in his lap, stubby fingers interlaced, and watched me through wide-rimmed glasses. The sorta Joe you'd never pick outta a crowd for anything, and about as menacing as a soggy dinner roll.

Unless, like me, you're somebody who can see the intensity in a person's aura, taste the emotion behind their words and their expressions.

And what I got from this guy was nothing. Like takin' a whiff or a gulp from a snifter of brandy and tasting water. He was either so controlled, or so *cold*, he damn near wasn't there.

In centuries upon centuries of walkin' this world, I can count the number of times that's happened without runnin' outta fingers. And okay, maybe there was something to him I was just missing, lost in the internal screaming of the car, the lingering pain of my injuries, and the smothering blanket of bad luck—but even if that were the case, it still made the man more of a cypher'n most.

"Mr. Oberon, is it?" Voice was as unremarkable as the rest of him. And hey, he got the name right. "I'm Saul Fleischer."

Yeah, I'd guessed as much. Flivver wasn't taking me to the sitdown, it *was* the sitdown.

"Pleased to meetcha. I've heard a lot about you."

"Oh, yes? Nothing too unpleasant, I hope."

I grunted, real noncommittal, since there was no good way to actually answer that.

He nodded as if I'd told him something important, then turned to gaze absently out the window.

"Miserable night, isn't it?"

"Just a little rain."

"This by you is rain? Feh. Rain comes in drops, and it's at least cleansing. This? This is just... damp. And it gets into everything. I'm sure it'll take nights for Nolan and his boys to dry their suits."

"So why have 'em standing around outside waitin' for me?"

"What, so *I* should get soaked instead? That's what I have people *for*, Mr. Oberon."

Were we really havin' this conversation? *Why* were we havin' this conversation?

"I'd have had you picked up at the train station," he continued, "so you didn't have to walk home in this. But, of course, we had no idea when you'd be coming back."

"So, what, you been sittin' around outside my place for three days?"

"Of course not. I've had someone watching the nearest train station. He phoned when he spotted you arriving. I was frankly a bit surprised we reached your office before you did, but I suppose you took your time in the walk."

I had, at that, since I still wasn't feelin' my best. Didn't seem the best thing to say, though. Instead, I asked, "So that was one of your people shadowing me?"

"Pardon?"

"On the walk."

Fleischer frowned, though I got the impression it was mostly for my sake.

"No. He reported your arrival, but that was all. If someone followed you, it wasn't one of mine. Neither are the two *gonifs* lurking in your office, waiting—I assume—for you to show up."

Huh. Interesting.

"I appreciate you mentioning that."

He waved a dismissive, "it was nothing" hand at me.

And again, why were we havin' this conversation? I wondered if Fleischer was sizin' me up somehow. I couldn't taste any magic in the air, but the same factors that coulda been impeding my read on him could even more easily keep me from noticing any sorta mystical examination, especially if it was subtle or came from an occult tradition I wasn't too familiar with. And I already knew Fleischer had *some* knowledge of the supernatural, since he'd sent Shea to Hruotlundt for one reason or another.

Yeah, the more I chewed it over, the more I became convinced that hadda be part of what was happening. If I could just get them to turn off the damn engine for a few minutes, gimme a chance to pull myself together...

"So tell me, Mr. Oberon, why the sudden interest in my business?"

So much for pulling myself together.

"Um, excuse me?"

Fleischer *tsk*ed at me. "It's a simple enough question. First, my people follow you from Fino Ottati's house, and when they try to ask you a few questions, there's a bit of a scuffle. Then you show up at Nolan's home claiming to be... What was it? A vacuum-cleaner salesman? Which, I should say, does not sound to me like a particularly well-planned cover story."

"It wasn't really meant for Nolan in the first place. But I was just following up some leads on a case. Shea didn't turn out to be part of it, so I moved on."

"And you see, if that'd been the end of it, I would believe this.

You showed up while he was working a few nights ago, asking questions, and then again when he was running an errand for me. I'm sure you can see how I might start to wonder."

"Sure, I can see. Ain't anything to wonder about, though. I really don't have any interest in your operation, Fleischer. Frankly, the less I have to do with any of you trouble boys, the happier I am."

"This from a man who visits the Ottatis as often as you do?"

Oh, but that car was startin' to feel *real* cramped all of a sudden.

"You gonna make me ask how you know that?"

"I keep an eye on my rivals. That includes anyone of import in the Outfit—and anyone who appears to be of import to *them*."

"Uh-huh. You been wastin' your time spyin' on me, then. Me'n Fino and Bianca are friends, not business partners. I worked a case for 'em once—a personal thing, not work-related. That's the extent of my 'involvement' with him, business-wise."

"Is that so? But you've also been in contact with Vince Scola and *his* people. That's two different Outfit *capos*; rather a high count for a man who doesn't share in their business interests, yes?"

"Oh, for the love of... That was also case-related! I'm a PI, in goddamn Chicago!"

"Please don't use that expression around me."

"Fine. Whatever. Point is, my job's *gonna* put me in contact with gangsters. Pretty much by definition. I try to keep it down, but it happens. Now, are we done?"

"You don't have a lot of respect for anyone, do you, Mr. Oberon?"

"I got respect out the wazoo. I just don't have much *patience* left."

"I see. Yes, we're done. Murray! Take us back to our guest's office."

The response came from over my shoulder.

"Right away, Mr. Fleischer."

I felt the flivver slow, begin to turn. On the square, I'd much have preferred to get out and walk, but tryin' to explain that woulda taken as long as the drive back, and probably caused offense I didn't really need to.

Unless he already knew what I was, of course. But if he *hadn't* been magically pokin' at me that whole way, I wasn't about to *tell* him.

"Mr. Oberon?" The Caddy pulled up to the curb, and I was all but lunging for the door before it stopped, but I made myself pause long enough to hear whatever threatening or cryptic farewell he meant to leave me with.

"Yeah?"

"Let's avoid anymore 'coincidental' meetings between you and any of my people, shall we? It would be unfortunate if I were to get the idea that you'd lied to me at all tonight."

Right. Threatening it was, then.

Noncommittal grunts are useful, so I gave him another one, and stepped outta the car. Nolan and the Uptown Boys disappeared from the stoop soon as I appeared—figure they had their own flivvers parked nearby—and then it was just me.

Pretty much as soon as I had the car outta my head, I started wondering about the whole conversation. Those were some softball questions he'd pitched at me; as far as bein' grilled went, I'd gotten the third degree worse from curious vendors at newsstands. So unless it was a distraction from something—and I had a hard time coming up with any idea *what*—I figured it *hadda* be about me bein' poked and prodded by subtle magics.

Which meant I hadda figure, for future reference, that Fleischer had a good sense of what I was. Swell. I needed that like I needed a hole in my head.

Ha. I kill me.

Shakin' my head, almost-healed hole and all, I unlocked the door and tromped tiredly down the stairs.

# CHAPTER TEN

I suppose I hadda thank Fleischer for the warning, at least. The two goons in my office wouldn'ta been too much trouble without it—even in my current state—but the advance notice sure made things smoother.

Between the lock on the front door and the echoes in the stairwell, I figured they heard me comin', which was just fine. I pressed my ear to the wall, to get a sense of where they were in the office, and heard one of 'em breathin' heavy just inches away. No imagination, these saps.

So, another quick sweep of my wand to pad my luck some, and then I didn't just open the door to my office; I slammed into it, hard, shoulder first. It swung wide, and woulda bounced off the wall if the dumb bunny hadn't been lurking behind it. So it bounced offa him, instead.

Goon number two was crouched behind my desk, aimin' the gleaming black barrel of a Colt my way. He hadn't quite been prepared for an entrance like I'd just made, though, so he froze up for a second.

Good. I been shot sufficiently for one week, thanks.

I got plenty of swift, but crossin' the office and clampin' mitts on the guy before he could squirt lead wasn't too likely even for me. Time for some, whaddaya call it? Creative problem-solving.

I spun away from the door, reachin' out to snag the hatstand. Grabbing it near the top, I took a few quick running steps and lunged, dropping almost to one knee and flippin' it over so I led with the base.

Even in a perfect lunge, the thing wasn't quite long enough to reach all the way over the desk. That was okay, though. I wasn't aiming at the bastard.

I *was* aiming at the heavy steel typewriter, which went neatly hurtling off the edge of the desk so *it* cracked hard into the guy's button.

Can't say I'm a hundred percent positive of a lot of things, but I'm pretty sure that typewriter's tasted more blood in its life than most of 'em do.

First guy was comin' out from behind the door, nose bloodied but otherwise not too much the worse for wear. I'm sure he had a heater in his coat, same as his buddy, but right now he had his fists wrapped around a baseball bat.

Another one. I'd had so many bats comin' at me lately I wondered if I had "Spalding" stitched across my forehead.

I tossed my end of the hatstand at his feet, plucked the bat out of his hands as he stumbled over it, and whacked him across the conk with it. Since I'd grabbed it by the fat end— and since I wasn't tryin' to kill the guy—I hit him with the handle, and not all that hard.

Then, because I *did* want him to *stay* hit, I picked him up by the collar and drove him headfirst into the side of the desk a couple times for good measure.

Took a few more minutes to drag 'em together, strip 'em of any weapons, then tie 'em back to back with belts and shoelaces. One of 'em was Irish as old whiskey, the other Italian as marinara. Not a combination you saw in Chicago's Mob. Plus, they were both decked out in cheap coats and slouch hats, and judging by the way they both smelled, if they'd been to a cleaner's in years it was to knock the place over, not to do laundry. Low-rent crooks, then. Street thugs or muscle-for-hire, probably, not Outfit or Northside.

Since I was stuck waiting for one or the other to wake up before I could take this any further, I wandered out to the payphone in the hall and, after a staring contest with the fucking monstrosity—it won, 'cause I ran out of patience, but I swear it was *this* close to lookin' away!—I dialed up the precinct. Pete was out on the beat, as I'd figured he would be, but I left a message with the desk sergeant.

A few more minutes, and I was about ready to start dumpin' cups of water onto the ginks until one of 'em sputtered, when the Italian guy started to come around. I poked him until he opened his peepers, and then shoved my willpower through his pupils like needles.

I've sometimes described what I do in people's heads as shuffling their thoughts like a deck of cards. These guys? It was more of a poker hand. Not the sharpest hammers in the shed, is what I'm sayin'.

And yet, I couldn't get a whole lot outta them. Oh, they knew they'd been sent to rough me up, maybe even rub me out if they had to, but they didn't seem real clear on who'd done the sending. They knew they hated my guts, personally, had been only too happy to take on the job, yet neither of 'em could give me a straight answer as to *why*, what I'd done to get 'em so good'n steamed, or even if we'd actually met before.

Golly-gee, why did *that* sound familiar?

Ramona again? Or McCall? I could ponder up motives for either of 'em; problem was, I could also come up with better reasons against it. Hmm.

Well, maybe they'd be able to tell me more later, given some time and distance for their scrambled noggins to unscramble. For now? Nothin' left to do but wait for Pete to return my call.

Since my guests didn't seem real taken by the idea of playin' cards with their hands tied behind their backs, I dealt out a row of piles for Solitaire on the desk where the typewriter would go back to, once I got around to cleaning it up, and settled in.

\* \* \*

Pete wasn't alone when he finally showed, a couple hours before dawn.

He finally came wanderin' down the steps to Soucek's basement, a pair of uniformed bulls in tow. Him bein' my friend, and appearances and procedure bein' what they are, Pete stepped aside and let the other two question me about what'd happened, why I had two saps beaten black and blue and bound next to my desk. I gave 'em the skinny, they agreed it was pretty clear-cut self-defense, and then dragged the grumbling goons back out to their radio car and vamoosed. Only when all that was done did Pete'n me sit down to bump gums over everything goin' down.

"To start with..." I tried to start with.

He didn't even let me get that far. "To start with, why don'tcha tell me why your map looks like you just went ten rounds with Barney Ross."

"You can see that?" Between the healin' I'd already done, and the unpredictable way each of you mugs sees somethin' a bit different when you give me the up-and-down, I didn't figure it was all that noticeable.

He snorted. "I spend enough time around you, Mick. You ain't the prettiest thing I see on a good day, but I *do* know you fairly well by now."

Maybe that was it, sure. And maybe Pete's other, uh, "problem" had somethin' to do with it. We were between full moons right now, and so far as I could tell he remained entirely normal and human 'cept for those three nights a month, but who could say for certain?

Didn't matter much, really. He'd seen it, so I went ahead and gave him the gist of what'd happened over the past few days.

"Jesus, Mick."

"Yeah."

"I thought this Ramona skirt was supposed to like you!"

"Well, I don't think she meant for me to get plugged…"

"Oh, that makes it *all* better."

He tugged a small metal flask outta his coat, took a deep gulp. Then he stood, walked over to the icebox, and tossed me a bottle of milk.

"Looks like you're runnin' low, Mick."

I nodded a thank-you, popped the lid.

"Been drinking a lot while I been waitin'."

"Hmm." He took his seat again, gazing idly at the bloody typewriter on the floor. "I think you've got somebody's tooth in your semicolon."

"Wouldn't surprise me."

"So what's your next step?"

"Well," I said around a swallow of cow juice, "that partly depends on what you got for me."

"Not a lot you hadn't already guessed." He flipped open his notebook, skimming back over the notes he'd copied down from department files back at the clubhouse. "They're both small fry. Get by mostly on mugging, knockin' over newsstands, some local protection rackets. Kinda goons most self-respecting mobsters only use as errand boys, if they bother with 'em at all."

In other words, all useless. I scowled into my milk.

"There is *one* bit stands out, though," he continued. "Could be a coincidence real easy, may not be anything hinky, but…"

"So, out with it. I'm the edge of my seat, here."

"You're leaning all the way back, Mick."

"I didn't say *which* edge. Spill already."

"Well, they were both under glass awaiting trial not a week ago. Various charges, nothing big, but enough to put 'em both over for a few years if they were convicted. And then the charges were dropped and they were sprung, just a few days back."

Now that *was* fascinating. As Pete'd said, could be a coincidence. Small-time crooks were bein' released all the time, to make room in an already packed judiciary for bigger fish. So it *could* just be that they were freshly back on the streets and lookin' for work, and that's how they got picked for the "ruin Mick's day" run.

Could be.

*Could.*

Damn. It was gonna be a while yet before there was any use tryin' to grill 'em again. I could probably have forced my way through the confusion of whatever Ramona or McCall or whoever had done to 'em—and maybe I should have—but I was still nervous about tryin' anything too heavy, magic-wise. If nothing else, it could do 'em some real damage, and I didn't hate the ginks enough to wanna leave 'em as drooling vegetables.

Well, they'd be cooling their heels for a while. I could afford to wait, chat 'em up in a day or two. In the meantime...

"C'mon, Pete." I was up and reaching for my coat before I realized I'd even made a decision.

"Uh..." He took one last swallow and shoved the flask back in his coat. "We going somewhere?"

"Yep. One of the only places I'm sure there've gotta be *some* answers to all of this. I've dug around there once already, but I think it's worth a second trip. Especially with an extra pair of eyes."

Not sure what he saw in my smile or my own peepers, but he actually wilted.

"I ain't gonna like whatever you got in mind, am I?"

"Well, you're a cop." I grinned even wider. "So you damn well better not."


"You were right, Mick. I don't like this at all."

"C'mon, Pete. What's a little B&E between friends?"

"On a first offense? Probably not more'n two or three years."

"See there? Nothin' to worry about."

Pete grumbled something rude I pretended not to hear, and stepped back to fidget and watch the hallway. Me, I was down on one knee, poking at the lock for the second time this week. No way for me to tell if Ramona'd been back here since my last visit, not from out here, but the wards on the lock were still down. If she *had* been back, she either hadn't taken—or *couldn't* take—the time'n effort to reset them.

Took just a few seconds to get that musical *click*, and then I pushed the door open and stood.

"You comin'?"

"I'd say I should stay and guard the hallway," Pete muttered, "but that still makes me an accomplice."

"Exactly. So come be a *good* accomplice, at least."

"I'd feel better if we had a warrant."

"Me, too, if it'd stop your constant bitching."

Not sure if it was his shoulder or his scowl that shoved me aside as he pushed past me into Ramona's apartment.

Everything stood more or less as I'd left it, including the piles of papers and scribblings and different envelopes addressed to different names on the nightstand. If Ramona *had* come back here after our encounter at the carnival, she hadn't left any obvious signs of it.

Which also meant there was no new evidence jumping into view, wavin' its hands at us and screamin' for attention. I took another look-see around the place while Pete sifted through those papers, and then I waited while *he* poked around some. All of which led us to nothing much. Still no sign of who Ramona's mystery boss was, or where we might find him.

Probably goes without saying that we didn't come across any stolen mummies, either. I'da mentioned something like that.

"What about this?" I jabbed one of the envelopes with a fingernail. "You recognize the handwriting, by any chance?"

"Sorry, Mick."

Guess I didn't expect anything else. It still nagged at me, though. I could *swear* I'd seen it before. Cursing softly—in Old Gaelic, 'cause why not?—I scooped up the whole pile and started cramming half-crumpled pieces into various pockets.

"Uh, Mick? What're you doing?"

"Taking these to study more closely later."

"You mean stealing them."

I almost missed a pocket due to shrugging at him.

"Book me."

"She's gonna know you were here!"

"She'll get wise to that—if she ain't already—soon as she sees the lock, Pete."

He rolled his hands and threw up his eyes, or maybe it was the other way around.

"Whatever. Do what you want."

"I was gonna. It's nice to have your support, though."

That task complete, I wandered across the apartment to stare at the blower.

"Hey, Pete?"

He grunted.

"You mind making a call or two?"

"Oh, now I'm useful?"

"I dunno, let's see."

Thankfully, it was just enough past dawn at this point that I figured there'd be people already at work in the various offices he'd need to speak to. I left him dialing around while I did yet more fruitless searching.

"Sorry, Mick," he said eventually, joining me in the dining room. "Everything about the place is in one of her fake names." He sorta gestured at me while he said that—or rather, I realized, at the papers I'd taken, where we'd first found those aliases. "Nothin' that leads to an employer."

Well, it'd been worth a try. But damn, I was gettin' frustrated! I'd known she was good, that she *hadda* be good, but if she turned out to be *too* good for me to track down or outsmart, I was gonna start takin' it personal.

"Could you get on the horn one more time?" I asked. "Find out if those two idiots who tried to jump me have been booked yet, and if we can grill 'em for a few?"

Yeah, I know. I said it'd be safer to wait a couple days, and it'd only been a few hours. Whaddaya want from me? I was gettin' desperate for a lead.

And oh, I got one.

"Uh, Mick?" Pete lowered the blower, puttin' one hand over the mouthpiece. "They ain't there."

Felt as if the air in the apartment got real thick all of a sudden.

"Define 'ain't there.'"

"I mean they're not at the station. Got diverted to the state pen en route. They're bein' processed and kept *there*."

Which meant a whole different set of procedures, under a whole different system. Different hoops to jump through in order to see 'em or question 'em, too. Sure, they'da gotten there eventually, but this quick? Totally bypassing county and city officials, a few days in the city slammer? On a simple assault charge? No way. Either somebody thought they needed protection—or somebody didn't want anyone to have easy access to 'em.

"Anyone" meaning *us*.

"Who gave the word to transfer 'em?" I demanded.

Pete raised the receiver again and repeated my question.

"Dunno," he told me. "Paperwork came down with all the proper seals through all the proper channels, is all guys at the front desk can tell me."

Hinkier and hinkier, as the man almost said.

"Pete... Who dropped the earlier charges on these two? Who arranged their release in the first place?"

Again Pete spoke and cajoled and commanded for another few minutes, sometimes stopping to wait while the desk sergeant on the other end picked up a different line to make *more* calls. When he finally put down the phone, his face was red from shouting and wrinkled in thought.

"You look like a shriveled apple," I told him.

"Nobody can answer the question, Mick. He said the

secretary at the courthouse told him that the records ain't complete. They know the order has to have come from someone legitimate, or the ginks wouldn't have been released in the first place, but whoever it was never got around to signing the damn paperwork."

"Gee, what a coincidence."

"Ain't it, though? What now?"

What now, indeed. Wheels in my noggin' were finally turning again. Guess they'd slipped back into place from where the bullet'd jarred them loose, because I felt like I was thinkin' clearly for the first time in days.

I'd already known that Ramona's boss was somebody important, somebody powerful, somebody with access to police and banking records. What I hadn't known until just now was that he actually had strings he could pull in the legal system, could make decisions affectin' prisoners and trials and the judiciary.

That by itself didn't prove much, didn't tell me much. But now that I knew, now that I was already thinking in that direction? That was the push I'd needed. I finally knew where I'd seen that handwriting before.

And a *whole lot* finally fell into place.

It wasn't enough to just suspect, of course, no matter how sure I was. I hadda know. You don't move against a guy with that sorta clout *without* knowing.

Which made our next stop City Hall.

I ain't gonna bore you with the specifics. Another train ride. Wanderin' from office to office, sometimes just askin' directions, sometimes throwing down a little mojo to get the answers I needed.

Then a lot more magic, even risking another backlash of bad luck (which, thankfully, didn't happen this time). Enough magic to get me'n Pete into rooms we shouldn't have been in, making sure to get the truth outta people we shouldn't have been talking to. Until I finally found and mind-whammied a secretary who'd been ordered to keep her mouth shut, but was able to tell me who'd given the order to drop the charges against my two recent unwanted visitors.

And yeah, it was exactly who I'd thought it would be. Exactly whose handwriting I'd thought I'd recognized.

My old client, whose case I'd wrapped up right before I'd first been hired to find Celia Ottati by her frightened mother, before I'd first met Bianca and Fino and poor, slumbering Adalina.

Assistant State's Attorney Dan Baskin.

# CHAPTER ELEVEN

I lost a big chunk of the day waitin' around climbing my thumb, since I wasn't about to grill Baskin about any of this in City Hall. Nah, this was gonna take privacy, and that meant doing squat until he got himself home. Well, it gave me time to check in with some folks elsewhere in the building who were kind enough to provide me the man's home address—whether they meant to or not. (I'm sure it'll shock you to learn that most of the lawyers workin' for the city in a place like Chicago don't publicize their addresses.)

Pete pointed out, correctly, that I had no way of guessin' how the chat with Baskin was goin' to go, if we'd be in any immediate danger afterward or if we'd have to go dashing off after some lead or other. I wasn't real thrilled with the idea of takin' my buddy's car—a beatup old Ford—instead of the train, but I hadda admit it was the wise thing to do. I just spent the whole trip tryin' to squeeze my head until it squished like a melon.

He, on the other hand, was even less thrilled about the notion of waiting in the car, down the block, when I went to confront Baskin. But he couldn't exactly argue that he should go with me, not when the man could end his career with a word in the wrong ear. Better he stay back, outta sight, and ready to come bustin' in if I yelled for help.

And yeah, I assured him I could yell so he'd hear me. He made some stupid joke about Fae sirens vs. police sirens. I said he was damn lucky I couldn't drive myself outta here in a hurry if I accidentally tripped and beat him senseless with his own shoes.

Then, that important bit of wisdom exchanged, I ankled on over to Baskin's doorstep.

The place was, uh... Well, it certainly consisted of a *lot* of bricks.

Yeah, Baskin had learned that much from the trouble boys he'd faced across the courtroom over the years. His place was big, real big, but not quite *too* big. Redbrick walls, white trim and shutters, neatly manicured lawn on a street where everyone else boasted the same. Nice enough to make you say, "Pretty fancy for a guy in his position," not *so* nice that you'd start to wonder if he was supplementing his income.

Unless you were suspicious as me, in which case you damn well *were* wondering if he was supplementing his income.

And also wondering what the hell kinda magical dinguses he might have locked up in there. How potent where they? Did he know how to use 'em? What sorta trouble was I potentially walkin' into?

Oh, and where in the house would I hide a millennia-old mummified body if *I* were an assistant state's attorney?

I rapped a couple knuckles on the door. Gave it a minute. Rapped again.

Baskin was no bunny. He wasn't just gonna throw the door open to any sap who came along. Your average Joe wouldn't have been sure he was even home. Wouldn't have heard the faint scuff of him sneaking up to glance out the peephole, or the soft choke when he saw who it was.

"C'mon, Baskin. I know you're in there. You make me break in, I'm gonna make damn sure the cops who come to arrest me see things you don't want 'em to. I just wanna talk a while. I ain't here to hurt you."

Probably.

Maybe.

Certainly not too bad, at least.

Took him a minute to decide whether or not to answer. I was gettin' ready to yell again—or maybe just do something scientifically impossible to the lock—when he finally shouted back.

"What do you want here, Oberon?"

"Uh, didn't I just say? You ain't hearing me too well. Must be all this door between us. How's about you open up and invite me in, and there'll be *less* door between us?"

"What if I don't want you in my home?"

"I'd be surprised if you did, frankly. I don't much wanna be here, either. We all got our crosses to bear. You gonna let me in now, or does your pride need you to protest a while longer?"

The door swung open, revealing a middle-aged mug with a five-dollar haircut, wearing a burgundy housecoat that probably cost more'n Pete's car, and carrying a double-barreled shotgun almost massive enough to qualify as artillery.

"Anyone ever tell you you're an ass?" he asked me.

"That a trick question, counselor? What's with the hardware? You go whale-hunting on the weekends?"

"I have a lot of enemies, Mr. Oberon."

"Seems like you'd want *many* gats, then, insteada one big one. Or do you expect 'em to line up for you? Because I'd pay to see that."

"Just come inside and close the damn door, would you?"

I went inside and closed the damn door. Learned a few different things the moment I did, too.

First, the house was warded. Not enough to keep me out, not near as painful as Orsola's protections had been. Just sort of a low-grade discomfort. Definitely woulda distracted me for a second or two if I'd come through the door fighting, maybe enough to have given Baskin a leg-up on whatever he woulda been doing in defense. Mostly, though, I figured it for an alarm; I'm sure somewhere in the house, a crystal was glowing or a taxidermied coyote was shouting a warning, or something similar. "Fae in the house! Fae in the house! Call an exterminator!"

Second, there was magic in the house beyond the wards. I mean, sure, I'd guessed there would be—"collector" and all, as Ramona'd told me—but it was good to confirm. Thing is, it didn't feel as strong as I'd expected. Either Baskin's collection was a lot smaller'n I thought, or he had enough occult knowledge to muffle some of it. Given the wards, probably the latter. Best I could tell from what emanations I *could* feel, the goods were upstairs.

And third, as a home decorator, Baskin made a good lawyer.

His sense of style focused on "inoffensive," fancy without the least trace of personality. Furniture mostly in whites and creams and grays, except where it was varnished hardwood; bog-standard china patterns; a few painted landscapes. About the only things that stood out were some newspaper articles, carefully clipped and framed, hanging in groups on this wall or that. I didn't even have to look to know they'd be stories about big court cases he'd won.

"Christ, Baskin. Couldya be any more of a stuffed shirt?"

Not that I was really payin' the slightest attention to the clippings, or much else in the house right then. Naw, I just didn't want him noticing what I *was* focused on. Woulda been too obvious and too threatening for me to make a grab for the L&G, and I hadda work slow and steady to make sure a stroke of bad luck didn't gum up the works, so I needed time...

His cheeks tightened around his teeth.

"Did you come all the way out here just to insult me?"

"Well, that ain't the *only* reason."

Shaking his head, he opened a glass cabinet and poured himself a lead crystal glassful of something vaguely golden.

"It's legal to own," he said defensively after a large sip. "Just not to buy."

"Yeah, I'm actually aware of how the law works."

"That remains to be seen." He finished off the drink in a quick gulp and went back to idly fingering the shotgun. "Quit stalling, Oberon. Why are you here?"

"Why don'tcha ask Ramona? I'm sure she can guess, if you can't."

"Who?"

And you know what? I couldn't taste the lie in his words. Don't get me wrong, I knew he *was* lyin', but it was weird not to be able to confirm it. Ain't unheard of for a human to be a good enough liar that I can't tell, but it ain't somethin' I run into every day, either.

Guess he'd pulled himself together a little with that drink.

"C'mon, Baskin. We really gotta go through the whole song and dance? I felt the wards when I walked in. I know the kinda stuff you're involved in. I can feel your collection from down here, even through all the efforts you've taken to veil it. I know you sent Ramona to try to snag the Spear of Lugh a while back, and to case Rounser's carnival so you could steal his mummy."

"You... You're mad! Certifiably insane!"

"You weren't surprised when I heard you through the front door. And you knew better'n to think threatening me with that hand-cannon was gonna stop me comin' in if I really wanted to."

"Maybe I just don't like the idea of violence if I can avoid it. Or I just don't want to have to clean up the mess and fill out the paperwork if I kill you."

Had it been long enough? Had I been focused enough? Time to find out.

"All right. Since I can sense everything anyway, let's just mosey on upstairs to your collection and I'll show you what I'm talkin' about."

That suggestion got twin shotgun barrels aimed my way *real* quick. It was almost disappointing how predictable that reaction was.

"No. I think this is about as much of my home as you're going to see tonight, Oberon."

"C'mon, bo. There's more'n just you and me riding on this." *A young girl's life and whole friggin' identity, for one*, though obviously I didn't say that. "Can we just skip over this part and go upst—?"

"No! It's time for you to leave, before—"

I mentally tugged on the mystical threads I'd been weavin' for the past few minutes, draining the luck outta the bean shooter Baskin was holdin' on me. A couple of unhealthy *clacks* echoed through the room, and the breach broke open on its own, the barrels swinging loose from the handle like a broken carrot.

"After you," I said.

Baskin glared at the gun, at me, then tossed the thing over behind the sofa and grumbled past me up the stairs.

"You wanna tell me why you let a couple goons outta the cooler to rough me up?" I asked him as we climbed.

He shrugged without turning.

"Where else was I going to get them? Would've taken a lot longer to find criminals out on the street."

Was he tryin' to make with the funny?

"That... ain't really how I meant the question."

"I guessed that might be the case."

We'd reached the second floor, now. The banister overlooked the sitting room we'd just come from; up here were a handful of doors, one of which was cracked open enough to show a claw-footed iron bathtub. The carpet and wallpaper upstairs were an off-cream, which is about the dumbest color for carpet and wallpaper imaginable. If you ain't gonna go white, at least go dark enough so it ain't gonna show dirt, yeah?

Oh, right. And I also recognized the lingering traces of familiar perfume and a natural musk. Ramona may notta been there now, or maybe she was hiding and focused on keepin' me from sensing her aura, but she damn well *was* here, and not too long ago.

"I knew they wouldn't be able to do you any real harm," he said, finally answering the question I'd actually asked, "let alone kill you. I just wanted you out of action for a few days."

"Long enough for you'n Ramona to finish whatever it is you got cooking? Weren't sure what she pulled was gonna keep me laid up long enough?"

"I'm sorry, I still don't know who you're referring to. Or what. If you were already injured, I assure you I had no idea."

"Uh-huh."

We'd stopped in front of a door that didn't look at all different from any of the others. Baskin obviously didn't wanna turn that knob. I wasn't gonna let him off the hook, but since I had another question, I gave him an excuse to put it off another minute.

"Tell me something, counselor. Did you already know about me when you hired me last year? 'Cause I'll tell ya, I certainly didn't get that impression."

Now he *did* face me. I didn't even have to try tasting his emotions; I could see in his face that he was measuring his answer, deciding if telling me the truth would spill any secrets or reveal any weaknesses he didn't want me knowing about.

"No," he said finally. "I don't know if I'd go so far as to say it's pure coincidence I hired you—I've come to see that the mystical has its own ways of shaping things..."

I nodded.

"...but no, at the time I had no idea you were anything more than what you seemed." Then, maybe thinking a friendlier approach might work out, he expanded on that. "Truth is, when we met, I was only just learning of the existence of the supernatural at all. When I was trying to retrieve those photos I eventually hired you to find, I came across some... interesting methods. That was my next step, if you'd failed."

Huh. And in little more than a year, he'd learned enough to construct wards, assemble enough of a collection to make himself a contender, acquire the services of someone like

Ramona, and get at least some notion of what I was and what I could do? Either he was lyin' through his teeth about when he got started, or he'd had some big-time help.

In any case, I offered up a glitzy smile like I believed every word and didn't have a question in my noggin, and gestured toward the door. He gave up a sigh in return—as though I was somehow gonna have forgotten that I wanted in there—and opened up.

Yeah, the room definitely had additional wards, meant to make its contents harder to detect. Soon as the door opened, the energies hit me like the burst of heat from a blast furnace. Wasn't the largest collection of mystical artifacts I'd ever seen, not by miles, but more'n I'd expected.

He'd divided the room—which was pretty sizable, probably occupying at least half of the second story—into a series of aisles via rows of half-height bookcases. Many of 'em were empty, or held random curios that looked interesting but held no power or intrinsic value. He owned a buncha books, most of 'em on the history or detail of various occult practices, from the Goetia to Vodoun to Kabbalah to Renaissance treatises on alchemy. A few were actual grimoires, spellbooks of this tradition or that; presumably Gina's stolen tome was supposed to have found a home among 'em. At the room's far end lay a cement slab with a rune-inscribed pentagram etched into it, makin' me wonder if Baskin had already been fiddling around with conjuring.

Gods help all of us if he had.

Other gewgaws on the shelves, and in a few glass display cases, radiated real power. A Grecian urn, cracked and discolored, hummed at a level too low for mortal ears with what mighta been the voice of the original potter's shade. An Austrian knife from the battlefields of the Great War was crusted and profanely empowered with old bloodstains in shades of brownish-violet, spilled from somethin' that sure as hell hadn't been human. A sliver of dried pumpkin rind from the Jack-o'-Lantern Gate, which hasn't opened since Washington was president. A protective talisman here, a shamanistic fetish there. Even a Fae wand, worn and a lot less potent than my L&G, with only a few traces of magic left. I saw one glass display, open and empty, that woulda been just the right size for a certain spear Ramona'd tried to acquire a short while back.

And off on a shelf in the rearmost case, a small pile of rags. All worn, tattered around the edges, some browned with age, some relatively new, some...

I froze, claws of ice scraping down my spine, each vertebra a key on an old, crumbling xylophone. I shivered where I stood, and I *don't fucking do that*. Somebody hadn't just walked over my grave, they'd soaked it in diseased blood and salted the earth.

Something in that heap of scraps and tatters was ugly. Profane. An oozing canker in the world. It wanted me dead; and not just dead, but damned.

I whirled, grabbing the top couple of rags and tossing 'em over my shoulder, ignoring Baskin's shouts. What I found was an old cleaning cloth, gray with dirt and oil. In the center of the fabric was a blotch of rust and filth where it'd once been wrapped around a hunk of... something. Something metal, obviously. Something, now that I looked closer, vaguely pistol-shaped.

*Fuck every heaven and hell.* I knew what I'd been sensing, what was chewing at me.

"Do you actually have it?" I was damn near shrieking, and I barely even noticed.

"Goddamn it, Oberon, what do you think you're—"

I had the collar of his robe in my fists and the man himself completely lifted off the floor.

"The Braddigan Gun! *Do you have it?*"

I don't think Baskin fully understood—I don't think *you* do—how close he came to dyin', in that moment. How near I was to turnin' everything I had, everything I *was*, loose on him, on that house, and damn the consequences. Some things are too horrible to be allowed loose in the world. In *any* world. I woulda killed him, a thousand more like him, Ramona, Pete—God help me—if it meant takin' that atrocity outta play.

Except...

"No! No, I don't have the damn thing! I acquired the rag and I thought maybe I could use that to *find* the gun, but it never worked!"

His panic carried the tang of truth in it, and while he mighta been a good enough liar to sometimes keep me from bein' positive if he was talkin' square or not, I was pretty sure he didn't have the skill to fake the taste of that much honesty.

I put him down, smoothed out his rumpled collar—rather polite of me, I thought—and took a long slant around the room. Yeah, as I'd figured, he had a buncha modern comforts scattered amongst the various dinguses on the shelves, so he could spend his time in here comfortably. I wandered across to another shelf, dropped the rag in an ashtray and picked up the rounded, brass-shelled cigarette lighter next to it.

"Hey! Don't you dare even think—!"

I dunno exactly what he saw in the expression I shot him, but while he didn't look remotely happy about it—steamed as a lobster dinner, in fact—he shut up quick.

Me, I made sure the oily, rusty rag had good'n caught, was already well on its way to cinders, before I even looked away from the ashtray.

And by the way? No. No, I ain't about to tell you one damn thing about the Braddigan Gun. Not what it is, not why I lost my head over it. Maybe one day, if I gotta, but... Fuck. Some things, I just damn well don't wanna talk about.

But the sensation I described to you—that I got just from the cloth it'd been wrapped in, not even from the vile thing itself—oughta give you some idea.

"So, is this why you're here?" Baskin snarled. "To just tear through my home and destroy my collection piece by piece?"

"I probably *oughta*, you incomparable moron! You got no friggin' idea what sorta power, what wonders and horrors, you've gathered here, do you? Hell, the fact you even *wanted* to find the gun is proof enough of *that*!"

Then, before the pressure I could see buildin' under his skin burst out through his yap in a form we'd both regret, I continued, "But no. I'm here lookin' for something in particular." Right about here I made a point of giving an obvious up-and-down to another of the display cases, a massive, wardrobe-sized thing lyin' on its side with a stone bench—what could only be described as a bier, really—inside it.

Baskin braced himself. No way he'd admit it until I forced the issue, but he knew what I was about to ask; ain't as though I was bein' remotely subtle.

So of course, I didn't ask. Not yet.

"Whaddaya know about Saul Fleischer?" Might as well try to learn somethin' useful while keeping the guy on his heels.

"Uh..." Yeah, definitely not what he'd expected. I hadda assume he was better at this in the courtroom. "What?"

"Fleischer. Saul. Northside Gang. Works for Moran."

"Yes, I... know who he is. Is *this* why—?"

"Way I figure, counselor, you keep an ear to the ground where trouble boys are concerned—and an even sharper ear when they're wrapped up in your—" I waved at the shelves. "—other interests. So tell me what you got on him that I ain't gonna find in a file in your office."

Baskin staggered to another cabinet, poured himself another glass from another bottle. He waved it at me, in what I guess was meant as an offer. I waved back, in what he guessed— correctly—was a "no, thanks."

"Fleischer definitely has some occult interests," he said, suddenly all too happy to be helpful. "I don't know much of the details, or how deep those interests—or his knowledge, or his skill—reach."

"Huh. You know what tradition he practices? Or traditions?"
If I knew for sure what to watch for, and if I wasn't recovering
from a head wound next time he and I met...

"He's Jewish. What do you think? He's a Kabbalist."

I shrugged at him. "Never presume, bo. I know of a rabbi
down in Galveston, Texas, who practices Haitian Voodoo. And
one of the most powerful Russian witches I ever met was Jewish."

"What, really?"

I smiled.

"Well, whatever. In this case, yeah. Kabbalah."

"Right. That's useful to know. Thank you."

"Of course. Was that all? If I'd known what you were
looking for, I'd have been happy to help without all the—"

"Well, that and I wanna know what you and Ramona did
with the mummy you stole."

It took a sec for his jaw to realize his brain wasn't tossin'
words through it anymore, and to finally stop waggling.

"We di—I don't know what you're talking about!" he finally
forced out.

"Uh-huh." I pointed back at that display case. "What's that
for, then?"

"It's not for anything in particular! I just had differently
sized cases built in case I wound up needing them!"

"Uh-huh," I said again. "I'll just keep on nosing around,
then. Ain't as though this house is all *that* humongous."

He was muttering again as I reached the door—not the one
back to the hall, but the nearest of several others that mighta
led to closets or different rooms—and it was only when my
mitt closed over the knob that I realized the bastard was
murmuring in Ancient Greek.

*You gotta be fucking kidding me.* He couldn't be that dippy,
could he? He wasn't really gonna try...?

He was.

I felt the house wards, and particularly the glyphs focused on
the collection itself, strengthening, reaching out to me, tryin' to

bind me in place with grasping fingers of old magics and barely constrained power. For the span of a few breaths, my stomach knotted, my soul quivered, in a faint but unmistakable echo of what I'd felt in times past when confronted with genuine, significant, hostile magics. Orsola Maldera's wards, f'rinstance.

And then I let go of the doorknob and turned back toward Daniel Baskin. Shoulders rigid, eyes unblinking. The whole second story trembled, just a little, as my own magic swept back over the runes, rushing up and over Baskin's chant in a backdraft of invisible flame. The lights flickered, dimmed; the display case that I'd figured was for the stolen mummy cracked across its nearest side.

"You stupid, *stupid* little man."

I drank the magics infusing his aura, his voice, leaving him gasping for breath, spitting words without meaning.

"You think because you've learned a few tricks, amassed a few relics, you know anything?"

I felt the power of one of the glyphs starting to slip through my own defenses, through a spiritual crack that shouldn't be there, wouldn't be there if not for the cloud of bad luck hovering around me. I channeled some of the power I'd just taken from Baskin back into it, shoring up the breach, sweeping the groping tendril of magic back the way it'd come. He choked, staggered back so that only the wall held him up. His glass tumbled from limp fingers to the carpet, spilling the last few gulps of whatever booze he'd been sipping.

"You think you *are* anything?"

What pain the wards had inflicted on me I now balled up in one mental fist, mixing in the lingering ache of the head wound, feeding both with the rest of what I'd taken from Baskin until they blended and flared in a psychic flame. It was probably just as well I hadn't taken the time to draw my wand; if I had, the agony might've been enough to kill an unprepared mortal.

As it was, when I thrust that pain into his thoughts and dreams, the wall wasn't enough to hold him any longer. He collapsed to the floor with a piercing scream, one arm bleeding as it crushed the fallen glass beneath it.

I knelt beside him, more myself, more in control, but still furious as a wet cat in an aviary.

"You have no goddamn idea what you've gotten into, do you, Baskin?" I let the worst of the pain I'd inflicted on him fade, just to be sure he could hear'n understand me. "You don't have the foggiest notion what's out there. What you're playin' with. You think you do. You think because you got someone to whisper forbidden knowledge in your ear that you're a force to be reckoned with. You thought that knowin' what to call me, that the name *aes sidhe*, meant you *knew* me. You're ignorant. You're a kid with a Tommy gun. 'Collector.' Like these are coins, or rare liqueurs, or fucking stamps? You don't even know enough to respect the power you've gathered around you.

"Where. Is. Ramona?" I poked his cheek with a fingertip. "Where's the mummy?"

He kept his trap zipped. I'll give him a few points for guts, even if the stifled moan at the back of his throat, or the fact he was lyin' in a sticky puddle of expensive hooch did sorta spoil the effect some.

"Okay, pal. Your call."

I stood, and now I *did* draw the L&G. He flinched, hard, but I wasn't aimin' at him this time.

"How many of these relics and dinguses are hot, counselor? How many people—or un-people—are out there, steamed and hunting for their missing toys? How many others would be *real* taken with the idea of acquiring a hoard like yours all in one fell swoop? Way I see it, that's the main purpose of all the wards you got inscribed around this room, this house. Gotta make sure every Tom, Dick, and Horrid with a nose for mojo can't find you in their sleep."

I picked a random direction, pointed the L&G, and started draining the luck and magic in its path, sweeping it back and forth. Not from any of the relics—I made sure to avoid those, or pass over 'em—but from the room itself.

The room... I don't wanna say it shook, 'cause it wasn't anythin' that physical; didn't flicker, 'cause it wasn't visual. But *something* shifted, something unseen, something I don't think most people could even have been aware of.

But I was. And Baskin was.

"How many of those wards can you lose?" I asked. "Can any of those folks and Fae you're afraid of sense this place yet?" I very deliberately raised the wand, then slowly lowered my arm to point at a different side of the room. "How many more can you spare?" I started gatherin' my will again...

"Enough! Dammit, Mick, enough. You've made your point."

She stood in a doorway, framed in the lamplight of what looked to be a pretty swanky bedroom. She wore a sheer bathrobe over a silken nightgown, a combination that, if I hadn't been through everything I had over the last week, mighta made me forget why I was here. As it was, all it did was make me wonder if that was the entire point, or if this was just what she wore to bed.

At Baskin's house.

Yeah, okay, that bothered me. Only a little, though.

"Ramona. Lookin' right at home for someone Baskin ain't ever heard of."

She crossed her arms and scowled fierce enough to scare off a rabid *cu sidhe*.

"You think you're so funny, don't you? You think you know everything!"

"Well, you're half right."

"Do you have *any idea* how much danger you might've put Daniel in just now?"

I carefully slid the L&G back into its holster under my coat.

"I'da looked pretty stupid if I hadn't. Melodramatic, even. You know how much I hate that."

"Goddamn it, Mick!"

"Go help your boss up, Ramona. Maybe fix him a drink; looks as if he could use one."

Wasn't so much giving her an order, really, as permission. Letting her know I wasn't gonna take it poorly if she moved to help. But hey, if phrasing it as a command irritated her more, I was feelin' petty enough to call it a bonus.

"I didn't know you could be this cruel," she whispered as she passed. I felt the disappointment, the sorrow, the heartbreak pouring off her in waves, tryin' to insinuate themselves into my head, my soul...

"Don't you fucking *dare*!" I put just enough mojo into my voice to make it thunder, saw her and Baskin both near jump outta their skins.

"First," I snarled, "you and me've been way too close for you to say that. You know damn well what I'm capable of.

"More to the point," and I jabbed a finger their way, making 'em both jump a second time, "you're the one who escalated this, doll. You're the one turned a crazed mob loose on me."

"I didn't know one of them had a gun! Mick, I swear to you—"

"So fucking what? You didn't know any of 'em *didn't*! Besides, couple lucky shots with a heavy enough club woulda done the same damage. You don't get to decide how much it's okay to hurt me, dammit! Or when it's okay to make me hurt anyone else! And then, just a few days later, what'd you do? You and your boob of a boss send a couple of droppers to try'n put me down again!"

"Hey!" Baskin, now back on his feet, tried to butt in. "Don't—"

"You! Close your head before I close it for you! And you!" Back to Ramona. "You had no friggin' idea what shape I mighta been in when you sent 'em. But you didn't let that stop you, did you?

"So don't you pull your emotional horse shit with me, sister. *You* took the gloves off. This, all of it, is on you."

Both of 'em looked shellshocked, but at least she didn't try to say anythin' else by way of excuses. Guess I'd made it clear there was nothin' *to* say.

"Good. That's what I wanted to hear. *Now*, let's try this again, from the top. Where's the mummy?"

"We don't have it, Mick," Ramona said, refusing to look me in the face. "We never did."

Okay, I admit, I wasn't anticipatin' that. It threw me for what felt like ten or twelve hours. "What?"

"It's true! We don't... I had to run after—after what happened at the carnival. Too crowded, too much attention, and after the gunshot, I knew the police wouldn't be long. Also, I... wasn't at my best. Worried over you, whether or not you choose to believe it. Anyway, I thought I'd lurk around outside until dark, when things had calmed down. I don't know how anyone else could have gotten in and stolen the body with so many people around, but when I finally did go back, it was already gone!"

It was a daffy story, unbelievable, but I *did* believe it. I heard it in her tone, tasted it in her aura. Ramona mighta been a swell liar most of the time, but she was off her game right now. Thrown by all that'd happened: me discoverin' her connection with Baskin, worry over him and over me both, confusion over someone beating her to the goods, more'n a little fear over what she'd just seen in me...

Maybe, on a better day, she coulda hidden all that from me. But no way even *she* coulda *faked* it all, not well enough to put one over on me. And in the midst of all that, I also tasted truth. She wasn't lyin' to me, not tonight. Not about this.

Which meant the only real meaningful observation I could make on the whole situation was, "Well, shit."

So who the hell had the damn thing? Fleischer was the obvious choice, but I didn't see Shea and his Uptown Boys bein' able to sneak past a whole mob of bulls and bystanders to heist anything as conspicuous as a dead body—and even if they *were* able, I had trouble imagining they'd be *willing*. No, it hadda be someone a lot sneakier, a lot subtler. That didn't rule Fleischer out—God knows who else he might have on the payroll—but it meant he wasn't a sure bet.

Damn. How many people wanted this stupid mummy? What the hell kinda mysteries or magic did it hold? How did—?

"Mick? How did you even know I was after the mummy in the first place?"

"Didn't, toots, not until I tracked you down to the carnival and saw the ads for the funhouse."

She was more puzzled than ever, now.

"You were looking for me? Why?"

Hmm. If she was already thrown tonight, maybe I could finagle some answers outta her I'd never been able to get. I tried to look real calm, real casual, but I was watchin' her close—physically and magically both—when I said, "Oh, your sister hired me to help bring you home."

You believe you've seen someone "go pale," that you've seen what I'm talkin' about. You haven't. You got no idea. Ramona went absolutely corpse-white, down to her lips. Her knees buckled, visibly, and what mighta been a word or a gasp or a breath died with a squeak as her throat closed tight as an angry fist.

That wasn't all. For just a heartbeat or two, the last of her mental and mystical control slipped, too. And I knew.

You gotta remember, Ramona'd been an enigma to me since day one. I hadn't been able to tell whether she was human or not, and even after I'd decided she couldn't be any old mortal, I was never able to pick up on what she *was*. That ain't normal; it takes a real good veil, some serious disguising mojo, to hide that kinda thing from me once I've started digging into it. But Ramona, she'd always managed.

Until now. I knew, and I almost wished I didn't.

*Succubus.*

Ramona was a friggin' *succubus*! I knew it hadda be my imagination, but I swore I could suddenly see a faint afterimage of horns and vast, membranous wings.

Guess she wasn't the only one not quite able to hide her reactions tonight. Whatever was showin' on my mug right then, or whatever she felt of my own reaction in that moment her defenses were down, she knew that I knew.

She straightened, got hold of herself, though she remained white enough you coulda waved her overhead to signal surrender.

"And that's why I never told you," she said, sorrowful but not remotely apologetic. "I've seen that reaction before."

"Can you blame me? Shit, it's *you* lot been spreadin' most of the legends about your own kind!"

"No. No, I suppose I can't. So what now?"

I stepped back to one of the lower bookcases, made sure I wasn't about to plant my keister on anythin' that was gonna break, stab me, and/or curse me, and hopped up to sit on it. It creaked, but held; Baskin winced, but also held.

"I've seen the rites for summoning and binding... demons, before." I almost couldn't bring myself to use the word in this context, but it's what they called themselves, and I didn't really have a better one, so... "That pentacle back there? Maybe that'd serve for summoning, but you don't look or behave like you're bound by any of the magics I know. So what's the story, sister?"

She tossed a silent question her boss's way, and it was Baskin who answered.

"You remember Winger?"

''Course I did. He was why I'd ever met Baskin at all. Corrupt Chicago committeeman who'd had pics of a more than revealing nature that coulda dropped our favorite Assistant State's Attorney in a whole deep pot of hot water. I nodded.

"Well, like I told you, I was just learning about all this, starting to study the occult, during that whole... misunderstanding. And it was right afterward that a man I was prosecuting managed to escape custody and skip town.

"Not a big deal. It happens sometimes, and there wasn't

a lot of security on this man—or that much of a manhunt afterward—as he wasn't especially dangerous. Just an embezzler and, on occasion, blackmailer."

Ah. I saw where *this* was goin'.

"Lemme guess. He's the guy who provided Winger with those pics."

"Got it in one. Obviously, I couldn't let him just run free. No, he didn't have the pictures, but he'd certainly seen them. I couldn't get the manpower, though, not with so many other, more dangerous criminals out there. So I... decided to pursue less traditional options."

"You panicked and summoned a creature from, for all you knew, the pits of hell."

"If you want to put it that way."

I wonder if he understood how damn lucky he'd gotten. How easy it was for the tiniest mistake or misstep in that sorta ritual to cost the summoner his soul, and set an unholy beast loose in the mortal world.

I didn't even bother askin' him why—assuming it was deliberate and not a happy accident—he'd called up a succubus instead of something a lot more overtly and obviously fearsome. In part because it wasn't tough to guess, and in part because, much as I was tryin' to keep my thoughts from dwellin' on that particular topic, the idea of the two of 'em makin' whoopee still made my gut squirm.

And I knew what direction Baskin's tastes ran; I *had* seen those pics, after all.

So okay, that explained how Ramona—or whatever her real name was—ended up workin' under... uh, workin' for him. And it explained a lot of his swift advancement in his occult practices; he had his own private tutor, with access to knowledge and powers that few humans ever could dream of.

But I still didn't know why she had the kinda freedom and free will she did, why she didn't show any of the signs of a traditional binding or "infernal" contract. Why...?

Wait a tick. Contract? Oh, for the love of...

"You *didn't!*" I shouted at him.

Baskin just blinked at me, confused, but Ramona started to laugh.

"I told you," she said to him. "Mick puts things together fast and makes these intuitive leaps. It's actually impressive, watching him work.

"Yes," she said, now turning back to me. "Daniel found me a loophole. A bargain spelled out so long ago that Latin was the newest style, and he found a loophole."

Somehow, I found the whole idea less exciting than she did.

"Leave it to the friggin' lawyers... Except, you ain't free. You're still runnin' Baskin's errands. And I remember our talk a few months ago. You couldn't tell me who you worked for. Literally *couldn't.*"

Her turn to nod. "We made a new deal. A separate contract—and yes, it included secrecy. He got me out of the binding, so I didn't have to go home when my term of service was complete. In return, I agreed to work for him for a decade. It's not particularly onerous, and it's not as though I'm getting any older. When the time's up, I'm free to go. Not many of us from my... neighborhood can say that."

"I'da thought your people'd have laws against that sorta thing. No way Baskin's the first to ever pull it off."

"We do," she admitted, taking the drink she'd poured Baskin from his hands and draining it. "If they ever drag me back..." She shuddered. "It doesn't bear thinking about.

"But the truth is, Mick, I'm nobody important. I figured I'd have to look over my shoulder now and again, but I honestly didn't expect them to send anyone after me!"

"Looks like you mighta blundered that one, Ramona."

"I don't know. Maybe. Or maybe it's more personal. We do a lot of squabbling and scrabbling for power back home. A lot of politics. Makes your Courts look downright cooperative."

I doubted that, but let it slide.

"It's entirely possible," she continued, "that whoever approached you isn't here officially, but is someone with a grudge who wants to see my shot at freedom destroyed. What'd you say her name was?"

"I didn't."

Then again, I couldn't see how it'd hurt, and this wasn't exactly a normal client-privilege sorta thing.

"McCall. Carmen."

Ramona frowned. "Don't know the name. Not that it matters; I'm sure it's an alias. Mick, I... I know you're angry with me, and you've got every right to be. You don't owe me anything. But please, please, you can't tell her where I am. You can't help her find me!"

Somehow, this didn't seem the time to clarify that my job wasn't just to *locate* Ramona but *deliver* her, neatly packaged with a bow on top.

"It ain't that simple, doll."

"What is she paying you? What could she *possibly* offer you that you'd even consider this?"

Kept my yap shut tight. No way I was answerin' *that*.

Unfortunately, though, Ramona's no bunny, and she *did* know me pretty well.

"Is she holding someone over you? Did she threaten Pete? Or something to do with Adalina?"

God*dammit*!

And again, either she saw somethin' I didn't want her to see, or she tasted somethin' in my own emotions. She was near as good as pluckin' that outta the air—or nearby auras—as I was.

"That's it, isn't it? Did she threaten to hurt the girl, Mick? Or..."

*Don't say it. Don't think of it.*

"Or promise to wake her?"

*Fuck.*

Through teeth clenched into a portcullis to keep words a lot uglier—or more dangerous—from escaping, I asked, "How do you even know about that?"

"I heard Sealgaire mention the name before he vanished, remember? Did you really think I was going to let that drop?"

"I'll kill him." Which we both knew was bunk, even if I could possibly find him, but it made me feel better to say it.

Barely.

"You managed to avoid talking much about her in front of me when we visited the Ottatis, but I heard the name. So once I knew there was more to her than just some sick kid, it wasn't too hard to dig up the fact that she's a changeling or, in a very general sense, the story of your investigation and of what happened to her. You'll have to tell me the specifics some day."

"Right. I'll be sure to pencil it in on my calendar. Gimme a ring when your home freezes over and we'll get into it." Then, because it didn't matter anymore, "An elixir. She promised an elixir that'll wake Adalina. So you can see why I can't just drop this for you."

"I think you not only *can* drop this, you will."

"Oh? Why's that, Ramona? You gonna try holding Adalina over me, too, now?"

"I don't think I'll have to, Mick. I think you already *know* why you can't go through with this, and it's not for *my* sake."

And again, all I could think was, *No. Don't you dare fucking say it.*

"If you know what I am, now, then you know what McCall is."

*Don't say it!*

"And you're a smart fella, Mick. You're already asking the questions, even if you don't want to admit it."

*You're right, I don't want to! So don't—*

"If Carmen McCall's a succubus like me, then you're already wondering... what's *in* the elixir?"

*Goddammit!*

"What's it going to do? Will it do what she promised? Even if it does, are there side-effects? Is it going to poison Adalina? Change her? Leave her open to possession?"

I didn't even remember standin', but I was on my feet, meathooks reaching out for the nearest thing I could break, and the lights were startin' to flicker again. I hadda force myself to stop, rein myself in before I fell back into... unpleasantries.

"So how desperate are you, Mick? What—*who*—are you prepared to risk on the word of a demon?"

# CHAPTER TWELVE

"Mick? Mick! Slow down a little!"

"What'sa matter, Pete?" I was storming along the sidewalk, headed for my office. The breeze kicked the tails of my coat and the occasional stray newspaper around my ankles, but at least it wasn't rainin' tonight. We'd parked his car a couple blocks back; I just hadn't been able to stand bein' inside that rolling torture chamber one second longer. "Your plates hurt? You should be able to keep up. I thought you were a beat cop."

"I don't mean the walk, dammit! I mean what you're telling me! She's a *succubus*?"

Part of me bein' so angry at everything had meant that, dealin' with the pain of being in the flivver, I hadn't been willing to jaw much on the road. So it was only when he'd parked and we'd hopped out that I'd started goin' into detail on what I'd learned at Baskin's place.

"That's what I said."

I did pause long enough to glance up at the street light I was passin' to check it didn't go out. I hadda make sure I was still in control; I'd been losin' it too easy of late.

"As in a demon. From the pits of Hell."

"So they tell me."

"And I thought *you* told *me* once that everythin' supernatural that wasn't human was Fae, or at least related."

"Yep."

"So how do *demons* fit into that?" The next street light and the headlamps of a passing car shone in his peepers as they went wide. "Shit, if there's a Hell, does that mean Heaven and God really exist? I mean really, *provably* exist? I gotta get my keister to church more often..."

"How the hell—pardon the expression—would I know that, Pete?"

"But, if demons—"

"Pete, *they* claim to be demons. They claim to come from the damn Pit, with lakes of fire and the souls of the damned and all that. Me and mine? We're pretty sure it's horsefeathers. They're just another nation of Fae."

"Really?" He sounded less than convinced.

"Really. Nastier'n most, even most Unseelie, and I'm sure wherever their home is, it ain't someplace you'd wanna take a new blushing bride on your honeymoon. They take strange forms and have stranger magics. But they're Fae."

"And you know this for sure."

"*Pretty* sure, I said."

"And if you're wrong?"

"Then we're all gonna look dumb."

I'm sure Pete woulda had somethin' smart to say to that, but we turned the last corner to see—surprise, surprise—someone sittin' on the stoop of Soucek's building. Probably waitin' for me, since most of the offices in the place were vacant, and none of the others kept the kinda hours I did.

"I need to start leavin' refreshments out," I muttered. "Maybe put in some furniture."

But on the square, when I came a few steps nearer and got a good slant on *who* was loitering there, it *was* a bit of a shock.

"Tsura?"

She bolted to her feet, almost guiltily.

"Mick! I'm glad you're finally here. I—" She stopped, peerin' over my shoulder, and I realized she was unhappy I wasn't alone.

"Look," I said, "this ain't a good time to—"

"Can we talk?"

"What part of 'ain't a good time' do you not—? Guh. Fine. Come in with us. When I'm done with—"

"No." She was damn near bouncin' in place. "No, I mean alone. Please, just for a minute."

Dammit, I couldn't handle this right now! I was too steamed, too worried, had too much to deal with!

"No, we can't! You wanna talk? Come in and wait your turn. You wanna make yourself useful? Tune in to whatever psychic radio you listen to and find me the missing mummy. Or McCall. Or Goswythe!" No way she even knew the names I was throwin' at her now, but that wasn't really the point. Not sure I *hadda* point.

I brushed past her, up the steps, and yanked the door open.

"You comin'?"

She crossed her arms and scowled, and otherwise stayed put.

"Suit yourself."

"Uh, Mick?" Pete asked as we tromped down the stairs to the basement level. "Who was—?"

"Don't worry about it."

Part of me was already feelin' a bit sheepish; this was the second time I'd barked at her that way without real cause. I was still too peeved and too caught up in more important stuff to go back out and talk to her, but if she was still there after I'd made the call...

Except I didn't have to make any calls. Soon as I set foot in the hallway, I sensed her, already in my office.

Again.

"Better locks. Definitely better locks."

Pete blinked. "Huh?"

"Maybe some wards. Yeah." I strode over and tossed open

the door to my place. "Ms. McCall."

"Mr. Oberon," she said, from my chair. Behind my desk. "Why is your typewriter lying on the floor?"

"It was tired."

"And the tooth?"

"It's the typewriter's teddy bear. What's in the elixir?"

She blinked, took a long drag off a cigarette in an ivory holder.

"Are you sure you want to talk about such things in front of your friend there?"

"If I didn't, I wouldn't have."

"Fair enough." Another puff. "But of course I can't tell you that. A little of this, a little of—"

"How about we skip to the part where I tell you I know you're a damn succubus and I'm more'n ready to commit some serious violence, and you give me a straight answer?"

"Oh." She slowly lowered the gasper, chewed her lip once or twice. I'd thrown her, but not very. "Oh," she said again. "Dear Ramona's been incautious, I see. That complicates things."

"You got plans to say anything *useful*, toots?"

"Fine. I'm still not going to give you the recipe for my elixir, *bo*. But I'll tell you the answer you're looking for is yes."

"Yes?"

"Yes." She grinned, which woulda been *less* disturbing if it hadn't been so pretty. "It requires a human soul."

There it was. The one thing I most hadn't wanted to hear, and the one thing I'd pretty well known I would. I dunno if demons can *really* steal or bargain for the soul or not, or if it's somethin' else about the life essence of mortals they collect and just call it the soul. But it *might* be the real deal—and even if it ain't, it'd still mean somebody's life sucked away and consumed to wake Adalina.

"And it doesn't matter," she purred. "You'll go through with this anyway, because you've no other choice. If you had any other way to wake the little tart, you'd have found it long before now. Besides, it's not as though *good* people have any truck with me and mine, is it?"

I wanna tell you I laughed in her face. That I didn't give it a second thought, that I'd never even have considered somethin' like that.

But every god help me, I did.

Just for a moment, I did.

I mean, she was right. What kinda sap gets himself mixed up in a hellish bargain for his own soul, anyway? I'd met a few, and I'll tell ya, Baskin was one of the *better* of the lot. Besides, it ain't like me refusin' to use the elixir was gonna unkill whatever poor fool she'd last rubbed out. Better *some* good come outta it, right?

Right?

Adalina... It'd been over a year, now. I didn't know what else to do for her. And she deserved so much better'n this, especially after...

After...

And that, *that* was when I came to my senses. When Adalina saved me from doin' something awful, from makin' the sorta choice I'd left the Seelie Court to escape.

Adalina lay on her bed, in an endless coma, because she'd almost died; battered and torn by her grandmother's spells until even her Fae magics and resilience shouldn't have been able to save her. She *should* have died, *expected* to die. Because she knew Orsola needed to be stopped, because it would save lives, sure, alla that.

But also because she refused to live as a monster.

It didn't matter if the price for Carmen McCall to wake her was one I'da been willing, in my worst moments, to pay. Adalina would never, ever have wanted it.

"You've got thirty seconds," I growled—*literally* growled—at McCall, "to get your ass outta my chair, outta my office, and outta my life. Otherwise, I am gonna either *make* you leave, or kill you. And by then I really, truly will not give a *fuck* which of those two outcomes we arrive at."

That unctuous smile slid off her face like wet mud on a hillside.

"You didn't... You can't!"

"I did. I can. Twenty-five seconds."

Now, she stood, the chair flyin' back so hard it bounced off the filing cabinet, but probably not so she could quietly leave like I'd asked.

"How *dare* you? Nobody says no to me!" Her fury was a series of explosions, blast after blast buffeting me from across the room. I squinted into 'em and didn't flinch.

"Twenty seconds."

She ranted, shrieking her rage in a voice that twisted and broke, in turns higher and lower and more heartbreaking and more horrifying than anything that ever came from human pipes. Claws she didn't have a few seconds ago gouged deep into the wood of my desk, sending out a geyser of splinters.

Well, nuts. No way *that* was gonna buff out.

"Ten. And if you'll take some friendly advice, maybe work on that temper."

"You can stop counting, Oberon." Just that quick, she was all smiles and calm again, which bugged me more'n all the screeching had done. "I'm not leaving until I'm good and ready."

I went for my wand before she'd finished speaking. If she wanted to make a tussle of it, I'd give her one—and I had every intention of hittin' hard and swift enough to win that fight before she knew the bell'd rung.

Except it was *my* bell that got rung. 'Cause what I didn't know is that her whole tantrum was a put-on, a distraction, at least in part. And that McCall'd started the fight before I set foot in the office.

The blow came from behind, hard, fast. Wasn't iron or magic, but a knock to the conk like that woulda put me on the floor, even if only briefly, at the best of times. Since it landed right on my wound, which was real near to healed but not *quite* faded yet, this wasn't the best of times.

My knees and palms hit the carpet; the L&G rolled under the desk, which actually surprised me some, since the room seemed to be spinnin' the other direction. I saw someone walk past me—just a pair of shoes and trouser cuffs, from my angle—and I didn't recognize 'em at first. I was too busy strugglin' to Humpty Dumpty my noggin back together, and tryin' to figure out who coulda slugged me. Who coulda...?

Aw, shit, no.

I forced myself to look up, and yeah, there he was. Pete stood beside McCall behind the desk like a good little puppy. (I never did find out for sure what he bashed me with, but I'm guessin' the butt of his service revolver.) She had her arm around him, her chin perched girlishly on his shoulder.

"Isn't he darling?" she said. "I could just eat him up with a spoon."

Wasn't Pete's fault. I knew that from the get-go. Didn't hold this against him at all, or at least I wouldn't in a minute when the ache subsided some.

McCall, though... Far as I was concerned, those two acceptable options for how to handle her had dropped to one, now. And "making her leave" wasn't the one I was still okay with.

'Course, it'd have to wait for a time where those claws weren't mere inches away from Pete's spine.

I struggled back to my feet. Didn't even bother tryin' to retrieve the L&G; no way she'da been okay with a move like that.

"When did...?" Nah, it didn't matter. She coulda gotten to Pete at any time in the past week. Or even before, if she'd planned this out far enough in advance to have him wrapped around her finger before she ever even approached me.

Damn succubi. I can respect a good plot or a good grudge, but you come at me direct. Goin' through my friends? Gettin' into their heads, their emotions, until they can't tell right from purple? That ain't kosher—and it ain't forgivable.

Meant she was well informed, though. And keeping a slant on me, so she'da known when it was safe to approach Pete and...

"It was you the whole time, wasn't it, McCall? All the different people digging around on me. Talkin' to folks I know, pinpointing who's more important to me than who? Never was any group." *Never was Goswythe*, I added silently. Damn, but I shouldn'ta let myself get so fixed on that notion! "Your whole spiel about findin' Ramona before 'they' did was just more smoke. All of it, just you wearin' different faces."

"Oh, I couldn't possibly know if it was *all* me," she cooed. "But certainly *most* of it." Crazy twist actually batted her lashes at me!

"So what now? You know everything I do, or you will once you'n Pete have the chance to barber for a few. You don't need me anymore—or him, either, once you got your information."

"Mick, Mick, Mick. You're adorable. I didn't hire you only to *find* my dear sister, remember? I hired you to *deliver* her. Signed and sealed."

Dammit.

"Yeah, but if you already know where to find her—"

"No. You're going to bring her to me. You're going to ensure that she's in no shape to resist, or interfere with me bringing her home. We have such... lovely entertainments planned for her 'welcome back' party.

"Until then, dear Pete's going to be keeping me company. Aren't you, love?"

Pete's answering grin was absolutely empty of anything resemblin' rational thought.

"You know how to reach me," she continued. "I do hope you'll come through for us. Soon. In fact, you have... Oh, what is it? Ten days? Eleven?"

I was reluctant to give her even this much satisfaction, but...

"'Til what?"

"Why, the next full moon, of course. Even *I* won't be able to keep dear Petey in check then. I'm afraid things could get... messy."

*Damn* her!

"So do get to it, Mick. I'm sure you'd absolutely hate to disappoint us."

Yeah. "Us." Not exactly bein' subtle with any of this, was she?

But it got the point across. My choice was between Ramona—who I wasn't exactly happy with, but I didn't wanna be responsible for her bein' slowly, *real* slowly, tortured to death—and my best friend. I watched the two of 'em march outta my office, arm in arm, and I couldn't think of a single goddamn thing I could do to get us outta this jam.

I got no idea how long I'd been starin' at the door, or past the door—seconds, minutes, an hour—when it opened again and Tsura stepped hesitantly in from the hallway.

"I saw them leave," she said.

"Swell."

"I sensed something about him, something on him, as soon as I saw you two. I just... didn't know what it was, or how to warn you while he was right there listening."

"Well, maybe you damn well shoulda—!" And just like that I stopped, temper and breath deflating. This woman'd done her best to help me, from the moment we met and she foresaw an inkling of what Ramona was about to pull... Plus she *had* done everything shorta takin' me by the arm and yanking me away from Pete to get me to talk privately, despite how much of a jerk I'd been to her last time we talked.

And here I was... what? Shoutin' at her that she hadn't tried hard enough?

Shit.

"I'm sorry. Why don'tcha take a seat? I, uh, can't offer you anythin' but milk..."

"Oh, um..." Y'know, when she wasn't playin' the carnival huckster, her smile was surprisingly kinda shy. It was sweet. "Milk would be great, actually."

Wasn't much of a grin I could work up right now, but I tried. Poured us both a glass, put mine aside to warm up a minute or three.

"Not that I'm objectin'," I said, "but why're you even here?"

"I didn't wanna leave things where we'd left off." She scooted her keister in the seat, like she couldn't quite get comfy—or else wasn't quite comfy with the answers she was givin'. "We're not exactly old pals or anything, but it didn't feel right."

"Yeah, but that ain't the whole of it, is it?"

More scooting. "Maybe I was curious. About everything going on. About you, Ramona, the mummy... This may be just another Thursday for you, but it's all new to me."

"Nah, this ain't normal, even for me." Then I thought over the past year and change. "Maybe every fifth or sixth Thursday, tops."

A soft snort, then that almost-but-not-quite-bashful smile again.

"But that still ain't the whole of it, Tsura."

And the smile was gone. "I don't know," she finally admitted. "It's... maybe there was premonition involved? I hate not knowing, but I just can't always tell. I think I mentioned that."

"Somethin' to that effect, anyway."

"Your friend's in deep trouble, isn't he?"

It didn't even feel much like a topic change, really. "Doesn't get a lot deeper. It's partly my fault—he's only behind the eight ball 'cause he *is* my friend—and I dunno how to help him. Not without someone else payin' a pretty awful price."

Quiet for a few, then, as we both took a few slugs of the white stuff.

Then she asked, "Do you wanna tell me about it?"

And y'know what? I did. Pretty much all of it, the whole ball of wax. Ramona and how dizzy I'd been over her durin' the hunt for Gáe Assail. My history with Baskin, and the kinda bastard he was provin' to be. My discovery of Ramona's connection with him; of her and McCall's true nature. Of the no-win bind

I was in with the two succubi and Pete. Even, believe it or not, the Ottatis and Adalina—partly because I'd decided Tsura could probably be trusted, but on the square? Mostly because, after her earlier vision of Adalina and Ramona's ease in findin' the girl, it seemed like she could find out easy enough on her own if she really had a mind to.

Sure, yeah, I focused on the last year or so, told her almost squat about me from before then. And it ain't as though I spilled *everything* from the recent past, or told her alla even my most recent secrets. Still'n all, by the time I wound down, I figure she probably knew more about yours truly than any full-blooded mortal in the Windy City other'n Pete himself.

Which is sayin' less than you might assume, since even Pete was ignorant about most of my life before the Depression or thereabouts, but... I guess even a self-exiled loner needs to open up to somebody now'n again.

When it was all said'n done, Tsura took another moment to polish off the last few drops in her glass. Then, in what I gotta confess was a pretty good imitation of me—or how I try to sound these days, anyway—said, "But that ain't the whole of it, is it?"

The sound I barked probably qualified as a laugh, though I wouldn'ta sworn to it.

"I'm steamed at myself," I admitted to her. "I been blind to too much. I shoulda tumbled a long time ago to what Ramona actually is..."

"Isn't that part of her emotional power, though? To manipulate you into *not* figuring it out?"

"Yeah, maybe, but there was a time I coulda seen through it anyway. I was too taken. Got too comfortable here in this world. This life. And then I got fixated on Goswythe. Spent so long diggin' around for the damn *phouka*, God only knows what clues I missed that coulda put me wise to McCall, coulda helped me protect Pete."

"And...?" she prodded.

*And?* And what? There was no *and*. Was there?

Except there was. Is this how it feels when I do that to some mortal sap? Sense or taste or just figure out they ain't singin' the whole song and keep pushing until they do? Because if so, it's *really* irritating.

(Which doesn't mean I'm gonna stop. Just means I don't much care for it bein' turned around on me.)

"Guess I'm... feelin' guilty, some. I had Adalina's cure in my paw, or near enough, and now it's gone. Poor girl's been out for over a year now, and I've been useless. I was so close..."

Tsura reached over the desk like she wanted to take my hand, then froze halfway—whether because she realized she couldn't reach, or suddenly wasn't sure it'd be a welcome gesture, I couldn't tell ya.

"But you never really *were* close, Mick. You said so yourself; it was never a cure you could have used, not in good conscience."

"If I hadn't known..."

"You couldn't have come this far, gotten so close to doing what McCall wants, *without* finding out. And not knowing wouldn't have made it right."

My sigh was for her sake, an easy way to convey what I was feeling.

"Yeah, I know that. Ain't how it *feels*, though."

"I understand."

*Yeah, sure. Everyone says they under—*

"Imagine how I feel every time something awful happens around me that I *didn't* sense or foresee in any way." Her voice was steady, but I could taste the tremblin' emotions pouring off her at the memories she'd just invoked. "A car accident. A mugging. It's always the same. *I should have done something.* I—I was actually grateful, in a small way, when I sensed what was about to happen to you. I know that's awful, and I don't mean I'm glad it happened, but..."

*Then again, sometimes somebody actually does.*

"It's okay," I told her. "I get it."

She gazed into her glass—wishing it were full, I think, just so drinking it would give her something to do. Then she said, "Why do you suppose she told you? That the elixir involved a soul?"

"Well, you just said. I couldn'ta come this far without gettin' suspicious. Once she knew I was wondering, she probably figured I wouldn't fully believe her if she said no—and she'da been right to worry—so I guess she just decided to get ahead of it. What with her havin' an ace up her sleeve already."

"That makes sense." And then, "I think you should go find the mummy."

This time, it absolutely *did* feel like a topic change.

"You're kiddin' me, right? I got bigger things to worry about right now than a missing stiff, however old he is. I gotta focus on gettin' Pete outta hot water before he cooks!"

"Yep. And you've, what? Come up with a brilliant plan to do that in the last minute and a half?"

"Uh..." As responses go, I thought it was fairly eloquent, myself.

"You still don't want Baskin getting his mitts on the thing, do you?"

"No, but—"

"And maybe finding it'll give you some leverage for bargaining with Ramona, which might give you a leg up on dealing with McCall."

"That's *thin*, Tsura. I mean, single-strand-of-capellini thin."

"Well, yeah. That's because it's just the sugar coating I'm using to get you to swallow this."

And that brings us back to "Uh."

"Look, Mick..." Now she did stand and come around the desk just so she could put a hand on my wrist. And I gotta say, no, the gesture wasn't unwelcome at all. "I say you should go look for the mummy because it's something you *can* do. Something that has to be done, something useful you can accomplish while you're coming up with some way to help your friend. Unless you really suppose you'll come up with a better answer sitting here twiddling your thumbs and trying to read solutions in the wallpaper?"

"Y'know," I said after a minute, "I'm startin' to feel that mortals really shouldn't ever actually figure anything out. Least not before I do. Makes you insufferable and it ain't good for my superiority complex."

There was that smile again, with a mischievous tint to it this time. She didn't even say a word, just handed me my hat and coat.

# CHAPTER THIRTEEN

Rounser's carnival was a whole different place this late at night. No crowds or wandering performers, just the occasional scuffed step of a hired security guard. Maybe one light in five was on, and the place sang with the tones of stray cats and night birds and crickets—but no pixies—accompanied on occasion by a loud snore from the wagons and tents where the carnies bunked.

The stench of the crowd, though, that lingered, as did the stink of various animals. And, if I'm bein' square, so did more'n a few unpleasant memories of the last time I'd been here.

The chintzy fence surrounding the property wouldn'ta kept out a determined tumbleweed, but I let Tsura guide me to a particular entrance—a wooden plank that rotated around the nail it hung on—rather'n finding my own way in. And no, I wasn't just bein' polite or makin' her feel useful. I was sure she hadda better idea of the security guards' rounds, or which of the performers were lighter sleepers. Yeah, I'da been able to handle any of 'em without too much trouble, but better to avoid discovery altogether, see?

I suppose it all shoulda felt creepy. The shallow pools of light huddled against the shadows; the creaking wood of two dozen slapdash buildings swaying in the wind, or the whistling of that wind between the slats; bright banners and painted murals, muted in the gloom. Weirdest of all was any attempt to look into the distance even when the light allowed. Buildings of different shapes and haphazard sizes threw off any sense of perspective, so you couldn't tell near from far.

I could certainly understand why some folks *woulda* found it unnerving. Even Tsura, who'd lived with the fair for a couple years now, jumped once or twice. Me, though? Having spent time in Unseelie territory in Elphame, this was duck soup.

And since this *was* easier for me than it woulda been for anyone else, I did my damndest not to bust a gut laughing at Tsura's face, or the tiny mouse squeak she made, when I suddenly grabbed her mid-step and hauled the both of us around into the thick shadow behind the soft drink and hot dog stand.

"Mick, what the fu—!"

It was a whisper, if a harsh one, but I still put a finger to her lips and shook my head. And there we waited, me'n her pressed against the stall that might well fall over if we leaned too hard. Until, finally, she heard the same footsteps I had, and understood.

"All right," I said when they'd eventually faded, "he's gone. Sorry if I startled you, I... Hey? You okay?" It was hard to spot in the dark, even for me, but lookin' down into her face, it sure seemed like she was blushing near enough to make her cheeks glow. And somehow, without even tasting the emotion in the air around her, I knew it wasn't embarrassment over me having spooked her.

"I'm... I'm fine. I just, um. Could... Could you move?"

Oh. Right.

I pushed myself away from the wall I'd basically squished her up against.

"Sorry," I said again. "Guess that was kinda int—"

Somethin' told me at the last second that *intimate* might not be the wisest choice of words right then. Tsura seemed a lot older in so many ways, I'd forgotten how young she was. I didn't figure she'd *actually* bolt like a frightened deer if I said it, but I wasn't positive.

"—rusive of me," I finished.

She mumbled something even my ears couldn't catch, and led the rest of the way to the funhouse at a near jog.

Gettin' inside the dump wasn't hard; the padlock was such a cheap piece of crap I coulda damn near picked it with the wand, magic notwithstanding. Gettin' to the mummy display itself, that was a bit trickier. None of the actual rides were runnin' this late, so we didn't have to navigate the bouncing "haunted" floor or slowly tilting rooms, and none of the walls—mirrored or otherwise—moved on us to make the silly little maze harder'n it needed to be. Still hadda navigate that maze, though, and deal with a few "ghosts" and "ghouls" that popped out at us when we stepped on hidden triggers lyin' along this hallway or across that threshold. Still hadda take a winding slide down to the dark lower floor, beneath the jaws of "the Devourer"—which was basically a wolf and a lion badly taxidermied together—and into a cut-rate Egyptian Underworld where the sandstone and granite were wallpaper, the hieroglyphics were meaningless scribbles, and the only spirits of the dead were rats who'd met their maker after chewin' on something toxic in the decorations.

(No, they hadn't dug a basement into the soil beneath the trailers. The entrance tunnel sloped up, so the "ground floor" was actually raised, leavin' room for... Y'know what? Skip it.)

Then, of course, we hadda deal with the light—or lack of it. I could manage well enough, since it wasn't *entirely* pitch black; I couldn't sprint around without tripping on things, but I could pick my way carefully without pickin' up any bruises. Tsura was another matter, though. Eventually, with a whole lotta fast-talkin' and cajolin', she let me into her noggin enough to jazz up her eyesight.

Honestly, I hadn't been sure I could do that, but I figured if I can manipulate mortal minds enough to make 'em see something that ain't there, or temporarily blind "em, it couldn't be *too* hard to go the other way with it, right? And hey, whaddaya know? It worked.

Though she got a tad flustered again with me starin' into her peepers for a minute and a half while I fiddled with things in her brain. I'm gonna go out on a limb and guess this was a chick who didn't have a whole lotta recent experience with the hombres, though of course I wasn't about to ask her.

It was kinda cute in an awkward sorta way. Maybe I *would* ask her, later. Wasn't a polite topic, or any of my business, but it might be fun to see her face or hear her try to answer.

Yeah, I'm a bastard sometimes.

Anyway, that neat trick got us through the intervening halls, full of more "Egyptian" décor so tacky I couldn't help but joke to Tsura that maybe the mummy just got offended and walked out on its own. Unfortunately, when we actually got to the "central chamber" where the ancient stiff'd actually been displayed, that amount of vision wasn't gonna cut it. We hadda be able to give the place a solid up'n down, dig for clues, anything the cops mighta missed or not understood.

So *then* we hadda stumble around, peering at and under and around the grotesque and/or stupid adornments, hunting for a light switch that we knew was gonna be well hidden from the payin' customers. We weren't *complete* bunnies, me'n Tsura; we'd known we were gonna need real light when we got this far, so I'd thrown the generator switch outside when we got here, makin' sure we'd have power when we needed it. (Carnival had enough machinery running, even at night, that I had *some* hope it wouldn't be noticed.) We just hadn't wanted to use it until there was no other choice. Even deep in the building as we were, there was always the risk someone might tumble to us once we brightened the place up.

But as I said, there was no choice anymore. It was Tsura who finally found the dingus, tucked away behind a "canopic jar" that I'm pretty sure was a Thermos with a layer of slapdash papier-mâché. Dull yellow lights sputtered on with an irritating hum, and I was finally able to take the place in.

I wasn't impressed.

At least Rounser'd kept this part of the funhouse closed, even though it hadda be costing him business. Dunno if that'd been his call or if the cops had basically ordered it, but either way it made my job easier.

Only a little, though. Maybe it'd been the bulls themselves, who hadn't considered bits of the broken display useful evidence, or maybe it was carnival staff, but a whole mess of ginks had tromped back and forth through the hall, slammin' their plates down on whatever got in their way. Bits of bandages and other wrappings—whether genuine or decorative I couldn't immediately say—had been kicked all around the chamber, many of 'em showin' clear shoe prints in grime and dirt. Some shards of glass from the case around the sarcophagus had been crushed so tiny they were nothin' but pinprick constellations glittering in the dull glow. The sarcophagus itself—which was wood and plaster—was covered in dust and powders from the investigation. It was intact, though, except for the lid, which had split in half like a stale loaf of bread.

Basically, now I could see it, I almost wished I couldn't. Hadn't the foggiest where to begin, or what I could possibly find in this mess once I did.

All right. Don't rush into it, Mick. Just think it through.

"Good God, where do we even start?"

Or maybe *talk* it through, long as Tsura was here anyway.

"Okay, kid. Who do we guess snatched the stupid thing?"

"Um... Well, you said it wasn't Ramona and Baskin, so we can rule them out..."

"Nope. I said they *said* it wasn't them and I believed 'em. But I been wrong before. They ain't top of the suspect list anymore, by a long shot, but we don't rule anyone out, savvy?"

"Oh. All right. Uh." She started to pace, stopped herself before she could trample anymore of the scene—or before I could *tell* her she was about to trample more of the scene. I jerked her an approving nod. "So, it *could* be anyone. No guarantee it's even somebody you know is involved in all this yet. But I'd think probably, um, Fleischer? That was his name, right? You said his people were casing us—uh, the carnival, I mean. That points to him, doesn't it?"

"Yeah. Yeah, it does. It don't entirely make sense, though."

Tsura blinked.

"There's a whole heap of occult and mystical traditions," I explained, "and they don't all play well together. Lotta occultists these days study more'n one practice, but others focus on just one. Far as I've heard, Fleischer's the latter sort. He's a strict Kabbalist, doesn't dabble in much of anything else. And the Book of Exodus notwithstanding, there ain't much overlap between Kabbalah and Egyptian *heka*. I don't see where he'd have too much use for anything he might get from the mummy's spellwork.

"Still'n all, though, I agree, he's the most probable suspect."

She smiled at me, clearly proud she'd gotten the right answer.

"Now forget all that," I told her.

"What?"

"You gotta study the evidence with an open mind. 'Sokay to have theories, but you gotta put 'em aside while you're hip-deep in investigating. You get too set on a theory, no matter how likely, you start missin' things that don't mesh with it."

"Like when you got fixated on... on what's-his-name? The shapeshifter?"

Yeah, thanks for that embarrassing reminder. Still...

"Goswythe. And yep, like that. Maybe later, when we *know* insteada guess, we go back and look for signs that we're right. But for now, we gotta study the evidence without preconception."

She humphed and stuck a fist on her hip.

"So why did you ask me who I thought was behind it in the first place?"

"Can't learn to put aside preconceptions if you don't have 'em, can you?"

"Fine, *professor*. Is there a written report, too?"

"Check back later in the semester. Now get to looking."

She looked. I looked. We found about equal amounts of bupkis.

"So, professor," she asked me, stretching her back and wiping a bit of sweat from her forehead with a sleeve, "what's lesson two?"

"Cheat."

It woulda taken a whole squadroom of cops half a day to reassemble the display case from the bits and pieces and shards scattered throughout the rest of the detritus. (Well, most of the case; some of the pieces, as I'd mentioned, were pretty much powder now. Nobody was reassembling *those*.) It took me'n Tsura about an hour and a half. 'Course, we only accomplished it that quick because I siphoned several buckets-worth of good luck from the rest of the funhouse around us. Tsura's coworkers were probably gonna have to fix up some of the machinery and replace some patches of rotted wood in the near future. (I did make sure to avoid too much damage to the slides or anythin' load-bearing. Wasn't looking to crush any children today.)

I also tried to get her to use her own gift, maybe peek into the future and see where some of the pieces were hidden, or how they fit together, but even after we were done, she couldn't say for sure if she'd managed to make that work or not. I figure it did, if only because she was fittin' some of those bits together faster'n I was for a little while.

Either way, though, clearin' some space on the floor and layin' the glass out so we could see at least a fair representation of how it'd looked before it got smashed all to hell made things a lot clearer.

"Mick?"

"I see it."

I didn't wanna see it, didn't wanna come to the conclusion it was pointin' at, but I saw it.

"What does—?"

"Hold that thought, sister." I knelt next to half of the broken sarcophagus lid. "This thing ain't closed all the time, is it? That'd make it hard for the rubes to actually see the mummy your boss's been advertising all over the place."

"No, it'll close for a few minutes, then open slowly. Loud creaking and all that. The whole 'mummy is about to rise from its tomb' sort of—" she stopped and shivered "—sort of nonsense."

"Right. Nonsense."

See, there'd be no need for whoever stole the mummy to break the lid. During the day, they coulda waited for it to open by itself. At night? Woulda been a lot quieter to force it open than to crack it in half. I mean, the mechanism's right there.

Then there was what Tsura and me'd both noticed with the glass. Yeah, it'd been tromped and kicked and shifted around, but puttin' the whole pane back together'd forced us to really pay attention to where the shards had all ended up. No way they'd *all* been moved, no matter how careless the bulls or the staff'd been. No way at least some of 'em hadn't stayed where they fell when the display first shattered.

And where they'd fallen was in a neat, radiating pattern *outward*. The glass, same as the lid, was smashed from the inside.

Goddamn it, I'd been *joking* when I suggested the friggin' thing got up and walked out on its own! Yes, I've said that the spirits of dead mortals are some of the few "supernatural" beasties out there that ain't necessarily related to the Fae, but this wasn't how ghosts or revenants or—or *anything* was supposed to work!

I was castin' about, searchin' the broken refuse and dusty corners for any other answer, any other possible interpretation, when somethin' else finally jumped out at me. Somethin' I'd already looked at a dozen times.

The tatters of wrapping lyin' around? The fake stuff they'd

used as part of the décor, I mean, not the real stuff the mummy'd been swathed in thousands of years ago. I was starin' straight at an unwound length of the material, draped over a corner of the sarcophagus—the texture, the fake aging and darkening that probably had more to do with ink and tea than passing years—when I realized I'd seen it before.

"*Fuck!*"

Tsura—who, to be fair, was probably strugglin' with the whole "millennia-old stiff may actually have gotten up and blown this joint of its own volition" angle more'n I was—just about jumped outta her toenails.

"What? *What?*"

"That damned broad put one over on me! Again!"

I'd been so careful, so friggin' clever, and I'd caught her out on so much, and she'd *still* slipped one by me!

"Mick, what are you talking about?"

I took a long, deep breath—not real calming for me, really, but sorta to reassure *her* I was simmerin' down some.

"When I was at Baskin's," I growled, "there was a pile of rags. One of 'em had been used to wrap the—to wrap a relic with some *seriously* bad mojo. Kinda thing I'd kill to keep outta the wrong hands, and in this case, the 'wrong' hands are just about *anyone's*. Turned out the dingus wasn't even there, though. Just the cloth that'd held it for a spell."

"I see," she said, makin' it real clear she didn't.

I bared my teeth in what I hoped she took for a grim smile.

"Ramona must've known I'd react badly to findin' that. And she used that against me." I bent down to pick up the scrap of faux-mummy wrap. "There was some of this in the pile, few layers down. Didn't even register with me. Probably never would've if I hadn't spent so much time in here surrounded by the stuff."

She perched herself on a "broken obelisk," sorta half-seated, half-leaning.

"I'm not sure I follow. Are you saying they have the mummy after all?"

"No." I was runnin' through it all in my head, now, tryin' to race ahead of a dozen possible thoughts at once. "But if the piece they have is really from the mummy, not fake like this one... Or hell, maybe even if it *is* fake, the stuff's been around the body for a while now, associated with it, that might be enough of a connection by itself, though the real thing'd certainly be a much stronger link to—"

"Mick! Make some fucking sense!"

"You tell people's mothers their fortunes with that mouth, doll?" Then, before she could completely explode, "What I'm sayin' is that they can maybe use the length of fabric they got to find the mummy. Almost certain if it's the real deal, but even if it ain't, there's all kinda rites and rituals and spells that'll lead them right to it."

"Oh. Well, but... doesn't that mean *we* can use *this* piece the same way?"

"*I* can't." At least, not without spending a few days it at and drawing on some truly prodigious quantities of luck, I couldn't. "But I may know somebody. Actually, I may know two somebodies." I tossed a rag at her.

Then, after a minute that took about an hour, "Anything?"

"No. But I told you, it—"

"It don't work that way. Yeah."

"Sorry. Maybe if it was an actual part of—"

"Yeah." I reached out, took it back. "Well, like I said, I know a dame. She ain't exactly the best in the business..." And I'd probably have to give her her grimoire back, if I wanted *any* shot of gettin' her to agree to this. "But she may be able to pull this off. We just gotta—"

The lights died with a last, strangled buzz and a dull *thump*.

"Uh..." Tsura said.

"Yeah."

"Did you do that?"

"Maybe. Amount of luck I was sucking up earlier? I coulda damaged the system. Might just be we busted a fuse or something."

"And if not?"

"Then somebody outside threw the main switch and is waitin' for us." I grinned, even though I wasn't sure if the fiddlin' I'd done behind her eyes was still good, if she could see me at all. "Wouldn't be mannerly to leave 'em standin' around, would it?"

She crossed her arms, almost but not quite huggin' herself.

"I could stand to be rude."

"You know any way outta here other'n the main door or the staff entrance?" I asked.

"No."

"Then I guess we go be polite. Aw, cheer up, kid. It was probably just my magic mixin' poorly with old equipment."

We made our way out, and guess what? It was *not* just my magic mixin' poorly with old equipment.

# CHAPTER FOURTEEN

"But are you sure...?"

"*Yes!*" I was fond of Tsura, really was, but *c'mon* already. "For the nine-hundred-and-fifty-third time, yes, I'm sure!"

"It's just, working with the carnival isn't the best job in the world, but it's all I have. I—"

I took her arm in mine—a gesture that looked completely innocent to the early mornin' pedestrians who'd started to flood the sidewalks over the past hour or so since dawn, but also let me steer her where I wanted to go. Ignorin' the expression I'm sure she was stabbin' at me, I guided us into the doorway of a small craft supplies and picture frames shop that hadn't opened for business yet. It was the closest we were gonna get to privacy without me draggin' her into an alley, and I wasn't quite steamed enough for that.

Yet.

"Listen, *Fedora*."

"Hey!"

"They're not gonna remember you. I promise."

"But they *know* me!"

The two ginks who'd been waitin' outside the funhouse had turned out to be a pair of the carnivals' roustabouts, broad-shouldered lugs who could easily have passed for a gorilla act if they'd just quit shavin' for a week or two. Apparently last night was their turn to walk security—and they'd noticed just the faintest trace of the light Tsura'n me had turned on, leaking through a split wooden board that'd probably been damaged when I vacuumed the last dregs of luck outta it.

What were the odds, right? *Damn, but this whole "curse of the mummy" bad fortune bit is gettin' real,* real *old.* Even if it was more an inconvenience than a genuine catastrophe, I was pretty well sick of it and ready for it to go away.

"Sister," I said, danglin' by a fingertip from the last inch of my patience, "I been doin' this since before the Roman Empire went the way of the dodo. I know what I'm doin' when it comes to gumming up people's thoughts and emotions and memories. They'll wake up knowin' they caught an intruder, they'll think they got pounded on some by goons even bigger'n they are, and that'll be the end of it. The most intimidating copper in the world could grill 'em on the subject from now until *I* grow old and die, and your name would never even come up."

She breathed in, deep, steadying herself.

"All right. I believe you. I do. I'm just... This is all new to me."

"Yeah, I got that." I forced a chuckle. "Ain't *all* new to you, though. Where'd you learn to throw a right hook like that?" One of the roustabouts was gonna wake up with more'n just the imaginary pain I'd stuck in their conks to back up the false memories.

"I work in a traveling carnival, Mick. We're strangers and outsiders, people figure we're all crooks, and some fellas want more than their fortunes told."

What she said didn't at all surprise me. How hot under the collar it made me, though, did. I don't much care for *anyone* treatin' people like those "fellas" did, especially since it put me in mind of some of the sins of my own ugly past.

I *really* didn't much care for somebody treatin' Tsura that way.

Nothin' I could do about it now, and we had more immediate problems. So I just jerked a nod, squeezed her arm once before lettin' it go, and got back to walking.

Morning traffic picked up, flivvers choked the air with squawking horns and stinking exhaust fumes, sidewalks slipped into their usual ebb and flow. The two of us were just comin' up on Gina's apartment building when Tsura stopped and spun to gaze through the window into some shop, snaggin' my hand in hers.

"That guy on the bench. He's watching the building."

"Yep. I saw him." Wasn't the same palooka who'd been pretending to read the paper the first time I'd wandered by, but he might as well've been. About the same build, planted in the same spot, could even be the same paper for all I knew. Only obvious difference was the color of his coat.

Alla which explained neatly how *I'd* tumbled to him, but...

"How'd you know?" I asked.

"Just did." She tapped a finger to her temple for emphasis. "There's another one, too. Down the street a ways."

"Hmm. Wait here a minute, wouldja?"

"What? Where are you—?"

I was already off, casually strollin' along the sidewalk, until I reached the bench. Bo didn't obviously look up when I sat down beside him, but I could see the tension in his shoulders. He figured I was *probably* just some guy, but he was ready in case I wasn't.

Good instincts. Too bad they wouldn't help.

"Who you workin' for?" I asked.

I mean, I knew *one* of these two mugs was Bumpy Scola's man, but I figured it might be wise to find out who else had peepers on the place.

He shifted his weight so he could get to his piece, turned to look my way, and that was that. I had him. Eggs in the coffee to get into his noggin once we'd locked eyes.

So I asked him again, and this time he answered.

"Nolan Shea."

Huh. "And why's he got you sittin' on this place?"

"Some skirt who lives here. She's some Outfit *gavone*'s main squeeze, or one of his squeezes, anyway. Shea said the boss wants to know who comes to see her."

"Why her? No way he's got enough manpower to watch over every moll in South Chicago."

"Dunno. Mr. Fleischer says do, we do."

Which said, to me, that Fleischer knew Gina was a witch. I couldn't come up with any other reason he'd set somebody to watching over her specifically, outta all the gangsters and gangsters' girls in the Outfit.

A few more questions, none of which provided any useful answers, and then he went to sleep. A short while later, I tapped on a car window to get Bumpy's goon's attention, and then he went to sleep, too. Only then, when nobody was watchin' us who didn't need to be, did I go back for Tsura and take her inside to meet Scola's pet witch.

Gina wasn't real eager to help us out at first, but it didn't take a whole lot of persuasion.

"Look, Mick, I'm grateful to you for bringing back my grimoire." In fact, since I'd walked in the door and handed it to her, she'd been cradling it like a lost pet. "But that was part of our deal to start with. I'm not looking to make you mad, but I don't owe you anything more, and I don't even *know* your squeeze here."

"Let me tell you something, sister..." Tsura began, soundin' exasperated. I shook my head, hard, and she clammed up, but I could *hear* her roll her eyes at me.

"And you ain't willing to just do me a favor?" I asked.

"Sorry. I'm wise to just enough of what's goin' down in the city to know I don't want any bigger part of it."

"And what if it wants a bigger part of you, Gina? You know Bumpy ain't the only one keeping a slant on you, right?"

"Yeah, you mentioned that."

"You ever figure out who?" Her expression was more'n answer enough. "'Cause they got peepers on your building right now. Well, not *now*, 'cause I put him in mind for a nap, but most of the time."

"So who is it?"

"Uh-uh. You want the rumble? Make with the ritual."

And so we'd ended up at her table again, with the bowls, mortar and pestle, and a bunch of the same this'n that as the last time I'd paid her a visit. Unfortunately, it didn't pan out quite the same way.

"I'm sorry," she said after the third time she'd dipped the fake mummy wrap in the chunky concoction she'd mixed, and the third time it'd come out not even wet, let alone soggy and waterlogged as it shoulda been. "It's just not taking. I tried, Mick. I really did!"

"'S'okay, Gina. I know you did. I was watchin'."

Hell. So what happened? Was it just that the faux wrapping didn't have a solid enough link with mummy dearest? Or was somethin' interfering on a mystical level? The bad-luck curse, maybe, or some kinda protection it'd cloaked itself with after it woke up?

"Y'know," I said to nobody in particular, "scryin' magic ain't too useful when everybody and their damn uncle's warded. When did this town become Grand Central Sorcery, anyway? I wanted to put up with *that* bullshit, I'da stayed in Elphame!"

Then, since there didn't seem much I could say—either to follow up on the rant, or in reply to the queer expressions the two ladies were castin' my way—I *harumphed* once for good measure, snatched up the length of fabric, and marched for the door.

The rest of the day was just as much of a waste of time.

I made the rounds of my contacts again: Franky, Lenai, and so forth. Half of 'em I still couldn't find, the other half knew nothin' about the mummy. If the dead geezer really was out there somewhere, he was lyin' dormy. Pretty slick for a guy who oughta be unfamiliar not only with the city and everything in it, but anything resembling a modern language.

And who most closely resembled a bandaged pork rind.

I'd tried, about mid-afternoon, to convince Tsura to go home, that she'd be a lot safer and probably happier not bein' any part of this. If nothin' else, I figured she might wanna sleep sometime soon. Calm, polite, everythin' I hadn't been as much as I shoulda been. She equally calmly and politely explained why it was the dumbest idea she'd ever heard, that could go a couple nights without snoozing if she had to, and that she wasn't goin' anywhere. (I still got no idea what she'd told Rounser about why she wasn't at work.)

To be frank, I didn't really want her to leave. I appreciated not bein' entirely alone on this, what with Pete bein'… indisposed. If nothin' else, it was an extra pair of shoulders to help me carry the frustration.

Plenty of *that* to go around, and no mistake!

Although it did make me wonder, since when do I not *want* to be alone? I like alone. When I ain't bein' influenced the way Ramona did—and I wasn't right then; I watched for it—alone's my favorite place.

The past year musta been *really* gettin' to me.

Come evening, we found ourselves back in my office, keisters planted in chairs—me behind my desk, her in my client chair—both intently studying the air in front of us. I had my heels crossed on the typewriter, which I still hadn't bothered to put back where it belonged. She was tappin' one foot on the carpet, which was so old and flattened by now it was pretty near to being a drumhead.

Eventually it got to be too much.

"You wanna knock that off?"

She jumped so hard the chair shook.

"What? Huh? What?"

"That." I pointed. "Knock it off."

"I'd hate to see how you treat a gal who *isn't* trying to help you." She turned her face away, staring—if I hadda guess—at the typewriter.

I felt like a jackass, and irritated that I felt like a jackass.

"Look, I'm sorry, I just... Couldn't you *not*...?"

"Some of us fidget! It's a thing we do. You know, humans?"

"Yeah, I do know. I just forget." Then, again, "Sorry."

She leaned back and crossed her arms, but at least she was lookin' at me again. And hey, her foot stopped.

"Mick, what are you gonna do if we *find* the stupid thing?"

"Friggin' hell, I dunno. Talk to it, I suppose? Try to figure out what a jobbie who's been dead for thousands of years even *wants*."

"You speak Ancient Egyptian?"

"I can *understand* it, given a minute. As for makin' *him* understand *me*... I got no idea. Although," I added, leanin' forward to rest my elbows on the desk, "he seems to be makin' his way around Chicago without drawin' attention, Maybe he's got his own means of understanding."

"You really can't even guess at what he can do?"

"Not even a little, kid. We're in uncharted waters, which is somethin' I don't often get to say. Ghosts and revenants are unpredictable at best, and this ain't like any of those I've dealt with."

"Well... Are we assuming he's following *some* kinda logic? Maybe we can puzzle out where he's going, or what he wants, or something?"

"Be easier if you just, y'know, *saw* where he was."

"Yes," she said flatly. "I'm sure it would be. Let me just find the 'on' switch. I'm sure I've got one somewhere."

So, yeah. Still a little touchy, she was. Can't say I hadn't given her good cause, though.

"Okay, so let's lay this out. Carnival's had the mummy for a while now, yeah?"

"Yep. Rounser bought him almost two years back, if I'm remembering right."

"And so far's we know, this is the first time he's woken up."

She snorted. "If he did before, he snuck out and back without telling anyone. Maybe he went for a coffee?"

"Assuming for the sake of argument he didn't, why now? What was it about Chicago that rang his alarm clock?"

Tsura's foot started to tap again. She blinked at it, half shrugged at me, and stopped again.

"Ramona? Or the Uptown Boys? Could he've sensed they were planning to take him?"

"Sure, that's possible. Or..." Hang on a minute. "You been to any cities with their own mummies in the last two years?"

"Um... 'Their own'...?"

"We got a few at the Field Museum. Part of the expanded Egyptology exhibit. Mummies, and also a heap of genuine Ancient Egyptian grave goods."

"You think those could have... could have called to him?" she asked.

"It's possible." Then, "I mean, *I* ain't sensed anything from 'em, but that don't mean somebody more in tune to that magic couldn't have."

You ever seen someone try to nod and shake their head at once? It's dizzying.

"I'm sorry, Mick. I honestly don't know. I don't *think* we have—we tend to hit smaller towns more than big cities—but I don't really get to go too far from the fairgrounds. If any of the cities' museums *did* have that kinda exhibit, I just can't say."

"Fair," I grunted. Not real helpful, but fair. "We should check into it, though."

"Mick, how do we know it was anything about Chicago at all? Maybe it was something to do with, I dunno, Egyptian astrology. Or a thousand other things."

"We don't. But until we rule it out, I'm gonna go on figurin' it ain't pure chance that he woke up here'n now. If only because that way means there's part of this we can puzzle out."

"Swell. So what do we *do*?"

Yeah.

"Tsura, you sure you don't wanna pack it in, head back home before this gets...? All right! All right, I just hadda ask!"

"Okay. You asked."

"For the luva Shakespeare, where'd you even learn to *make* an expression like that?"

"I'm... Did you just say—?"

"So," I interrupted, "our missing mummy has some notion how to get around a modern city. But I gotta guess he ain't gonna be real comfortable with Chicago, and he knows that the more he interacts with people, the more he risks exposure."

"That makes sense," Tsura said, scowling, "but if he's gone into hiding, how're we gonna find him?"

"Way I figure it, he's either not too far from the carnival, or he's in the vicinity of the Field. Even if it wasn't somethin' in the museum that woke him, there could be all kindsa things there callin' to him. At the very least, some of the stuff there'd feel more familiar to him, more like home."

"You're guessing," she accused me.

"You'd be surprised how much of detective work is just guessing from among the most likely options until somethin' pans out."

"Fantastic."

She was up and pacing, now, which was somehow still less aggravating than her foot-tapping had been.

"Even if you're right, you're still talking about a few dozen blocks of possible hiding places."

"You ain't wrong. We need a way to pinpoint the damn thing, or at least narrow down the area some."

She smirked at me. "So do you know any Ancient Egyptian bloodhounds?"

I froze, 'cept for a long, slow grin.

"You know what, sister? I don't, but I might just have an angle on the next best thing..."

\* \* \*

You wanna hear about another of my excursions to Elphame? Well, tough. I ain't gonna tell you.

Aw, don't worry about it. You ain't missin' anything. I won't tell you 'cause there's nothin' worth telling. No trouble. No surprise ambush. No politicking. No run-ins with the Unseelie, or anyone in the Seelie Court who particularly wants me whacked. Not even a starin' match with Slachaun the pugnacious spriggan. I went—alone; I wasn't gonna *literally* pull Tsura further into my world—I found who I needed to talk to, we came back. Easy as pie.

It was night by the time my new Fae pal and I got to the Field Museum—where I was startin' to feel as though I maybe oughta be payin' rent, often as I'd been in there lately. And somebody was sittin' on the front steps, waitin' for me.

"Um," I said.

Tsura, who wasn't supposed to be there, leaned forward, crossed her hands under her chin, and gave me a smile I can only describe as fluttery.

"I thought you might *forget* to call me like you said you would."

"I was gonna."

No, I really was. I'd just wanted to figure out what kinda danger we were walkin' into, first.

And maybe go ahead and deal with it, so she wouldn't be walkin' into it at all.

"Well, now you don't have to. Isn't that convenient?"

"How'd you even know when and where I was gonna... Oh. That was about to be a dumb question, wasn't it?"

"Don't sell yourself short, Mick. It already was."

I couldn't help it. I chuckled.

"Your powers pick the most aggravating times to kick in."

"Don't I know it. Mick, I get you're trying to protect me. It's sweet. But don't ditch me again."

"All right, kid. You got it."

She stood, and finally gestured to my new pal.

"Just so you know, it wasn't a serious suggestion. And also, that's not a bloodhound."

Oh, this was gonna be a fun explanation. I wasn't sure what was gonna set her noggin spinning more—me gettin' in there and letting her see the "dog" for what he really was, or her learning what I had planned for the evening's next activity.

A little while and an important (if illegal) errand later, we started our search. Went around the block, and slowly worked our way out. Two blocks out, then three, and so on. We didn't really need to bother with goin' farther east, since there wasn't much left between us and Lake Michigan, but in every other direction... Well, this was gonna take a while, even with our "hired help."

I wondered what he looked like to the late-night pedestrians. He got himself a few stares, but they were of the same kind that any dog as big and shaggy as him woulda gotten. He was *not* drawin' the sorta attention he woulda been if the mortals could actually see he was a luminous, aquatic green.

"Anything yet, Gwal?" I'd waited until there was nobody within earshot of the three of us. Didn't figure even the most open-minded Chicagoan would take the conversation too well.

Gwalchmai *wroofed* somethin' deep in his chest. "Do you think I'm going to forget to mention it if I *do* smell something, Oberon? It's not as though I'm out here for the fun of it!" He paused, snuffling at a passing alley. "Why do *they* think we're out here?" he asked, aiming his nose at a couple across the street.

"Far as they know, we're just out walkin' our dog."

"Walking?"

"Y'know, lookin' for a tree for you to mark. Or a fire hydrant."

"*What?* That's humiliating! What kind of sideshow are you making of me?"

I shrugged. "Just what's expected here, Gwal. Same as the leash."

"This is why I never come here. I hate the mortal world. Your payment better be worth all this."

Tsura made a noise like she was chokin' on marbles. Her blinkers were a little wild.

"I think something's wrong with your mate, Oberon."

"She's not my mate."

"Why not?"

"Just... keep sniffin'." I dropped back a step or two, payin' out the leash. "You okay, kid?" I asked Tsura.

"Do all dogs from Elphame talk?" she asked, breathless.

"I am *not* a dog!" Gwal huffed from up ahead.

Yeah, that wasn't an argument I wanted to let happen.

"I told you," I reminded her. "He's *cu sidhe*. Fae, like me. Just... built a little different."

"I am no more a *dog* than Oberon is a *human*."

"Let it be, Gwal. She gets it."

"Hmph."

"And he can just sniff the mummy out?"

Wow, she really was shaken. We'd been through this already. Though I shoulda realized it wasn't all sinkin' in. She'd been too busy tryin' to wrap her noodle around the idea of Gwalchmai.

To be fair, the fact that we'd been breakin' into the Field Museum at the time had also had her real on edge.

"*Heka* ain't exactly common in Chicago," I told her. (Again.) "And the *cu sidhe* can 'smell' magic—sense it a lot more precisely'n I can. Gwal here couldn't just snuffle up any old mojo, but now he's got a nose for Egyptian magics, and there ain't many sources of that around here. If the mummy's usin' any of it at all, there's at least a chance Gwal can pick up on it."

"And that's why you broke into the goddamn *museum*? So he could use the relics there as... as scent articles?"

"Among other reasons." I'd also had to pick somethin' up from the workrooms downstairs, somethin' I'd remembered seein' back when I was hunting for the Spear of Lugh. "That's really eatin' at you, ain't it?"

"You *broke into the Field Museum*!"

"So you just said."

"And that doesn't bother you at all?"

All I could do was shrug. "Ain't as though it's my first time."

Tsura began muttering in Greek. I made an effort *not* to translate it in my head; I didn't figure I'd be any happier knowing.

On the square, for all my nonchalance, it'd never been—and still wasn't—a sure thing. I'd come *this* close to trippin' the alarm; they'd added some new triggers since last year, and the luck I'd drawn on to bypass the ones I knew about hadn't covered those. Then, despite listenin' with more'n human ears, me'n Gwal had somehow both managed to mistime the security guard's patrol, and I'd hadda make him take a nap. He'd finally dropped about half a second before he coulda fired off a slug from his piece, which woulda made hiding the fact that somebody'd been there all but impossible.

Bad luck. It kept on poppin' up, rearin' its head just enough to remind me it was hauntin' me. I know the curse ain't technically the mummy's fault—it's somethin' the priests who entombed him did, not anythin' he chose—but he was still startin' to seriously get under my skin.

Whole thing made me nervous, too. Gwal's sniffer was good, but it wasn't infallible and it could only smell so far. We could cover the area around the museum—and then around the carnival, if that didn't pan out—but if the mummy wasn't where I'd guessed, or if he'd found a way to mute his magic, there was nothin' even the *cu sidhe* could do to dig him up. I was relyin' on luck—as little of it as I could arrange, but some—at a time where me'n luck weren't exactly on speakin' terms.

Then we hit 8th, near State, and Gwalchmai's head jerked up. I could see his nose wigglin' fast enough to shatter glass, and his tail started thumpin' near hard enough to knock him over.

*Cu sidhe* ain't dogs, but they *do* have a lot in common.

"You got somethin'?"

He looked at me like I was a special kinda bunny and broke

into a slow trot. Well, slow for him. Me'n Tsura hadda jog some to keep up.

*Where* he took us was a narrow stone building up on LaSalle, with a couple flagpoles—empty, now, since it was dark out—and a pretty modern revolving door up front, with broad windows to either side. Place even had a doorman, though his uniform was maybe a tad worn, the glass behind him just a little in need of cleaning.

"This can't be right," Tsura protested.

"You wanna tell Gwal he followed the wrong trail, be my guest. He *probably* won't bite you too bad."

I mean, this place was no Drake or Morrison. You wouldn't find the upper-crust tourists stayin' here, or the town's high'n mighty livin' on the top floors. But it was a nice place, respectable, sure as hell not *cheap*. And way fancier than the kinda rundown flophouse we'd expected to find our fugitive dead guy, on the off chance he was stayin' anywhere near other people at all. In a dive, people don't look at you twice; it'd be a lot easier for him to stay unnoticed. Here? I wasn't entirely sure how he'd even gotten through the door.

In other words, this was hinky. Big time. And when you're lookin' for a mummy who got up and walked away, possibly in order to avoid the succubus tryin' to steal him? Well, then, it takes a lot to even *get* to "hinky."

'Course, there was another difficulty, too.

"Pretty sure a place this hoity-toity ain't gonna allow us to bring our 'dog.'"

Gwal snorted. "Stupid humans. But hey, I found you the place."

"Yes, you did. Um, would you be willing to share the scent?"

"Oh, fine."

I crouched, me'n the *cu sidhe* locking eyes, sharing thoughts. Took some real willpower to let him in even that far; I ain't ever been fond of people getting into my noodle, and recent experience with Ramona'n McCall had only strengthened that.

Still, I bit back the instinct to resist long enough to get from him a pretty good feel for the magic he'd picked up. Might take wandering the halls for a while, but now I *should* be able to feel the *heka* when I got close enough, even if the mummy wasn't usin' it for much of anything.

"All right, Oberon. Pay up."

Well, he'd more than earned it. I reached into a flogger pocket and pulled out the other reason we'd sneaked into the Field. I wasn't entirely sure what kinda bone it actually was, though I guessed some sorta primate. What mattered was that, one, it was older'n dirt, and two, bore the last lingering trace of ancient magics. If I hadda take a stab at it, I'da guessed it was part of an old shamanistic fetish.

Gwal clamped his jaws around it, growling with excitement—a sound still not as loud as the *thwapping* of his tail.

"So," I said, wipin' *cu sidhe* drool from my fingers, "you gonna need me to get you back home?"

"Don' fink fo," he answered around the once-in-a-century treat. "Got fome people to vivit while I'm here. Vey can pobably fend me home."

"All right. That doesn't work out, come by my office in a couple days. I'll open a passage for you." I stuck out a hand. "Pleasure doing business with you."

He rolled his eyes, bumped a wet nose into my palm, and trotted off, bone clenched tight in his teeth and tail threatening to hurl him off the sidewalk with each delighted wag.

Tsura squeezed the bridge of her nose between two fingers.

"Every time I start to think that things can't possibly get any weirder around you..."

"Oh, I got an easy solution to that," I told her.

"Let me guess. Stop ever thinking that things can't get weirder?"

"Bingo. Works for me, anyway. Shall we?"

# CHAPTER FIFTEEN

I jerked a nod to the doorman, slid around the revolving door, and then decided there might be a quicker way to find our quarry than trooping aimlessly up and down the halls like an idiot. Instead I sauntered up to the counter, with its not-quite-hardwood veneer and not-quite-marble top, and poked at the brass service bell until somebody finally emerged from the back room. He was a middle-aged hombre in neat glad rags with a halfway decent toupee and a smile that looked about as genuine.

"How can I help you tonight, sir?" He put *just* enough weight on "tonight" to convey that he wasn't real thrilled with the idea of checkin' anyone new in so late. His words also tasted like he wasn't real sure he approved of Tsura'n me just in general.

Fine by me. I wasn't gonna lose any sleep over his opinion.

"I hope you can," I said. "I'm lookin' for a guest. Woulda checked in within the last few days." This woulda been easier if I knew exactly how the stiff was blending in, but... "Probably somethin' off about him. Maybe how he was dressed, or—"

"I'm sorry, sir," he said, clearly not sorry at all. "It's against hotel policy to discuss our clientele. Now, if that's all..."

So I cursed once under my breath and did it the other way,

juggling his thoughts and feelings until the ones I wanted—trust and compliance, mostly—landed at the top of the heap. I asked again and got what I wanted.

Yeah, some weird, sloppily dressed little fella'd come in a few nights ago, even later'n this. My new friend wouldn't have checked him in, especially since he had a peculiar accent and smelled funny—obviously some filthy foreigner, he confided in me, makin' me wanna sock his teeth out—but somebody higher up in management had overruled him. Guy hadn't made so much as a peep since, 'cept on his second night, to politely request housekeeping stay outta his room.

Once I got him to spill which room that was—339, if for some reason you're curious—I stepped back outta his head and made for the stairs.

Tsura and I ended up in a hallway with cream-colored walls and slightly scuffed red carpeting, standing next to a potted plant and staring at the mummy's door.

"Do we knock?" she asked.

I actually wasn't sure *what* the best way to handle this was. Bust in? Good way to attract attention, and probably ruled out a peaceful sit-down. On the other hand, if he was already in a hostile mood, did we wanna give him any advance warning we were here? I still didn't know what he wanted, what kinda mojo he had available, or... much of anythin' else really.

"I think..."

I dunno how I woulda ended that sentence, frankly, but it turned out not to matter.

"I know that you stand outside my door." Voice was rough, hoarse, not real strong—like a wheezing old man, 'cept without the wheezing—but it still carried clear enough. It also spoke English with an accent I'd never heard in all my years. "You may as well step inside. We should not be so discourteous as to wake my neighbors while we decide whether or not we must do battle."

"Well," I said to Tsura after a minute, "I guess I can't argue with that."

"I could." She didn't, though.

I tried the door, found it unlocked, and went in, Tsura followin' close behind.

First thing to hit was the scent, both physical and spiritual. The former, a bizarre combination of spices and incense, resin and sand, unwashed sweat—from the stolen clothes, I'd expect—and a hint of decay so faint I doubt Tsura could even smell it. The latter? Magic, deep, old, but not like anything I knew. Came from all around, yeah, but also, for no good reason, from below. And I don't mean like "the floor" or "the carpet," but *way* below. A supernatural below.

Underworld below.

The man, if that's even the right word, sat cross-legged on the edge of the bed, watchin' us. The shoes he'd swiped were too big, his pants rolled up at the cuff so they didn't drag, and I could tell even with him sittin' that his coat woulda swept the floor behind him. Not surprisin', any of that; folks today were a bit taller than they'd been in his time. His fingers, barely protruding from his sleeves, were worn and leathery like smoked meat, and his mug looked much the same. Wrinkled, brown, rough, gaunt and bony—but like an old man who'd spent his life outside, not like somebody who'd been entombed before the Old Testament was a best-seller.

Only thing about him that really looked dead was the empty sockets; just fallen black holes where his peepers shoulda been. But in poor lighting or the shadow of a broad hat—or hell, if he just made a point of lookin' down at his feet—it wouldn'ta been obvious.

"You don't look like a pork rind after all," I said.

Tsura choked.

"I do not know what this means." When the mummy spoke, a faint gust swept across the room, carryin' the aroma of ancient dust. Strangely, that tremulous voice was exactly as clear—no louder, no softer—as it'd been through the closed door.

"Yeah, you're probably better off that way. Are we gonna hafta fight?"

"Did you come seeking to engage me in battle?"

"Not unless I gotta."

"Then let us not."

"Uh... 'kay."

He rose, then, and bowed. Every move he made was stiff, and I coulda sworn I heard a faint crack or snap with each motion.

"I am called Nessumontu."

"Mick Oberon. This is Tsura Sava."

"I am honored. Although I am already passingly familiar with Tsura Sava."

"You are?" she'n I both asked.

"Indeed. You rarely entered the structure in which I have recently traveled, but you did so a time or two, and you often passed nearby."

Tsura frowned. "I... don't understand. Are—were you *aware* the whole time?"

"Not all of me, and not at all times. My *ka* remained awake to experience the world and watch over me."

"*Ka?*"

Oh. Of course. "The Egyptians believed the soul had multiple parts," I explained. "The *ka* was sorta a duplicate of the person as a whole, and it hung around the world of the living to continue some aspects of life—and also to protect the body for the sake of the rest of the soul in the Underworld." I stopped, glancin' over at Nessumontu. "That more or less right?"

"It is rather an extreme oversimplification, but so long as we lack opportunity for detailed discussion of faith and philosophy, it will suffice."

"Uh, thanks. So I'm guessin' that's how you picked up English, too? And why you're not having a total ing-bing over how different this world is from the one you knew?"

"Ah... If I understand you properly, then yes, you are correct."

"You did that on purpose!" Tsura whispered.

Well, yeah. Wanted to see how well he'd picked up the language.

"I... Look, we're all standin' around like a buncha mannequins. Can we sit?"

"Be welcome." He lowered himself back to exactly where he'd been, again with the strange creaking.

Oh, right. Probably the wrapping, hidden beneath the stolen rags. Sure, it all started as fabric, but after the resins to protect it had set for a few thousand years, a whole lotta it musta been stiff as plaster.

Tsura took a chair upholstered in a shade of orange I can only describe as "rodent vomit after binging on carrots." I planted my keister on the desk, pushin' the lamp aside to make room.

"I think maybe you oughta tell us what's goin' down," I said. "Why you're even awake, alla that."

"Why should I tell you this? I appreciate that you appear not to be my enemy, but neither are you my friend."

After all the damn work I'd put into finding him, I sure as hell felt *entitled* to hear the whole rumble! But he had no way to know that, of course, and it might notta meant much to him even if he had.

"Look, pal, there's more people'n just me gunnin' for you, and I'm one of the friendlier of the bunch. You got no reason to believe me, but I'm interested in keepin' their mitts offa you. So what's it gonna hurt to sing for me? If I'm tellin' you the truth, you're helpin' both of us. If I ain't, well, I already found you. Knowin' how you ended up here isn't gonna make you any *more* found."

"This is true enough," he agreed. "I awakened fully several days ago, when my *ka* sensed the presence of something unnatural in the vicinity of my new resting place. Had it passed by only the once, it might perhaps have gone unnoticed, but it returned time and again. It felt not entirely unlike you do,

Mick Oberon, but with several fundamental differences."

"Ramona." It wasn't even a guess.

"You know this individual?"

"She's one of the others comin' after you, on behalf of someone I *really* don't want gettin' hold of you."

"I do not, either. Your culture has no respect for the deceased. I will not hold either of the two of you accountable for actions you yourselves did not take, but think not that I am either ignorant of, or content with, my current existence as... *entertainment*."

Tsura swallowed hard and blushed, obviously ashamed on her boss's behalf. Her own, too, even though it ain't as if she'd played any deliberate part in it. I patted her knee in sympathy, but now wasn't the time to get sidetracked.

"Yeah. For what it's worth, I ain't thrilled with a lot of modern society either. But to be square, I'm a lot more concerned with these people havin' access to your magics than with how much respect they would or wouldn't show you."

"As am I. This is the primary reason I returned to my *ha* and awakened myself entirely back to the land of the living."

"The body," I whispered to Tsura before she could ask. Then, to Nessumontu, "You mind if I ask what you can do? What spells and magics you carry? What kinda threat do you actually pose if someone snatches you up?"

"The extent and power of my *heka* I will not tell you, Mick Oberon. I have no cause to trust you anywhere near to *that* extent. Besides, they cannot force me to practice my rites and spells on their behalf if I choose not to."

Okay, I hadda admit that was fair, at least the first part. Didn't know how true the second half was, but I let it go.

"As to what they might do or learn, however, that is another tale." He opened his coat, tapping a finger on the stiff and age-hardened wrappings I'd figured were there. "I was a sorcerer of some power in life, and my burial rites were appropriate to one of my standing. The spells and benedictions are many, and

I cannot know how easily or how well modern sorcerers might master them.

"The preponderance of them, of course, deal with life and death. Preservation. Protection. The Underworld. Much of the *heka* has faded from them over the many years, but one sufficiently knowledgeable and skilled might use them to ward off a death that should come, or to curse the healthy with a death that should not. They might hear again the voices of those who have gone forth by day, calling them from the realm of the dead and learning secrets the living must never know. It may even be that such a one could use these spells as the basis of an even greater one, to raise the recently deceased back to life."

"Um..." Tsura said, hugging herself.

"Yeah," I agreed. "I don't want anybody in this rotten town anywhere *near* that kinda mojo."

"Understand that the worst of this is possibility, not certainty," Nessumontu continued. "It would require one with sufficient mastery of *heka* to extrapolate from the simpler, base spells inscribed upon my burial raiments. I know not if any such even exist in this day. I have sensed enough of the unnatural beings in your city, however, to beware the possibility, however remote. It sounds as though you and I are in accord on this."

"Better believe we are."

He nodded—loudly, thanks to the resin. I wondered if that was somethin' he'd picked up lately, or if the gesture meant the same three thousand years ago on the other side of the world as it did here.

Either way, he continued spinnin' his yarn.

"I decided immediately that I could not remain in the vicinity of the bazaar." By which I figured he meant the carnival. "If the presence I had sensed indeed represented a threat, then that would have been the first place it would resume its hunt for me. Of course, I knew nothing of this city, precious little even of this world. I had to flee, but where to?

"I opened my senses to the ebb and flow of *heka* and the energies of my past life, of ages gone by. It was those that drew me to your museum."

Yep. I'd guessed pretty near the mark on that one, it seemed.

"The curators there are far more skilled and respectful in their treatment of the dead than those of the bazaar, though still greatly lacking. I thought to find relics of power that might aid me, perhaps even another such as I—another whose *ka* remained with sufficient might to call the remainder of its being from the Underworld—but it was not to be. No power remained to any of them, either in body or *ib*, nor were any of the grave goods possessed of useful *heka*."

"Um, if you don't mind that I keep asking..." Tsura began.

"The *ib* is the heart," I said. "Part of the soul and body both. It's removed during mummification and placed in somethin' called a canopic jar."

"*Those* I've heard of, at least." She forced a weak smile. "Guess you can't get into one without a *canop*ener?"

Me'n the stiff both stared at her.

"I do not understand," Nessumontu said.

"You don't wanna. And *you*, kid..."

"I'm sorry. I'm nervous."

"You sure you'n Pete ain't related?"

"What?"

"Never mind." Back to the mummy. "Please go on."

"I do not know that I've much more to tell. I took the opportunity to study bits of history between my time and this one, and then departed the museum. I have done little but remain here and attempt to stay inconspicuous."

Which brought up a question I hadda ask, but Tsura beat me to the punch with a different one.

"So how come Ramona and Baskin haven't found him? If they have that scrap of wrapping..."

Nessumontu frowned—or maybe scowled; it was hard to tell one expression from another on that mug—but said nothin'.

Maybe he wasn't too keen on the notion that somebody else had a piece of him, though he hadda know it was a possibility.

"Maybe the magics haven't worked. I'm sure you've got wards or protections, of some sort, right?" I asked.

"Indeed."

"Or maybe they got some idea where he is but aren't sure what to do about it. Remember, Baskin thought he was gettin' a nice, cooperative corpse with nifty occult secrets scribbled on it. If he'n Ramona have figured out that they're dealin' with someone who has the option of deciding not to cooperate—a potential prisoner, not a prize—it coulda gummed up their entire operation."

Tsura was tappin' that foot again. I'd hoped she might leave that particular fidget behind at my office.

"Still, do you suppose maybe we ought to take this somewhere else? All three of us, I mean? *We* found him here, so it's possible someone else—"

"I will not leave this place, Tsura Sava," Nessumontu insisted. "I have protections here beyond my own, means of hiding myself to which I would have no access elsewhere."

*That* was a tidy segue into the question I'd been wantin' to ask if ever there was one.

"Let's talk about that, pal. How'd you even wind up here? Ain't exactly the sorta place I'd expect to attract a wanderin' mummy. How'd you know about it? Pay for it? Why'd you pick it? Why'd somebody in the back office order the desk clerk to admit you?"

Just once, while he was ponderin' on how much to tell me, Nessumontu drummed his fingers on his knee. It was the most human thing I'd seen him do, and it reminded me how little any of us—mortal or Fae—ever really changed.

"As I was departing the museum," he said, "I encountered one of your city's sorcerers."

What?

"What?" Tsura asked, startled.

"Yes. I cannot say how he located me, but perhaps it is to do with his particular practices. He demonstrated for me some of his magics, and they are quite dissimilar from the *heka* I know. He recognized me for what I am, and after convincing me that he intended me no malice, he arranged this place for me. Here, he suggested, I might stay safely until we could determine a way to prevent any in this city from obtaining the spells I carry. Just as you do, he fears such a possibility." The mummy scowled, then—and yeah, this time it definitely *was* a scowl. You ever see a dead guy scowl? It ain't attractive. "The rivalries between sorcerers and beings of the Otherworld here must be severe indeed."

"They can be," I muttered. I had a sinkin' feeling in my gut over all this. I mean "The *Lusitania* shakin' hands with the *Titanic*"-levels of sinkin'. "How'd he persuade you to trust him?"

"Primarily by making it very clear that, had he wished me harm—or to claim me for himself—he might have done so immediately. He was well warded against mystical attack, and he had with him a great many heavily armed men. I am not intimately familiar with the weapons of your world, nor—as I have told you—with his form of magic. Neither do I know precisely how readily I might be harmed as one newly returned to the world of the living. For all that, I must say, had he intended me any ill, I was as vulnerable to it then as ever I would be."

Funny, that didn't sound real convincing to *me*.

"Don't suppose you'd care to share this Good Samaritan sorcerer's name with me?"

"I do not believe so."

Figured. "Anythin' you can tell me about his mojo, at least?"

"Mojo?"

"His magic. Tradition. Practices."

"Only that I recognized many of its precepts as rooted in numerology."

Yep. That sinkin' feeling? Now good'n truly sunk.

See, for him to recognize even that much, he hadda be familiar with the base language behind the symbology and incantations of the practice. I already knew it wasn't Egyptian, since he'd said it wasn't a *heka*-based practice. So what other languages would a dead guy from his era know in passing?

Sanskrit? Ancient Greek? Sure, yeah, possible, but I didn't know too many guys in Chicago who made use of those, for the occult or otherwise.

Hebrew, though...

"Kabbalah," I said.

Tsura sucked in a breath. "That's bad."

"Yeah. I mean, sure, there's any number of Kabbalists who're perfectly good eggs, but we only know one who's already stuck his schnozz into Nessumontu's business. And he *ain't* a perfectly good egg."

I *still* couldn't work out *why*, though. Nessumontu's spells were about useless to a pure Kabbalist. The traditions weren't at all compatible. That was the same reason I hadn't wanted to put Fleischer at the top of my suspect list earlier. Still, I'd have to puzzle out "why" later on, since it was pretty clear now that he was, indeed, my "who."

"That's why they sent him to stay at this hotel, instead of someplace he'd stand out less!" Maybe Tsura was no Second City native, but she was no bunny, either. She knew how the Mob boys liked to handle things. "He's probably part owner, or has something on the owners."

Yep. Wasn't as if a guy like Fleischer woulda had much interest in any place much crummier than this one. Hell, just 'cause the place wasn't real swanky meant we were already on the low end of the sorta hotel he'd...

Oh. Fuck me.

Dunno what she saw on my face, but she saw *somethin'*.

"Mick, what's wrong?"

"If this is Fleischer's place, he's got eyes and ears on staff. We—"

*"They're here!"*

To me, the teensy *clank* of a key in the lock sounded louder'n any gong—but these guys were good, and I'd been tightly wrapped up in tryin' to piece everything together. Without Tsura's warning giving me an extra half-heartbeat to move...

I yanked the L&G from my coat as the door flew open with a bang, rebounding off the wall. I got a quick glimpse of three or more thug-shaped heaps of flesh and suit, all of 'em carrying even uglier masses of wood and steel, barrels rising.

I fired first, siphoning huge swathes of luck from the lot of 'em, though I didn't have time to aim as precisely as I woulda preferred. Only one of the choppers failed completely, trigger clicking and hammer thumping without effect. The other two opened up, squirting a hailstorm of lead that chewed through walls and furniture until the whole room was obscured in a cloud of smoke, wood dust, and splinters. The goons shootin' at us managed to get in each other's way, though, thanks to their sudden lack of fortune, jostlin' elbows and missing anything that woulda felt the impact.

Whole buncha those slugs woulda been in my back and ribs without Tsura's premonition. Right. No more trying to ditch the oracle.

If we both lived through this, anyway.

I was already movin'—well, *still* movin' really—before the gunmen could fire a second volley. Nessumontu was gonna have to look out for himself. I came outta the spin snaggin' Tsura's hand, yanked her to me for a better grip around her waist, and lunged. A stream of slugs followed us as we bounced over the bed, sending up geysers of fabric, feathers, the occasional spring. Even as we tumbled off the edge and onto the floor on the opposite side, I was weavin' the luck I'd just stolen into a quilt all around us. Then, lyin' on top of Tsura—I may not care much for bein' shot, but it ain't as bad for me as it'd be for her—I reached out and dragged the already perforated mattress over so it provided a little extra cover while still leavin' me room to pop up and squeeze off a few blasts of my own, if I had the chance.

"You havin' fun yet?" I asked her, quietly as I could while still bein' heard over the thunder of the Chicago typewriters. "Ain't this so much better'n the carnival?"

She didn't answer with anything more'n frightened panting. Shocking, I know.

Wouldn't be true to say there was no pause in the barrage of the Tommy guns; not even those monsters, with their hundred-round drums, can keep their rate of fire up indefinitely. These guys were good, though. They traded off bursts, never lettin' either their sprays or their breaks between 'em fall into predictable patterns. Woulda been a roll of the dice for me to poke my head out'n shoot back, and with the way those dice'd been loaded against me lately, I didn't wanna chance it. Sure, I coulda burned up some of the good luck I'd gathered to do it, but right now I was more concerned with usin' it to keep Tsura from gettin' fulla holes.

Thing is, I ain't addle-pated. The shootin' they were doin' now? They weren't tryin' to hit anything in particular. I mighta quit the business of war before you lot invented automatic weapons, but I understand the basics of battle and I keep my ears open. So yeah, I recognize suppressive fire when I'm under it.

They coulda chewed through the bedframe and the mattress to get to us if they'd meant to kill, but that woulda forced me to respond, shoot back no matter the risk. This? This was about keepin' us pinned, so we couldn't interfere.

But interfere in what?

Ain't easy to tune out an a cappella trio of Tommies, especially when you got hearing sensitive as mine, but I buckled down and worked at it. Sure enough, there it was, just audible in the tiny gasps for air between slugs. Two voices, raised in competing chants.

One of 'em was a tongue I'd never heard, but even if I

hadn't recognized Nessumontu's raspy pipes, I'da pegged it as Ancient Egyptian.

The other was Hebrew. And yep, I knew that voice, too, even though I'd only heard it the once.

A few bits of translation started to filter through the cacophony in my noggin. An Egyptian god here, an Old Testament angel there, a whole heap of words of power.

And I could tell without question, by the bitter tang of mojo in every syllable, the weight and flavor of the building magics, who was gonna come out ahead.

Mighta been different if the royal stiff had been at the top of his game, insteada comin' off a long stretch of being dead. If he'd been prepared and ready for this contest. If Fleischer hadn't been studyin' for this particular exam since before the pair of 'em ever met, hadn't arrived bustin' at the seams with protective wards already active.

If he hadn't been sharp enough to order his thugs to keep me from steppin' in to lend a hand or a bit of luck.

If, if, friggin' if.

A final torrent of lead from all three Tommies to keep us cowerin', and a sudden surge of pure mystical power combined to ring my skull like a church bell. Even when the guns and the chanting fell silent and nothin' remained but the fading sound of beating feet, it took me long seconds before I pulled it together enough to carefully peek up over the shredded mattress.

Sure enough, nothin' but an empty room and the sounds of screaming phone calls to the police from up'n down the hall. Fleischer and his boys were gone—and Nessumontu with 'em.

# CHAPTER SIXTEEN

"Heya, fellas. Nice evening, ain't it?"

The two ginks in question, both of 'em loitering around Baskin's front porch, gave me a couple half-nods—one whole nod between 'em, I guess?—and heavy-lidded glowers. Other'n the colors of their coats and slouch caps, they more or less looked identical.

They were also both cops. I'd hung around with Pete'n his fellows enough to recognize the look. Off-duty, but definitely bulls.

Made sense, though. Where else was my favorite ASA gonna go for hirin' some extra security? And I'd known well before I showed up that he *would* have extra security. It musta been one of the first things he'd done after my visit of... Lessee, I guess three nights ago, now.

Since they didn't appear inclined to say anythin' in response, I went on.

"You don't mind if I just wander up and knock on the door, do ya?"

"'Fraid we do," the one on the left said.

"Move on," the other one added, openin' his coat just enough for me to see he was packin'.

Great.

"Look," I said, closing by a single step and keepin' my mitts well out to my sides, "I just wanna—"

They both moved, not toward as I mighta expected, and not back as though to clear themselves room to skin leather and start shootin', but to the side. Away from each other.

And somehow, even though I coulda come up with half a dozen different reasons for it, I just knew why.

*They were makin' sure I couldn't look one of 'em straight in the eyes without turnin' my back to the other.*

I couldn't guess just how much Baskin had told them, or what they'd believed of it, but they were takin' his instructions serious enough. I was gonna hafta add "keepin' other people's secrets" to the list of topics I wanted to jaw with him about.

I watched both of 'em, the stubble on their chins and the whites of their blinkers bathed in waves of light from passing flivvers on the street behind me. Their shadows danced over the front of the house, walkin' patrol even while the guys themselves stood still.

"I'm not here to cause any trouble, dammit. I just need to talk to Ramona Webb. She's a... friend of Mr. Baskin's. She may be here, and if she ain't, he'll know where I can reach her. That's it."

"Leave now," the second one growled at me, "or trouble's what you're gonna have, want it or not."

Another car passed, slightly out-of-tune engine rattling our teeth as it passed, and this time the light lingered on the two bulls a little longer. Guess the driver slowed, wantin' to see what was goin' on with we three ginks standin' around on the lawn.

And that right there was my answer.

I grinned, makin' real sure it was broad enough they could see my pearly whites in the glint of the house lights.

"All right. Say we got trouble. What then?"

Thankfully, they didn't blink *quite* in unison. That woulda been too much. Definitely wasn't the response they'd been expectin' though.

"We got ourselves three possibilities." I raised three fingers on one paw, started tickin' 'em off with the other. "First—and by far the most likely, even though you're gonna be too proud to believe it—is I put you both down and go knock on the damn door anyway."

They both puffed up at that, but I went on before they could interrupt.

"Second, and *least* likely, is you put me down and arrest me, but not without a long scuffle that's gonna leave the both of you black'n blue for a good long while—and that's gonna be a loud enough to pull every one of Baskin's neighbors to the window.

"And third is that, after a while of what looks like option one or option two, one of you pulls a gat and shoots me. At which point you're gonna have a lot more of the neighbors running to either the window or the horn, and you'n Mr. Baskin are gonna be up to your neck in questions."

It was the first cop who responded.

"Look, bo, just move along, wouldja?" It was closer to a plea than an order this time.

I didn't. I wasn't done.

"Option one ends the same as if you'd just let me go on by—for me, anyway. Not so comfortably for you. You figure out what the other two options got in common?" I didn't wait for 'em to answer. "Attention. A *lot* of it. Attention that ain't gonna do you two, and *sure* as shootin' ain't gonna do Baskin, any good at all.

"So, how about this? One of you stays out here with me, to make sure I'm bein' a good boy, and the other can go on up to the house and explain to Miss Webb or Baskin—like I just explained to you—why they really oughta offer me a few minutes of their time."

I won't go into the runnin' back and forth or the exchange of messages that followed, but the end result was the two goons retreatin' to the front room, where they could keep a slant on us from between the curtains, while me'n Ramona gabbed for a bit on the front lawn.

"You have a real knack for making a nuisance of yourself," she accused me.

"I should hope so. I been practicing."

To that she just grunted and fidgeted a bit, fingering the fabric of her skirt. Definitely right on the edge; she musta been seriously tired. I mean *all* in.

"No luck finding the mummy, huh?" I asked her.

She *hissed* at me.

"Nope. You don't get to be steamed at me for diggin' him up first. Not after the horse shit you pulled with the wrapping."

"We had to make sure you didn't find—"

"Save it sister. It don't matter now, anyway. Guess you've heard about the 'showing' comin' up?"

She sighed, nodded. "Yeah. We've heard. Daniel's in a panic trying to figure out what to *do* about it."

That's what I'd spent the last couple of days on, see? Well, not *all* of the last couple days. First there'd been an hour or two spent makin' sure Tsura was okay. I mean, girl had plenty of tough, more'n most people I knew, but she'd never been shot at before, let alone by a trio of choppers from across the damn room. Ain't *any* amount of tough makes you ready for your first Chicago lightning-storm.

Except... She was more or less fine. Shaken up, some, but nothin' more.

I couldn't explain it. *She* couldn't explain it. Somethin' about her gift, telling her she'd be okay? Hadn't stopped her bein' scared when the lead was flying. Somethin' else?

I didn't understand that girl.

But she'd gone back to the carnival to recuperate for a bit, surrounded by familiar sights'n sounds'n people—and maybe to keep her job, since I *still* didn't know what excuses she'd been givin', or how patient Rounser actually was. Me, I'd set out to learn what was goin' down, and where.

And *why*. Fleischer couldn't make a damn bit of use outta Nessumontu's spells, so why...?

I'd been stompin' along the sidewalk, dodging other pedestrians and kickin' old, greasy napkins off my Oxfords while I pondered. The day was warm, the breeze was gentle, and I didn't give a fig for any of it due to the gray skies and thunder in my thoughts. I nearly bumped headlong into a passel of schlubs headin' out to lunch, lurched to a stop ready to shout somethin' more or less obscene at 'em, and it was right then I noticed the building they were leavin'.

A bank. They worked at a bank.

That's when it all hit me like a fallin' piano. Made of anvils. And I *did* spend a good couple minutes muttering some vile curses, imprecations, and profanities—in about half a dozen languages—but all directed at me, not the folks I'd just about run into.

Because I'd done it again, without even realizin' it. Even after gettin' fixated on the idea of Goswythe, and warnin' Tsura not to get locked into any one angle when studying the situation, I'd gone and done it myself.

All this time—from the moment I'd first suspected Fleischer's involvement, let alone confirmed it—I'd been huntin' for a motive rooted in the mystical. The motive of an occultist. But Saul Fleischer *wasn't* just an occultist: first and foremost the mug was a *gangster*. Alla his skills in magic, his occult knowledge, were tools in his criminal cupboard, not an end unto themselves.

Which meant I shoulda been lookin' for the usual gangster motive: money.

Fleischer never intended to keep the damn mummy, but to *sell* him!

Once *that* little piece finally fell into place, at least I had a handle on what needed doing next. It took time and a lotta burnt shoe leather, but it was just a matter of tracking down how and where the sale was gonna take place. Sure, Fleischer'd wanna be careful who got wind of it, but the word hadda get out through Chicago's magical community. Don't do anybody any good to sell somethin', no matter how valuable, if none of the potential buyers know about it, you dig?

So yeah, I'd tracked down Four-Leaf Franky, who knew a guy, who knew another guy, who'd heard of a girl, who knew of a non-human thing, who knew a guy... Took the better part of a day and a half, but I'd finally tumbled to the time and place.

And then I'd come here, lookin' for Ramona, which brings you pretty well up to date.

"Well, *Daniel's* gonna hafta be disappointed," I told her. "See, you're gonna be there to help *me* recover Nessumontu. Or, well, I guess 'rescue' might be a better word. Important part, though, is helping *me*. Not Baskin."

She laughed softly. "Mick, you know I still care for you, and if I could help you both, I would. But—"

I looked around, edged a couple steps to my right as though I was fidgeting. I mean, she knows I don't fidget, but the show wasn't *for* her.

"No 'but,' doll. If you're there, you'll be backin' me up."

Dunno if it was just my tone or if she caught the "if" buried in there, but her expression cooled by thirty degrees or more.

"And why will I be doing that, exactl—?"

I had my wand in my hand before the "y," and because I'd made a point of "accidentally" puttin' her partly between me'n the window, I was pretty sure nobody inside the house had seen me draw.

"Because I am completely fucking through playing games with you, Ramona." The porch light dimmed, then—just a little, since we were a ways away, but neither of us missed it. I felt the lawn pressin' against the soles of my shoes, tryin' to writhe, and the grass around me turned a late-spring green even as it flattened, caught in some unseen storm. I wasn't *quite* as near losin' control as I was lettin' on, but Ramona hadda know I was serious.

And maybe I wasn't *as* far from losin' control as I'da preferred.

"This is only happenin' because bastards like Fleischer and Baskin can't keep their mitts offa what ain't theirs, and Baskin's only a player because of *you*. I mighta gotten to Nessumontu in time, warned him off or found him before Fleischer did, if you hadn't sicced that damn mob on me! Pete's in danger because McCall knew about my connection to *you*—and I had no clue what I hadda protect myself against because you could never be bothered to tell me what the fuck you *are*."

"Mick—"

"So you are going to help me put this right, Ramona—you are going to do everything I need you to do, to make sure *nobody* walks away with Nessumontu, your boss absolutely included—or so help me, I swear by my ancestors and every last one of the Tuatha Dé Danann that I will deliver you *giftwrapped* to Carmen McCall or die trying!"

Everything the two of us had been through together, I'd never seen her make anything even *close* to an expression like this one. I read a dozen conflicting emotions on her map, tasted 'em in her aura—but more even than that, I saw her own control startin' to slip. Her features were shiftin' beneath her skin—subtle, slow, unnoticeable to anyone without my senses—and I saw the shoulders of her dress bunch and fold as she struggled to keep webbed, barb-tipped wings from sprouting across her back.

"You'd really do this?" I swear I heard two or three different voices in her words.

"I don't make an oath like that one for funsies, sister."

"And are you so damn sure I can't put you down, Mick?"

She clenched her fists, opened up wide—and her fingers were tipped not with nails, now, but black and pitted talons.

I tightened my grip on the L&G.

"Maybe you can. But not without takin' a whole *mess* of hurt in the process. Even if you do beat me, even if you *croak* me, you're gonna be suffering for a good long while afterward. And when I go missing? McCall's gonna come for you herself, and you ain't gonna be in any state to fight *her* off, not after tusslin' with me. I may lose, Ramona, but you *can't* win. Not by fightin' me, you can't."

I wondered at first if she wasn't gonna test me on that score. One more surge of leather and bone movin' under her clothes, one sharp screech as talon scraped against talon... Then both were just gone, and it was Ramona—just Ramona, as she'd looked the day we met—standing in fronta me.

"Goddamn you, Mick. This isn't you. I can't believe—"

"Don't. Just don't. You started this, and my best friend's payin' the price. You get zilch for sympathy from me now. I don't *want* this, but don't think for a second I ain't serious."

"I don't."

She hung her head, scarlet locks fallin' in front of her face, though whether any of it was genuine or if it was more of her "woe is me" human act, I wouldn't begin to guess.

"All right. What do you want me to do?"

"First off, don't breathe a word of this to Baskin. Not just for my sake, either. You do, he's gonna order you to do somethin' dippy that we're both of us gonna regret, see?"

"Yeah. I see."

On that, at least, I could probably trust her. If she decided to move against me or put her own spin on what I told her to do—and I'm not dumb enough to assume she wouldn't—she'd wanna be able to choose her own time, her own tactics. Baskin? He still didn't really comprehend the waters he swam in. She didn't want him callin' her play any more than I did.

As to the rest? Well, I just hadda hope I could either keep her on board with the plan, or anticipate what she'd do when she veered off-script.

"So," I told her, "here's what we're gonna do..."

\* \* \*

"Wow. Looking pretty sharp there, Mick," Tsura said as I stepped outta the bathroom. I'd known she was there; I heard her come into the office while I was adjustin' my tie in the mirror.

What, did you think I *only* had cheap, wrinkly glad rags? Most of 'em, sure, but I own a nice suit or two for special occasions.

"Thanks, doll. You, too."

She really did.

The deep blue number, with broad sleeves and a slim skirt, wasn't exactly formal, but it was close; damn sight fancier'n anythin' I'd seen her in before. She cleaned up nice, a lot nicer'n you'd expect if you only ever saw her in her gypsy fortune-teller getup. Tsura was never gonna stop the conversation when she sauntered into a room the way Ramona did, but she was definitely the kinda gal you'd remember afterward, that'd make you wonder if you'd been focused on the wrong dame.

Tsura's answerin' smile was almost bashful, as was the way she ran her palms down the sides of her skirt. I dunno how much of that was in response to the compliment, small and casual as it was, or to what she said next.

"Mick, I'm... The other night..."

"We been through this," I said, slidin' my wand into the holster and makin' sure it didn't throw off the lines of this swankier coat too bad. "There's nothin' to apologize for."

"I should've seen them coming sooner. And I wasn't much good once the shooting started."

"You warned me before they showed, gave me time to *not* get my spine blown to pieces. That's good enough for my book. After that, hell, anybody woulda been scared. I ain't that easy to bump off, and I been shot at more times than I can count, and *I* was scared." Well, a little.

"Still, I'm sorry I was so—"

I pointed a finger at her.

"Quit it! Trust me, kid, you're doin' fine. Better'n most people would be, under the circumstances."

"You swear?"

"Cross my heart."

"Okay." She abruptly looked up, and her grin wasn't shy anymore. "Long as you remember that before you try giving me the 'This is gonna be dangerous, maybe you shouldn't come along' speech."

Wasn't just her looks that were sharp, that one. I probably wouldn't have given her that spiel tonight; she really *had* saved my bacon at the hotel. But I *had* thought about it, a little.

And no, I didn't think she'd engineered the whole conversation to get there—her nerves were genuine—but she sure wasn't slow on her feet.

All I said, though, was, "Noted. Gimme one minute."

I wandered out into the hall, over to my favorite device in the whole damn world. I snarled at the blower, it snarled back, and I made the call I hadda make—as quickly as I could possibly get it done.

"Right," I said, pokin' my head back into the office. "Shall we?"

She handed me my hat—I scowled at it, but the getup woulda looked incomplete, and conspicuous, without it—and we were off. Just another Chicago couple, out for a night on the town.

After a while, as we got near the L, she said, "So, um, you might've already explained this that night. I don't... entirely remember the specifics of the conversation we had after we fled the hotel."

"'Fled'?" I protested. "I don't flee."

"We dusted out in a rush before the police could respond to all the shooting. What would you call it?"

"A daring escape."

She snorted. "Fine. After our daring escape from the hotel, then."

We stopped long enough for me to slide a handful of coins over the counter to a bored young cat in a starched uniform, and then wandered up to the platform to wait for the next train.

"All right, what am I explaining to you?"

"The hotel. Why'd Fleischer put Nessumontu up there at all? Why not just take him when they first ran into him? He said himself the 'sorcerer' had enough power and enough men to at least take a shot at it."

At this hour on a weekday, in my part of town, the platform wasn't too terribly packed, so it was eggs in the coffee to find us a spot we could talk—at a hush, at least—without any chance of bein' overheard. Sure, any random mug who *did* happen to eavesdrop on our conversation'd probably just assume we'd gone whacky, as opposed to actually believin' a word of it, but even so...

"You gotta remember," I told her, "nobody had the slightest idea Nessumontu himself might have an opinion on any of this. Far as Baskin, Fleischer, or anyone else knew, they were plannin' a heist, not a kidnapping."

"So, he... What? Wasn't ready?" The screech of the brakes and the nauseating scent of scraping, sparking iron put the kibosh on the conversation long enough for us to board, and then find a couple seats at least half a car away from anyone else. The L lurched into motion, I acknowledged and then put aside my usual train headache, and the world was nothin' but constant rocking and more metallic screeches.

Well, that and a quick poke at my elbow.

"Huh? Oh, right. Yeah, wasn't ready. I mean, you're gonna want a whole different set of locks and whatnot if you're tryin' to keep a mummy from gettin' up and takin' the run-out than if you're tryin' to keep others from gettin' *to* him, right?"

"Makes sense."

"And it ain't just about the locks or guards or doors. You're talkin' magics, too. It's one thing to ward a relic so it ain't easy for others to detect it. It's a whole 'nother kettle of horses to bind a walking-dead guy so he can't break free, or draw on whatever mojo he might possess. Between researchin' what he'd need and then actually sketchin' the glyphs and circles, casting the rituals? I'm frankly surprised it didn't take Fleischer even longer to set up. Come to think of it, he may *not've* been ready. Us showin' up at the hotel probably forced his hand. Might mean things ain't as secure as he'd have hoped."

Tsura frowned. "Or maybe the three days it's taken him to set up the showing were enough to shore all that up."

"Or maybe that, too."

"So did our rushing him actually help us in any way?"

"No idea, kid."

She jabbed my arm with a finger again, this time a little harder than an attention-getting poke.

"Anyone ever tell you how reassuring you are?"

Wow. Déjà vu.

"No, but you ain't the first to ask me."

We spent the next ten minutes lost in thought, me ponderin' my history with Ramona and everything I'd felt—or thought I'd felt—for her, Tsura contemplating whatever a scared-but-determined fake-carnival-gypsy descendant of the Greek oracles might contemplate.

My life is filled with some weirdly specific questions.

And regrets.

I spent part of the ride prayin', though I ain't positive to whom, that this wouldn't be one of 'em.

This was gonna be dangerous, and not just to life'n limb. Even the best victory I could imagine had us comin' outta this with some powerful and violent people steamed at us. Tsura said she understood all that, but did she really? Her clairvoyance was useful and she was a smart cookie, but none of that meant she *really* knew what she was gettin' into. And Pete? Pete hadn't been allowed to choose at all. He'd been dragged into this, and made to think it was what he wanted. Maybe it woulda been better for everyone if I'd stayed the loner I'd been for decades.

Too late now.

*Hope you know what you're doin', Tsura. Hope I do, too.*

# CHAPTER SEVENTEEN

It was comin' up on eleven when we got where we were goin', arm in arm so we'd look all respectable.

The warehouse was a hunkering, square monstrosity, fat'n lazy as buildings go. Dirty red walls, flat roof, big honkin' windows so dark and thick they were no more transparent than the bricks. The loading platforms, sittin' at truck height, were closed up tight, locked, and guarded by men openly carryin' Tommies or double-barreled street sweepers. Broad steps led up to the door, which looked to be the only easy way in—also guarded by goons packin' big gats. On the steps stood a handful of other guests, dressed to the nines, waitin' their turn to enter.

"Why aren't the cops all over this?" Tsura whispered, peepers dancin' between the hardware and the formalwear.

"Fleischer probably paid someone off. Ain't exactly uncommon. Since Prohibition, I been to illegal shindigs much more conspicuous than this."

"My faith in your city's law enforcement is withering by leaps and bounds."

"Welcome to Chicago."

We were among the last people to climb the steps. The two tuxedo-clad goons workin' the door took one look at me and went for their roscoes. They didn't draw, but the meaning was clear as crystal. The few other guests still lingerin' outside stepped back, wisely gettin' outta the way of whatever was comin'.

"I guess Fleischer told 'em to watch out for me," I groused.

"You think?" Tsura's tone was tightly pinched; she was keepin' her cool, but only with a fingertip grip.

"Take it easy."

I smiled real big, though I decided at the last second not to wave; they mighta taken it wrong.

"Evening, boys."

"Boss don't want any trouble here tonight, uh, O'Brien," one of 'em snarled at me. "So we're supposed to give you the chance to walk away. But you ain't comin' in."

"O'Brien?" my "date" whispered.

"You wouldn't believe how often I get that. I could tell you stories..."

"Maybe another time, huh?"

"Come on, pal," I said, more loudly. We were just a few long paces away, now. "I ain't here to start anything. But we got as much right to examine the goods and make an offer as anyone, don't we?"

"I told you, you ain't comin' in. And that's close enough!" Gink half-lifted his shotgun, but it was already too late.

See, he was right; I *was* close enough.

"We got as much right," I repeated, starin' into and past his pupils, pluckin' at the strings of his brain, "to examine the goods and make an offer as anyone else does."

"Yeah," he agreed, real thoughtful now. "I suppose you do."

"What?" his buddy demanded. "Stan, what the hell are you—?"

More smiling, more eye-contact, more whammy.

"I think Stan's got a point, don't you?"

"He does, sure. Just don't gum anything up in there, willya? You'll get us in trouble."

"Wouldn't dream of it," I assured him before leading Tsura

past the both of 'em and into the warehouse itself.

"That's creepy," she said.

"Is it? Well, they're creeps, so that's okay."

She decided not to respond to that. Too blinded by my impeccable logic, no doubt.

Inside was all echoes and shadows and the scent of old wood dust, the ceiling and the far walls soaked in gloom. We made our way straight through the massive building in a path formed by a line of dim overhead lights, accompanied by the ring of our own footsteps and the hum of distant conversation. I could *just* hear the occasional breath, taste the edges of an aura, enough to know that those pockets of darkness hid more of Fleischer's goons. I didn't bother tryin' for an exact count, since the only two numbers that woulda mattered were "enough to make a difference" and "not."

At the far end, everybody had gathered in an amorphous cloud of formal rags, mostly blacks and blues and browns for the gents, more of a rainbow for the ladies. Rows of chairs had been set up facin' a raised work area-cum-stage, which was currently blocked off by heavy curtains. Even from a ways away, I could tell that a handful of 'em weren't near as human as they looked.

One of those not-humans broke away from the pocket of conversation she'd been part of, much to the disappointment of everyone else, and moved to meet us.

"Mick."

"Ramona." Her dress was slit just a bit too high, cut just a bit too low, to be entirely proper. "You're lookin'... predatory."

"How kind of you to notice." She raised an eyebrow at Tsura. "New pet?"

"Funny. I—"

Tsura's fingers tightened on my arm hard enough to make a halfway decent tourniquet. Her cheeks'd gone a sharp red, and her breath was comin' fast and uneven.

"Turn it off, Ramona," I growled.

"Hmm? I'm sure I don't know what you—"

"Turn it *off*."

Ramona sighed, tossed me a smile with no goodwill in it, and just like that Tsura's breathin' evened out. Didn't seem she was gonna stop blushin' any time soon, though; I tried to look like I didn't notice.

"Don't muck around in my friends' emotions, sister," I warned her. "Not *ever*."

"Sure, whatever." Ramona glanced back at the assembled audience. "You ready to tell me what it is I'm to do here, Mick? Your plans were pretty vague beyond 'Help me make sure nobody walks away with the mummy.'"

"I prefer 'open-ended for maximum flexibility.' You know, maybe help me convince a few guys they got better things to spend their money on. Or back me up if things get violent. That sorta thing. Don't worry. I'll let you know if I need you, and when—unless what I need you to do is so obvious I don't *have* to let you know."

"That is impressively unhelpful."

"Oh, good. I rehearsed it for just that effect."

She turned without another word and made her way back toward the chairs.

"Mick...?"

I reached down and patted Tsura's hand.

"That's what she does, kid. And she can do it to almost anyone. It's how McCall got to Pete. Don't let it eat at you."

She forced herself to smile. "You remember how I said I was ready for all of this?"

All I could think to do was offer another pat.

Not that Ramona was remotely the only soul here I recognized, though of course I didn't know *everybody*. Fenway was a shrewd, grossly overweight mug who I knew occasionally worked as a middleman for Hruotlundt. Lairgneigh, who woulda sent half the room screamin' if they could see through her human-seemin' to what she actually was, represented *someone* in Chicago's Seelie Court, though it mighta been any one of a handful. She sneered at me as I drew near, so I tossed her a friendly wave. Got another, much darker sneer from a boggart I didn't know personally, and didn't want to. I wondered if he was here for Eudeagh, "Queen Mob" of the Unseelie Court herself.

And there were plenty of others, men and women who either were, or who represented, a wide swathe of Chicago's supernatural and/or occultist population. I'd be lying if I told you I didn't give passin' thought to solving a whole mess of the city's (and my) problems by barring the door and settin' the place on fire.

"Isn't that the witch?" Tsura asked, sorta pointing over my shoulder with her chin. "Gina?"

I didn't need to look; now that I felt for it, I could taste her aura among all the others.

"Yep. Not surprising, really. If Scola heard about the showin', she's the one he'da sent to check it out."

"I thought... Aren't they part of rival gangs?"

"Fleischer woulda guaranteed this to be neutral ground. If he wants the best price on Nessumontu, he's gotta make sure those kinda beefs are left at the door."

"I... guess that makes sense." She sounded doubtful.

Meanwhile, though, I'd gotten a whiff of somebody *else* I knew, somebody whose presence I *did* find a bit surprising.

"Speakin' of rival gangs..." I steered Tsura around the edge of the growin' throng. "How's it hangin', Archie?"

You remember Archie "Echoes" Caristo, don'tcha? Thin, hair greased back slick enough I'm amazed he can keep a hat on, real irritating verbal tic? Important mostly 'cause of who he works for?

"Oberon." He clamped his cigarette in his teeth to free up the hand that'd held it, reached out and shook mine. "What're you doin' here?"

"Window-shopping. Peeked inside and realized I hadn't

picked me up a summer mummy for this year."

"Summer mummy. Cute. Who's the tomato?"

"Tsura," she answered for herself, followed by a *long* string of Greek. She smiled through it all, and her *tone* was polite enough...

Archie looked back at me.

"It's a traditional greeting," I lied blandly. "She's pleased to meet you."

"Pleased to meet me?" He sounded more'n a touch doubtful. "Took that long to say it?"

"Well, it loses something in translation."

"Loses... Right."

I leaned in some.

"Archie, what're *you* doin' here?"

He tossed a suspicious glance over his shoulder.

"Boss got wind of this, wanted me to look into it."

"Fino wants to buy a mummy?" That didn't sound right.

"Probably not. Pretty sure even if he did, lotta these *gavones* would outbid us. But he... Well, y'know, with everything around his momma's death, and everything with Adalina... He's keepin' a closer watch on the weird hocus-pocus shit goin' on in this city."

Great. That was all I needed. Still, I couldn't blame the guy. Wasn't as though I'd had any luck wakin' his changeling daughter up, myself.

And, of course, thinkin' about *that* reminded me why I was even here, which brought a whole new wave of guilty anger.

"You know, Oberon... The boss'n me, we had no idea you had any kinda angle on this. I'm sure Fino woulda talked to you, at least let you know we were looking, made sure it didn't gum up anything you had going, if he knew."

"Not a problem. No reason he *shoulda* known, and it's not gonna mess up anything for me. Um, except..."

Damn. Wouldn't mess up anything for *me*.

"Archie, I'm gonna make a *real* strong suggestion here."

"Yeah?"

"Leave. Don't make a show of it, don't tell anybody why. Just go."

"Just go?" Now he was suspicious; I could taste it in his words. "Why? You got somethin' going you don't want the boss to hear about?"

"Oh, for the love of... No, that ain't it. Fino's a friend..." Well, sorta. "And he wouldn't want anything happenin' to you."

Archie stiffened, and just that quick, he was dangerous. He coulda had a gat in his fist, or his fist in a face, in half a heartbeat.

"You expectin' this place to get hot?"

"As hell."

"As hell." He nodded. "You need backup?"

That... was actually touching, in a mobster sorta way.

"I appreciate that, Archie." I really did, too. "But no. Just get your ass outta here so I don't gotta explain to Fino why it got filled with lead. Please."

Took him a minute to decide if he trusted me or if I was hidin' something, but in the end he nodded one more time, tipped his hat, and slowly—still mingling, actin' a lot more subtle than I'da given him credit for—made his way back toward the long hall of shadows that led to the exit.

After that, it was a few more minutes of mingling—which, in a shindig like this, was about one-fifth actually yappin' with people and four-fifths tossin' nasty expressions at ginks you either didn't know or didn't much care for. I spent most of the time tryin' to keep a slant on the boggart, since he seemed the most likely to try pullin' a fast one before the show even got rolling. I mean, most boggarts I've met can't take much of anyone or anything with 'em when they pull that "disappearing down their own gullet" act, but you're never certain with those bastards. Maybe this one had some means of dragging a mummy with him, for all I knew.

But nope, he behaved himself, as did everyone else, despite some nasty glares. Eventually, the overhead lights dimmed, the ones over the makeshift stage flipped on with a loud snap, and we all figured that was our cue to plunk our keisters down. Me'n Tsura sat at the back, since what I needed now was mostly to stay unnoticed and kill some time before the shit started flyin'.

The curtain rustled and waggled. A couple'a muffled curses sounded from behind it, followed by a dull thump. Then they rustled again and slid open.

Behind 'em, Nessumontu faced us, leaning back on a shallowly angled slab. His arms lay across his chest in typical "old dead guy" fashion; the light and leathery crags of his mug made it impossible to tell if his blinkers—well, his empty sockets—were open or shut.

He was incased in a box of thick glass, each pane deeply etched with binding circles, glyphs, Hebrew letters, and similar scribblings. As I've said, I ain't too familiar with Kabbalah, but I recognized the power inherent in the work. To say nothin' of the fact that the glass was so fat it could probably take a couple high-caliber slugs before it even started to crack.

And standin' next to it, dressed in a sharp tux, was...

Not Fleischer. Huh.

"All right, you... ladies and gentlemen," Nolan Shea, *capo* of the Uptown Boys, said, steppin' forward. "Let's quiet down and get to—"

"Where's your boss?" someone in the audience demanded.

I actually heard Shea's teeth grind.

"Mr. Fleischer's got more important business to attend to. I'll be runnin' this show."

A few folks grumbled, probably puffed up and offended that the big guy wasn't catering to 'em personally, but nobody got up'n left.

Me, I didn't entirely buy it. No matter how precisely he'd designed Nessumontu's cage, there was always the chance of somethin' queering the deal. Unless any of the Uptown Boys were also Kabbalists, which I didn't suppose was too likely, he'd wanna be nearby to shore things up if necessary.

On the other hand, *claimin'* he wasn't here and hangin' back outta sight, so he could either step in or take the run-out, depending on which seemed the better idea... Yeah, *that* I could see.

Given what was comin', my guess was that he'd make tracks faster'n a hummingbird with its tail feathers on fire.

Shea dove into his spiel and I leaned back in my seat, just waitin'. He basically went through everything I already knew—the nature of the spells inscribed on Nessumontu's wrappings, their potential to commune with, and just *maybe* even wake, the dead, alla that. How it'd take a lotta occult knowledge and study of Egyptian traditions to even begin to make sense of it all, but that the power'd be more'n worth the effort to anyone willing to make it.

He *also* admitted that the mummy was conscious, only held in mystical slumber by the case he was in, but that Fleischer knew how to rip the lingering spirit from the stiff if the buyer didn't have the means of doing so himself—and would be happy to provide either that service, or the case itself, if the buyer wanted to keep the mummy alive, for an extra fee.

Can I tell you again just how much I frickin' hate mobsters? They even ruin *magic*.

I'm paraphrasin' here, of course. Shea's speechifying went on a good while. It had to. Yeah, we were all here for a showing, to see the merchandise, but nobody was gonna be able to actually get in there, open up the bandages and read for themselves. This wasn't an open auction; everyone got one chance to make a secret offer, once the showing was complete. A whole lotta Fleischer's potential profit on this deal relied on Shea convincing everybody that the stiff was worth a whole *heap* of kale. So believe you me, the gink was doin' the hard sell, hittin' every possible use and advantage he could come up with.

Me, I was startin' to get antsy. The special guest star shoulda arrived by now, and the notion that she might not show was only slightly more discomforting, at this point, than the notion that I might have to listen to the entire damn sales pitch before she did.

When Shea suddenly jerked to a halt at the sound of clicking footsteps comin' our way through the darkness at the front door, I almost jumped outta my chair and screamed hallelujah.

More'n one set of footsteps, actually, which I'd expected. Demanded, even. But the fact it was more'n *two* threw me a sec.

"Hey! Assholes!" So much for Shea's efforts to sound classy. "I thought I told you idiots not to let anyone else in once we got started! What're you—?"

"Oh, you'll have to forgive them," McCall cooed. "I'm afraid they've really got their minds on other matters right now."

She strutted into the light, swishing enough to make even Medusa's ex-beau sit up and take notice. Pete followed half a pace behind, dazed and disheveled. He hadn't shaved since I'd seen him last, and now he was close enough for me to tell with half a sniff that he hadn't showered at all in that time, either. Looked a little wan, too, like he hadn't been eating much.

I almost bit through my tongue, keepin' my temper under control. I didn't need to call that kinda heat, not yet. But right in that moment? I coulda razed the whole building and everyone in it—'cept Pete and Tsura—if I could be sure of getting the damn succubus with 'em.

Trailin' behind them, like a buncha dazed ducklings, were the guards who were supposed to have kept 'em out. Yeah.

"And you'll have to forgive *me* my little interruption," she continued, smiling broadly. "I just have a quick appointment to keep, and then you all can get right back to bidding on your dead—"

"You *bitch*!"

McCall's jaw dropped as Ramona shot from her seat.

"You... But... You're supposed to be...!"

All hell broke loose.

I'd gone for the L&G as soon as McCall started speakin', slowly rising from my chair. I was *fully* aware I'd only have an instant before she realized that I musta broken our deal if Ramona wasn't unconscious, bound, or otherwise trussed up and ready for shipping. No way I was gonna let Pete suffer for that.

So even as she was gawpin' at Ramona, I fired a burst of magic at Pete, carefully aimed and tightly controlled, draining luck from around his feet'n ankles and filtering it up into the rest of his aura.

My buddy toppled like somebody'd yanked the rug out from under him, just in time to avoid the furious swipe McCall suddenly directed his way. She had just enough time to glare at me with all the hatred of the Pit, and then she had more immediate concerns.

You gotta understand somethin', 'cause you've only ever heard about Ramona and McCall bein' charming or manipulative. It's what they do. They're good at it. But sometimes, a plan breaks down, instinct and frustration sweep aside all planning, all façades, all thought—and it's only then you see 'em for what they are.

Raging. Bestial. Nothin' feminine, nothin' human, not even anythin' Fae.

Maybe it's true, maybe it ain't, but when it comes to wrath, hatred, there's a reason we call 'em *demons*.

With the shrieking of the damned, Ramona took to the air of the cavernous warehouse, all semblance of humanity fallin' away, and McCall leapt to meet her. Those pitted, metallic black talons—not iron, but near as painful; I knew that from old experience—extended until they were longer'n the fingers that held 'em. Hair and flesh split, pushed aside by sprouting horns, and the rest of their skin turned red; not blushing, not even like a sunburn, but as if the blood underneath it *boiled*. Pupils expanded until their eyes were nothin' but bloodshot black, and fabric shredded to make way for broad, thunderous wings of membranous leather and bone. Beneath and around the raging demons, the air grew thick with choking sulfur.

They slammed together overhead, thrashing and clawing and even *chewing*, held aloft by somethin' more than those wings. Skin split, rotted at the unholy touch of those talons, healed almost as quickly only to split again. Blood rained across the center of the room, burning holes in fabric and flesh so that other screams rose to join theirs.

People scattered, scrambled, upturning chairs and knockin' each other over in their mad dash to get away from the brawling demons. It was a cauldron of bubbling chaos that only got worse when Shea shouted "Oberon!" and several of his goons appeared behind him from backstage, roscoes raised.

Guess it was too much to hope that he'da missed me in all the hubbub.

"You're behind this, ain'tcha, you bastard!" he accused.

"What? No!" Well, I mean, yeah, sorta. But... "I ain't the threat here, Shea! Don't be a—"

"Fill him fulla daylight!"

Wouldja believe I *really* wanted to yell back, "It's nighttime!" as I dived for cover behind the last row of chairs? Yeah; yeah, you probably would. I didn't, though, and he wouldn'ta heard me over the roar of the Tommies even if I had. I rolled, wand clenched tight, slugs and wooden splinters whippin' up a storm overhead.

Other guns shot back, a few of the jumpier sorts in the audience instinctively returning fire. I tried to get a slant on all of it, figure out where might be safe for a spell, who was shootin' at who, where Tsura'd gotten to in the chaos...

Then, from the bloody brawl overhead, McCall managed to shout out a clear, if inhuman-sounding, "Kill Staten!" And I had no more time for pondering.

One blast with the wand, sweepin' the stage, random and haphazard, slammin' Shea and his boys with as much misfortune as I could manage. Then I scrambled upright and ran, sprintin' hard as I could across the warehouse, winding the luck I'd just stolen around me. I ducked, weaved, everything I could manage to stay a hard target. Between that and the extra luck, I managed not to catch any lead, though a few of the shots came pretty near and I was gonna have to consign yet another coat to the trash.

The second group of guards, the ones McCall'd mickeyed on her way in, saw me comin'.

Good; I'd meant 'em to.

What the succubi do, it's emotional, not mind control. Their victims can still think for 'emselves, they just *want* to make the demon dames happy. Which meant that these guys were only too willin' to whack Pete, but they weren't gonna ignore oncomin' danger to do it.

So instead they turned their guns on me. Hooray?

Fortunately, they hadn't been *too* far away, and they couldn't have expected me to close as quick as I did; I'm faster'n you mugs when I put my mind to it. Soon as I knew I had their attention (and their aim), I dove, hit the ground at a roll that probably woulda shattered a collarbone if I'd been human; couldn't afford to do it any slower, since I still had the ginks across the room squirtin' lead at me, too. I popped right back up and fired the L&G again. Put everything I could into it, as much of my magic as the thing could handle. Two of the guns stopped workin' outright, bullets jamming, springs breaking. One got off a single shot before his own gat gummed up, and the fourth guy dropped to the floor, writhin' and clutching his chest. Guess he had a bum ticker, or somethin' else that made a sudden loss of luck dangerous.

Hadn't planned for that to happen. I mean, he *probably* deserved it, bein' a trouble boy and all, but... Of course, given what was comin' next, he mighta got off easy.

I threw myself into their midst—not punchin' or tacklin' or anything, just pushing through 'em. That was all it took.

I'd done all this at a sprint, see? Shea'n his boys on stage firin' at me the whole way. Fast as it all happened, with all the luck I'd sucked from *both* groups of trouble boys? Only one way it coulda ended.

The three goons I'd just run through danced and spasmed and screamed as their own buddies' fusillade of slugs ripped through 'em, and then dropped into a bloody heap in my wake.

Again, I didn't feel *too* bad for 'em; live by the gat, die by the gat. But I mighta been a little less casual if Pete hadn't been the one at stake.

For three or four breaths, everything fell silent—the guns, the shoutin', all of it. Well, all of it but the screaming succubi tearing flesh from bone, but they were way up near the ceiling and for a minute somehow felt even farther away than that.

"You..." The bulging veins in Shea's head and neck seemed to be blockin' his throat. "You...!"

"Why'd you hafta go and open up on me, Shea? This was only ever about the mummy. It didn't need to get personal. None of your people hadda get hurt."

Yeah, okay, it was never gonna go down *that* easy. But I really had hoped to avoid anythin' *this* bloody. Didn't matter now, though. Made no difference that they'd shot first, or that it'd technically been their own choppers that'd cut down their pals. Uptown Boys were dead, and so far as Shea and the others were concerned, it was my fault.

I wondered briefly if Fleischer was watchin' from some hidden vantage or if he'd dusted out the moment the fireworks started. But then, even if for some whacky reason he'd *wanted* to call Shea off at this point, I doubt he coulda done it.

More of the Uptown Boys had converged from where they'd been standing guard at the warehouse's other entrances. Every one of 'em was packin' somethin' heavy, and every one of 'em was angry enough to kill. It was gonna be tough as hell tryin' to get to Pete and drag him to cover before they opened fire, or maybe I should just dive for it on my own, trust that their fury would keep 'em focused on me and they wouldn't notice the other guy McCall had walked in with...

And then I saw Tsura, approaching the stage just behind the last of Shea's goons. It was the strangest thing (and this is me talkin'), too. At random times, she'd just stop, breakin' stride for a second or three before moving again. Or she'd suddenly stagger left, even though it took her off track. It was only after a good few seconds of this that I realized she was changin' direction any time one of the trouble boys looked back or otherwise came near to spottin' her. Except, she was doin' it *before they looked*! Every move, every pause, kept her from comin' outta the shadows or otherwise appearing where Shea's guys *would* have seen her.

When her gift *did* decide to kick in, it didn't mess around.

So even as Shea's throat started working again and he was halfway through ordering his men to put so many holes in me I coulda been a fishing net, Tsura crept up on the gink farthest in back and whacked him over the noggin with what looked like a Colt semi-auto that I guessed someone'd dropped in the last minute or two. Even from here, my *aes sidhe* ears heard the crunch of bone, and I saw her flinch, her cheeks pale, but she didn't let it slow her. Tough broad, that one. She dropped the pistol, reachin' down to replace it with somethin' bigger.

I dove for the flimsy cover of the chairs again, now completely abandoned, skiddin' across the floor so fast my pants tore down the outside of one leg. The Uptown Boys started pluggin' away at me, again filling the room with enough lead to sink a battleship. And Tsura opened up, too.

Not at the gangsters, but at the glyph-inscribed glass.

I was right. The glass was thick enough, sturdy enough, to take a few high-caliber slugs.

Then again, the drum of a Tommy holds a helluva lot more'n "a few." And even though the recoil set her staggering, she held on long enough.

Nobody heard her, not at first. Hers was just another gun in the firing squad, a single instrument in the pounding, cacophonic symphony. It was only a piercing *crack*, shrill enough to be painful even over the roscoes, near high enough for the sound itself to have shattered small, that a few of the thugs took their fingers off the trigger long enough to look around.

When they did, it was just in time to see the case detonate in a blizzard of thick wedges of glass. They sounded like an avalanche as they fell to the platform, some of 'em sharp and heavy enough to gouge furrows in the concrete.

Everybody turned to stare, peepers gone wide, and again the guns went silent—but this time it didn't matter. 'Cause the sound that followed? There ain't a heater in the world, or any dozen heaters, that it wouldn't have drowned out and blown away.

It was the bellow of an earthquake given voice. A tornado tearing down an empty, endless alley. The roar of the dead, echoing through the caverns of the world's foundations.

The mummy awoke, and whatever rage wore that millennia-leathered flesh sure as hell wasn't the Nessumontu we'd met earlier.

Lifeless hands lashed out, heavy and unyielding as stones, to shatter skulls. Ancient fingers clenched with immortal strength, crushing throats and various bones. His voice—booming, endless, never pausing for breath—shifted from wordless scream to chants that I didn't have the chance to translate in my head. I recognized the names of Egyptian gods of several dynasties, though. Anhur. Osiris. Montu. Set.

With that last, his voice grew louder still, and with it came a great wind, blasting two of Shea's boys from their feet. One tumbled off the platform, landing on one shoulder with a pained cry; the other cracked hard against the far wall and made no other sound at all.

I tore my gaze offa the mummy, dashed back toward where Pete was crawling across the floor, tryin' to find cover while still keeping his peepers trained on the other scuffle, the one happenin' up near the ceiling...

Tommy guns clattered and I glanced back, saw Nessumontu

stagger as slugs tore chunks outta dead flesh. They couldn't kill him easy—there wasn't exactly anythin' to kill—but it might be they could take him apart to where the pieces of his soul couldn't stick around, or at least didn't have a functional body to work with.

But Nessumontu raised his chant again. I recognized the name of Sekhmet, among others, and that dead skin began to bulge. Scorpions skittered outta the mummy's open wounds, tuggin' the injuries shut with their claws before piercing 'em with stingers and then going stiff, dying and hardening into horrible stitches.

I jumped one of the bloody Uptown Boy bodies—I could just hear enough of a faint gurgling in his chest to know he wasn't quite dead yet, but it wasn't gonna be long—and skidded to a halt next to Pete. He sure seemed out of it, dazed by everything that'd happened, but I still reached out with one hand to pin him tight to the floor by his shoulder. No tellin' what orders McCall mighta given him before they got here, or just how complete her hold on him might be.

Tsura appeared outta nowhere beside me, leanin' in to hold down his other arm. She was gasping for breath and looked more shocked at what she'd done than I was, but she jerked me a solid nod.

Tough broad. Think I said that already.

The guns still roared, but on both sides now. I dunno how he'd gotten hold of 'em, though "magic" seemed a pretty good bet, but Nessumontu clutched a chopper in each hand. No way most humans woulda had the strength to fire 'em that way and maintain any control, but the mummy wasn't relying on human strength, and he'd picked up the principles *real* damn quick. He marched across the stage, ignoring the dust-flinging impacts that dug into him. Strips of wrapping trailing behind him, he returned bursts of fire in turn. And with every step he took, more Uptown Boys fell.

Gettin' into Pete's noodle shoulda been duck soup, given

how well I know him. Between the distractions and the noise, though, along with the ambient magics and especially the shroud of outside emotion the succubus had wrapped him in, it took every speck of concentration I could muster, along with a boost from my wand. A couple times he tried to break free, though whether he was fightin' my mojo or just throwing an ing-bing over everything going on, I couldn't tell ya. Between the two of us, though, Tsura'n me managed to hold him pretty still. And eventually, I broke through. I couldn't just yank McCall's influence outta him. That woulda taken more time than I could spare right now. But I was able to bury it pretty deep, bringin' the real Pete Staten back to the surface.

"Wha...? Mick? What the hell...?"

"No time. You... Hang on."

I twisted around, aimed the L&G at a clump of Shea's thugs and fired. Gats jammed, footing slipped, and basically they were sitting ducks for Nessumontu.

"Right. No time. You got your service piece on you?"

"I... What?"

"Your revolver, Pete. You got it?"

"Uh, yeah... Coat pocket..."

I reached in, grabbed it.

"Tsura, get him outta here."

"But—"

"Kid, you done spectacular. Better'n I coulda hoped. I'm impressed, and I'm grateful. And I'll be even more grateful if you get my friend outta here. Please."

She ducked under his arm, took his weight on her shoulders to help him up, and they were off. Me, I took a few seconds I probably couldn't spare to get a handle on everything.

Shea and his last few guys were putting up a good fight, and it was *possible* they might yet do enough damage to Nessumontu to put him down, but it didn't look probable. If nothin' else, he could wait a tiny bit longer while I took care of somethin' a tad more immediate.

The battle overhead was furious as ever, but it'd slowed. Ramona and McCall were both coated in blood, spattering the walls in crimson with every flap of a wing, every slash of a talon, every spitting scream. Ribbons of flesh hung worse'n Nessumontu's wrappings. Holes gaped in the membrane of their wings, showin' the ceiling above, and in patches of torn clothing and flesh, revealing raw meat and glistening bone.

I felt sick. I knew the fight was gonna be brutal, and I'd felt no compunction about helpin' Pete before Ramona—still didn't—but I had no idea it was gonna get *that* nasty. That either of 'em was still aloft, was a testament to... I dunno— how strong succubi are? The fury and hate they felt for each other? Somethin'.

Whatever the case, though, I didn't mean to let McCall win this. I was steamed at Ramona, but she wasn't the one who'd taken Pete.

I crossed my wrists so I could level the L&G and Pete's roscoe at the same target, carefully tracked the spinning, thrashing pair across the ceiling, cocked back the hammer while ignoring the twinge in my mitt that came from using the damn thing...

And stopped.

Maybe it was somethin' in the succubi's own mojo throwin' mine off. Maybe it was that same sporadic bad luck I'd been suffering for weeks now. But I could just *feel* that my aim was off, that even all the luck I'd sucked outta the thugs and stored in the wand wasn't gonna be enough for me to make this shot with any level of certainty.

I hadda get closer. A *lot* closer.

Dammit.

I ran. I put everything I had into it, building up a head of steam only your best Olympic sprinters mighta come close to matching. I blasted past most of the rows of chairs, used the last as a stairstep, and I was up onto the platform, still goin' flat out. I kept my head down, hunched tight as I could without slowing, as I passed behind Nessumontu. Wound a bit of luck around me to avoid gettin' clipped by any of the Uptowners still standing...

Wasn't enough, not with the specter of bad fortune doggin' my steps.

I felt the slug pass through my thigh, takin' skin and muscle—to say nothin' of a chunk of ragged pants leg—with it. I let myself scream, just once, with the shock and pain, and I couldn't help but stagger a pace or two, but I'd be damned if I was gonna let it slow me. Took everything I had, every ounce of will and another surge of magic into my own aura to strengthen the limb and dull the burning, but my drumstick was gonna hold up because I frickin' well *needed* it to hold up.

For just a few more steps...

A few more tough, agonizing steps, as I hit the slab Nessumontu'd been lyin' on, almost slipping on the shattered glass. One foot on the stone, then the next, chargin' uphill now, the makeshift bier rockin' under me, threatening to send me toppling, until I finally reached the top on my good leg and leapt.

Bullets flashed past under me, ricocheting off the stone; a couple chips embedded themselves in the heels of my Oxfords. I stretched out with my empty hand, reaching for the heavy light fixture hangin' overhead. Fingers clenched around the metal rim, started to slide, tightened, gripped, slipped again...

From my other hand, wrapped around pistol and wand both, I poured every last bit of luck still stored in the wand—to help me catch myself and to make sure the fixture's brackets, already startin' to creak and whine, held my weight.

It held. Unbelievably—and, I was horrifyingly aware, *briefly*—it all held.

Meant I had time for one shot. Since I'd just drained the L&G, a single *unaugmented* shot.

I don't use guns much. It'd been a long time since I'd pulled a trigger. And the two succubi were still spinning and thrashing around each other like cannibal cats, making for one helluva tough target.

On the other hand, I been around a *long* time, and I fought in a lotta different eras, a lotta different wars. I don't carry because I don't like to, not because I can't.

I hung there like a tranquilized monkey, gently rockin' back and forth, sighting down the barrel of the revolver, watchin' as wings and arms and bloody backs flashed past me...

*Bang.*

McCall shrieked, arching backwards as the round tore through a shoulder blade right at the joint of a wing. Wasn't iron or enchanted or anything, so it wouldn'ta been a crippling wound under most circumstances, but... these circumstances were a damn sight far from "most."

I saw her bend back, saw Ramona lunge, bloody teeth bared, and then the luck I'd pumped into the fixture ran out. Brackets snapped, my grip slipped, and *wham*!

I was lyin flat on the floor, new agony tearin' through me as several heavy shards of glass punched through my coat and into my back—agony that only got worse as the heavy round fixture landed on top of me. I felt my ribs bruise, and the bulb, which shattered on impact, gouged another semicircle into my skin. Groaning, I shoved it off and rolled over, wincing as every motion tugged at the wounds.

McCall hit the platform a few feet away, hard enough to shake the concrete. Her whole face was a mess of lacerations, her throat open to the air. She choked on spurting blood. Ramona landed beside her, staggering a little but upright. Carefully she knelt down beside her "sister."

I knew I wanted to turn away from what was about to happen, but I couldn't make my body move fast enough.

Ramona slowly drove the talons of her pointer and middle fingers through McCall's eyes, digging deep but curving downward, driving into the bone above the mouth rather than through into the brain. McCall screamed like I'd never heard, thrashin' and flailing to get away, to grab Ramona's arm and make her stop, but she couldn't find the control or the strength.

Then she couldn't even scream as Ramona slid the claws on her *other* hand up under McCall's chin, until she had a good, solid grip inside the muscle and bone.

And then she pulled her hands, one hooked in the upper half of McCall's skull, one in the lower, in opposite directions.

I shut my eyes just in time to avoid seeing the results, but I couldn't shut my ears to the horrible *crack* or the moist tearing sounds that followed.

Instead I finally turned over and dragged myself to my feet. The pain was already subsiding some, though I wasn't gonna be able to heal right until I got those damn shards outta me. Still, between those and the gunshot, I was pretty proud of the fact that I wasn't limping *too* bad as I made my way over to Nessumontu, where he stood over the lone survivor of the once fearsome Uptown Boys gang.

Nolan Shea, of course. He was nursin' a mangled left arm and his mug was pale with shock and pain, but he'd probably make it.

"How you doin', old man?" I asked the mummy. Hey, there ain't a lotta people I can honestly call that, y'know?

"In more than a small amount of discomfort, in truth. I think, however, far better than I would have been without your assistance, Mick Oberon. Thank you."

"Yeah, well. You're welcome. I didn't realize you had that kinda power, though. How'd they even take you in the first place?"

"Surprise. And I cannot invoke such *heka* easily. I have been gathering strength every moment I was encased in their cage of glass, and it will be some time before I can even contemplate doing so again. I require rest."

"You'n me, both. I—"

Shea interrupted us with a deliberate cough.

"Gloat all you want, Oberon. You're a dead man."

"I wasn't gloating. You'd know if I was—"

"Fleischer's gonna come for you. You won't see it comin', but you're already a corpse. You just..." Another cough, then a pained wheeze as he clutched at his arm. "You just don't—"

"Shea." I took a step, stood over him. "Fleischer's long gone, isn't he? Dusted outta here soon as this whole mess started, I figure."

"Yep. You won't find him. But he'll find—"

"Means he knows I was part of what happened here, but he don't know how much, or what exactly I did. Not what happened, not in any detail. And there ain't anybody who *did* see the whole thing who's gonna be able to tell him."

"What? Yeah, there—"

I wonder if he saw it coming.

I stepped back away from the corpse—didn't need blood and brain on my shoes—and slid Pete's gat into a coat pocket. Then I turned to meet Nessumontu's questioning gaze.

"I ain't proud of that," I told him. Wasn't lyin', either. Killing that casually don't sit right with me at all. Especially not after... some of what I've done in the past. "But I can't afford to let Fleischer find out the details of what happened here, and I *sure* can't have him hearin' it from someone who already had a grudge against me and woulda painted it even worse than it was. As it is, he's another new enemy I can't afford, especially given the kinda power he can bring to bear. So anything I can do to keep him in the dark, make me less of a priority to him..."

"You need not justify yourself to me, Mick Oberon."

"Oh, but you fucking well do to *me*, you bastard!"

Ramona staggered up from behind me, still drenched in blood. She'd resumed human form, so I couldn't see how bad her wings mighta been mangled, but she still bore rents and gashes across nearly every inch of exposed flesh. Some of 'em had already started to close, but it was gonna be a good long while before she was anywhere near whole. She took another step, winced, and angrily tore a flap of hanging skin off her arm.

"You've looked better, doll. But then, pretty sure so have—"

"How did she know I was here, Mick?"

I thought about lyin', but really, what was the point?

"I called her. Told her I'd lured you here with the promise of the mummy, that if she met me here with Pete, I'd have you trussed up out back and ready for delivery."

From her expression, that didn't come as a surprise, but she was *not* happy about it. Her forehead bulged as her horns tried to emerge again.

"You betrayed me!"

"Not at all. My deal with McCall was that I serve you up helpless and ready to be dragged home. I didn't. Hell, I helped you beat her, or didn't you notice me pluggin' her in the back?"

"*Look* at me! Look at what she did to me! Because of *you*!"

"You'll heal. And it's better than her draggin' you home, ain't it? Or havin' to look over your shoulder for the rest of your life?"

"Are you trying to tell me you did this *for me*? Because that's a load of horse shit even for you, Mick!"

"No. I did this for him..." I pointed a thumb at Nessumontu. "But mostly for Pete. Who wouldn'ta been dragged into any of this if not for McCall. You might wanna remember this, just in case you ever feel the urge to threaten any of my friends."

"So I was here as a... what? Distraction? I was just a pawn in your plan?"

"If that *were* the case," I told her, tryin' hard not to growl it, "it'd make us about even, wouldn't it?"

Horns burst free, talons extended again... And just as quickly retracted. Ramona spun on her heel and stalked off into the shadows, leavin' a trail of wet, squelching footprints behind her.

I wondered where things might stand next time we bumped into each other.

And apparently I wasn't the only one.

"I fear assisting me has made you several new enemies this day," Nessumontu said.

"Eh, I'm used to it. What's next for you?"

"I? I shall return to the bazaar, at least for a time. It is...

not the most dignified of resting places, but it will allow me time to recuperate—and to prepare the spells necessary to safeguard myself from events such as these repeating themselves in the future. Do you believe Tsura Sava might be willing to assist in watching over me until such time as I have completed those preparations?"

Huh. I hadn't even thought about the fact that she'd be leavin' when the carnival did. Found I didn't much care for the notion. But, "Yeah. I mean, I'll ask, but I'm sure she would."

"I owe you both a great debt, Mick Oberon. Is there anything I might do for you, before I return to my slumber?"

"Nah, I don't..."

*Wait a minute.*

"Actually, pal..." I stepped over, draped my arm around his shoulders. He looked puzzled, least as much as he could without peepers in his head, but didn't move. "There just might be."

# CHAPTER EIGHTEEN

"Don't do it, Mick."

It'd been the first thing she'd said to me, after Nessumontu and me'd slipped outta the warehouse and found her hiding with Pete in a neighboring alleyway.

"Huh?"

"What you're planning. Don't do it."

"You don't even *know* what I'm—"

"It doesn't matter." She'd looked just as upset, just as scared, as she had back when the bullets and the blood were flyin'. "I don't have to. I've sensed it, felt it. Whatever it is... it's terrifying. Dreadful. Please, Mick, for God's sake, don't do it."

I almost listened.

I trusted her; she'd earned that, and more, over the past days. To hear her react this strongly, almost begging, made my blood run cold.

But in the end, I couldn't. I'd worked too hard, owed too much to too many people, not to try. Not now, when I could finally give back a life that'd been stolen too many times already.

Which is why I was standin', the next evening, in a bedroom that'd gotten *real* crowded. Lacy sheets matched lacy curtains, all kinda pretty gewgaws sat on the shelves, and I could barely even see any of it through the thick, suffocating haze of emotion. Agonizing hope and an almost comfortable fear. Soft sobs and rasping breaths, nervous sweat and the subtle tang of a mother's tears.

It was maybe just as well that Tsura, caught up in the lingering worry of her vision, had refused to come into the house, let alone the room, instead waiting outside and pacing the lawn. We couldn't have fit another soul in here.

I'd squeezed myself into a far corner, tryin' to keep outta the way. Archie waited next to me, rollin' an unlit cigarette between two fingers, peepers locked on his boss and friend. Fino and Bianca Ottati held each other tight, her arm around his waist, his around her shoulder. She wept openly; he was praying under his breath in Italian. Celia stood across from them in the doorway, steadyin' herself with one hand on the jamb.

Between 'em, lyin' flat in the same bed she hadn't left in over a year, lay the slumbering Adalina. And over her, arms outstretched and entering the second half-hour of his unbroken chant, stood Nessumontu.

*Spells of protection, revival... and* awakening.

I'd found the mummy some less conspicuous clothing, a complete suit and greatcoat, as well as a pair of cheaters with real dark lenses to hide his suspicious lack of eyes. It made him look kinda hinky, wearing 'em inside, but less so than the alternative. Besides, the Ottatis didn't much care who the fella was, if he could do what we all hoped he could do.

Archie was, under the circumstances, a little more suspicious.

"Where'd you say you found this mug?" he whispered at me.

"Just an old acquaintance," I answered.

"Old acquaintance. Right."

Well, it was true. We were acquainted, and he was *real* old, so...

"Why?" I asked.

"Just... if this don't work... I don't wanna see the boss disappointed again. I dunno if he can take it."

"Trust me, Archie, I don't wanna see that either. I—"

A deep, desperate, rasping breath sounded from beneath the heavy quilt. Nessumontu's chant trailed off and the entire room fell silent.

For an instant only. Then everybody in the room who wasn't centuries old cried out at once as Adalina bolted upright!

Bianca was already lunging in to wrap her daughter in her arms, Fino half a step behind, and I hadda practically leap across the room to bar their path.

"Hang on! Let's make sure she's okay before we—"

Adalina screamed, and I mean *screamed*. It was piercing, like gettin' Ramona's talons through the eardrums. One hand lashed out, grabbin' me by the sleeve and hauling me in and around so we were near face-to-face. The girl's peculiar Fae lineage made her ugly, even somehow alien, but there'd always been a kind humanity behind the bulging, widely spaced eyes and twisted, gawping mouth.

Not now. Now I couldn't tell who—or what—I was facin'.

The painful scream dropped to a more manageable volume and for an endless few seconds she shouted at me, spouting what musta seemed an enraged gibberish to everyone else in the room. But finally, *finally* she wound down, let go of my coat and fell back on her pillows.

Again there was silence. I don't think the Ottatis were even breathin'. And then...

"Mama? Daddy? What... What happened?"

This time I didn't try to stop 'em. The entire family, both parents and her sorta-sister, were on the bed, near smotherin' Adalina in hugs and tearful kisses. So far as they were concerned, whatever'd just happened was already over and done, a moment of trauma and confusion as their baby girl finally awoke.

Me, I stepped back away from 'em, and it's a good thing everyone there already knew what I was, 'cause I totally forgot to blink, to fidget, to do anythin' to make myself look even slightly human.

'Cause I was the only one there who knew that what Adalina'd been spouting *wasn't* random nonsense. That for just a minute, there'd been someone else there, someone other'n a scared and confused girl.

It hadn't been a single language, see, but a combination, switchin' from one to the next as she shouted. I'd recognized several. Old Gaelic. Old Polish. Old East Norse, of all peculiar things.

And because of the constant switchin', I hadn't been able to understand most of it. Each language was gone, replaced by another, before my brain could start translatin'. But I'd caught just a snippet of meaning, at the very tail end.

Somethin' about being woken too soon. About not being ready.

I turned my back on the sobbing, grateful family to stare out the window. Tsura, alone on the lawn, looked up just in time to catch my gaze.

All three of us were outside, now, loitering around the porch and watchin' as one of Fino's boys pulled up at the curb in the Shark's burgundy LaSalle, ready to chauffeur Tsura and the mummy—which sounds like a duo act, come to think of it— back to the carnival. Nessumontu'd already refused any sorta real payment, and he'd been pretty anxious to get outta there once the grateful hugs had started flyin' around the room. We got us a few weird glances from neighboring windows, or so the twitching curtains suggested, but I figure anyone livin' near Fino's place was used to odd visitors at odd hours.

Me, I was makin' small talk with Nessumontu mostly, askin' about plans we'd already discussed and some historical tidbits I was curious about. It beat dwelling on what'd just happened in Adalina's room, or what the repercussions might be—or on the fact that I'd actually made me a new friend, someone without a hidden agenda and who wasn't tryin' to hold magical influence over me, and she wasn't gonna be stickin' around.

Almost as an afterthought, since he *would* be leavin' in a few more days, I asked, "What about the curse? How far you think you'll need to get before it fades?"

You ever see a fella with no peepers blink in confusion? It's disturbing.

"I beg your pardon?"

"The curse? You know the... bad luck?" My stomach was suddenly sinkin' toward my toes.

"I have no protective curse on me, Mick Oberon. I might once have, but if so, it has faded in the many years since I was taken from my proper tomb. This is one of the reasons I must prepare so many new defenses for myself."

Yep, toes. And then even lower. If Nessumontu wasn't the source of my recent misfortunes, unwitting or otherwise, then where the *hell...*?

Tsura reached out, brushing Nessumontu's arm.

"Could you give us a minute, please?"

The stiff nodded, uh, stiffly.

"I shall wait in the vehicle." Then, the way he'd seen so many of us do it, he stuck out a hand to me. I took it, and he turned and wandered toward the car.

"Well," I said, a bit reluctant, "I guess this is it."

"I've never been as scared in my life as I was in the last few days," she said. "But your world is... amazing. I'm sorry to leave it, though I won't mind not getting shot at for a while. Thank you, Mick."

"You did good, kid. I'm actually gonna miss you."

"Shocking," she said playfully.

"*I'm* stunned, yeah."

She smirked up at me. "I'll be back, Mick. Chicago's one of our regular stops. And what's a couple years to a guy like you?"

"Yeah." Wasn't as comforting as she'd meant it.

"Listen, um..." Her voice got low, suddenly serious. "That shapeshifter you mentioned. The, uh, *phouka*? Goswythe?"

Not what I was expectin' to hear.

"Uh, yeah?"

"You asked me to try to focus on him, see if I could sense anything."

"Sure, but that was when I thought—"

"I know, but... I did. Sense something, I mean."

"Yeah?" Didn't know how much it mattered, now, but it'd be nice not to have him hangin' over me anymore. "So where is he?"

"Dead."

Whoa.

"You certain, doll? It ain't easy to kill any of us, and *phouka* can be harder'n most."

"I'm sure, Mick. Or as sure as I can be, anyway. None of my visions come with money-back guarantees."

Well. Well, well, well. That was a load off. I mean, it'd be nice to know when, how, alla that—not just outta curiosity, but in case whatever zotzed him was a threat. But for the most part, it was good news.

"But that's not all."

I shoulda known.

"What else?" I asked.

"I got... flashes. Images. Of stone angels. Crucifixes. Last rites, a sense of the sacred."

Now I stepped fully back so I could look her clear in the face.

"What're you saying, Tsura?"

"I'm saying Goswythe got a Catholic burial, Mick. Full ceremony, the works."

"That—that don't make any sense!" How the hell would a damn *phouka* end up buried with completed rites on church ground?

"I don't know what to say. It's what I see. I thought you should know."

"Thank you."

There were more goodbyes, even a brief hug, but sorry as I was to see her go, I was too preoccupied to give any of it my full attention. This was supposed to have been a night of answers, and all I had was a new bucketful of questions.

Fortunately, I had a vague idea where I might go to find myself at least some shreds of understanding.

If I kept showin' up here, I was gonna need to ask for my own key. One way or the other, though, I *didn't* intend to be here again for a good long while.

What state I left the place, though, was up to her.

"No! God, no, I wouldn't do something like that!" Gina was backin' away across her living room, setting the chairs rocking as she bumped into 'em. Her limp hair and the smell of sweat made me think she probably hadn't showered, or gotten much sleep, since she'd fled the horror show at Fleischer's shindig.

"You sure, Gina? You don't come clean, this ain't gonna go easy for you."

"I swear to God, Mick! I've never hexed you! No spells, no curses, nothing!"

I believed her. Woulda even if I couldn't taste the truth mixed in with her desperation. Frankly, I hadn't really figured it was her even before I'd showed up at her door; I just didn't know of any other witches I'd bumped into lately. (I'd given a brief thought to the idea that Baskin'd done it, but I'd seen him in action. No way he had the skills to hex me without me sensing it, not yet.)

I wasn't gonna tell her that, though. I still hadda learn more, she was one of the few people I knew who might be able to tell me, and I didn't have time to mess around.

"Prove it," I demanded. "Find the hex on me. Tell me everything you can."

Took a few minutes for her to gather her ingredients, and then to calm down and concentrate enough to cast her spells. Eventually, though, I'd been splashed with more herbal oils than I cared to think about and she had her answers.

"It's definitely there," she told me. "Subtle, hidden. Your own power, your own aura, make it hard to spot. If I hadn't been specifically looking for it..."

"Any way to tell who cursed me?"

"Not exactly. Not any way I know, at least. But it's someone good. *Real* good. The skill it'd take to wind the hex into your own essence this way, to hide it... You're not looking for any dabbler, I'll tell you that."

Great. So now what? Who the hell had I offended that bad? As I said, couldn't be Baskin; not only was he not experienced enough, but the bad luck had started well before the two of us had even known we were involved in the same mess. So that also ruled out him havin' hired anybody. I had more'n a few enemies among the Fae, and some of 'em mighta had the skills to pull this off, or the resources to hire somebody who could, but why now? I hadn't dealt with any of 'em in a while. Fleischer? Again, this all predated the two of us lockin' horns. I just didn't know anybody who had the power to make this happen and who hated me enough to go through the hassle. Nobody still alive, anyw—

Oh, no. Oh, *fuck* no.

"Blower," I hissed at Gina.

"Sorry, what?"

"*Where's your goddamn phone?!*"

She squeaked somethin' incomprehensible and pointed. I stalked across the room, grabbed it, dialed. I didn't even *notice* the burning and buzzing in my ear, not this time.

"It's Mick." I'd known Pete'd be home. He'd managed not to get fired from the force, but he was on probation for taking sick time—his excuse for the days he'd missed while under McCall's thumb—without callin' in.

"Listen, I need... Yeah, I know you're sorry. I told you, ain't your fault. Listen, I... Dammit, Pete, *listen*! I need you to meet me. Yes, *now*." I told him Gina's address. "Get here fast as you can.

"And Pete? Bring lanterns. And shovels."

I wanted to be wrong. I needed to be wrong.

*Please, God, let me be wrong.*

\* \* \*

You waitin' for me to say it? I wasn't wrong.

Me'n Pete stood deep in a newly opened grave, covered in dirt and—in his case—hours' worth of sweat. Our coats were draped over the tombstone above, our work lit by the lanterns placed beside it. We still had an hour or two before dawn; probably not long enough to get the hole filled back in, least not neatly, but I couldn't really find it in me to care. We'd been at it so long that the crickets were chirpin' again, having gotten used to our presence and the sounds we made.

The two of us, we were lookin' downward at the coffin we'd—much to Pete's dismay—forced open, using one of the spades as a crowbar. Of course, he hadn't been happy about *any* of this, and I think it was only the guilt he felt for beaning me while under McCall's influence that'd gotten him to go along with the whole Igor act. Now, though, he was more befuddled than anything.

"I don't get it, Mick. Why would anybody bury animal bones like this?"

"They wouldn't." I idly poked around with the shovel, shovin' aside a tiny sorta-canine skull, a femur way too small to be human. "But these ain't animal bones."

"Huh?"

"They're *phouka*. When one of 'em dies, some of the bones revert to animal shapes, while others just fade away entirely."

"Wait, *phouka* like...? Is this that Goswen guy you been gunnin' for all these months?"

"Goswythe. Yeah."

I hadn't told him why we were here. Hadn't wanted to talk about it, really even think about it much, until I was sure.

"That makes even less sense. Who'd bury—?"

"Nobody. But..."

Dammit, I shoulda seen this comin'. Shoulda made sure, even back then. The blackout... The surge of magic that'd put me under for just a minute, right after everything went down? I shoulda suspected *something*. It woulda been just long enough to make the swap...

"Mick, talk to me, dammit. Spill! What's going on?"

"Transformation magic ain't easy, Pete. Tryin' to turn something into something else? Those are some of the most potent, most difficult spells any human can try to master. And it don't last long, either, not without pumping even *more* mojo into it."

"Um... Okay."

"So if you were, say, tryin' to convince people you were dead? Wanted to transform a corpse to look like you? Real hard, especially if you were badly hurt. And if it turned back before the funeral, before 'you' were safely six feet under? Catastrophe.

"But a natural shapeshifter like a *phouka*? They're already chock fulla that kinda magic. It'd be easier, so much easier, than tryin' to pull the stunt with any other corpse. And it'd last longer, too. Definitely long enough to get it buried. Long enough that you could be damn sure everyone, even the *aes sidhe* PI who's supposed to be suspicious of everything, was well and truly convinced you're dead."

That's why Goswythe'd never shown back up, after the brawl in my office. He was already dead, stashed away just in case *she* needed him...

"Who? For God's sake, Mick, who're we talkin' about here?"

I told you, I hadn't wanted to talk about it, think about it—or, for that matter, to answer any of the questions I knew Pete woulda asked—until I was sure.

Now I was.

I planted my palms in the dirt and clambered outta the grave, steppin' over to the stone where I'd draped my coat—very deliberately—to hide the inscription. And without a word I brushed it aside, lettin' it fall to the soil, lettin' Pete read the words carved into the unyielding marble.

*Orsola Maldera*
*Beloved mother, grandmother,*
*And faithful servant of God.*

# FAE PRONUNCIATION GUIDE

Áebinn [**ey**-b*uh*n]
*aes sidhe* [eys shee]
Ahreadbhar [ah-**rad**-bawr]
*bagiennik* [**baig**-yen-nik]
*bean nighe* [ban **nee**-yeh]
*bean sidhe* [ban shee]
*boggart* [**boh**-gahrt]
*buggane* [**buh**-geyn]
*brounie* [**brooh**-nee]
Claíomh Solais [**kleev**-soh-**lish**]
*clurichaun* [**kloor**-*uh*-kawn]
*coblynau* [kawb-**lee**-naw]
Credne [**kred**-naw]
*cu sidhe* [koo shee]
*dullahan* [**dool**-*uh*-han]
*dvergar* [**dver**-gahr]
Elphame [**elf**-eym]
Eudeagh [ee-**yood**-*uh*]
*firbolg* [**fir**-bohlg]
Gae Assail [**gey** ahs-**seyl**]
*gancanagh* [**gan**-kan-aw]
*ghillie dhu* [**ghil**-lee doo]
*glaistig* [**gley**-shtig]
Goswythe [**gawz**-weeth]
Grangullie [gran-**gull**-ee]
Grindylow [**grin**-dee-lo]

*haltija* [hawl-**tee**-yah]
Hesperides [he-**sper**-i-deez]
Hruotlundt [**hroht**-loondt]
*huldra* [**hool**-dr*uh*]
Ielveith [ahy-**el**-veyth]
*kobold* [**koh**-bold]
Lairgneigh [**Leyrg**-nigh[1]]
Laurelline [**Lor**-el-leen]
*leanan sidhe* [le-**an**-uhn shee]
*ljósálfar* [**lyohs**-ahl-fahr]
Luchtaine [**lookh**[2]-teyn]
Lugh mac Ethnenn [**lugh**[1] mak **ehn**-nen]
*mari-morgan* [**mar**-ee **mor**-gan]
Oberon [**oh**-ber-ron]
*phouka* [**poo**-k*uh*]
Raighallan [**rag**-hawl-**lawn**]
*Rusalka* [roo-**sawl**-k*uh*]
Rycine [rhy-**see**-ne]
Sealgaire [sal-**gayr**]
Seelie [**see**-lee]
Sien Bheara [shahyn **beer**-*uh*]
Slachaun [**slah**-shawn]
*sluagh* [**sloo**-ah]
*spriggan* [**sprig**-*uh*n]
Téimhneach [tey-**im**-nach[1]]

Tír na nÓg [**teer** na **nog**]
Tuatha Dé Danann [too-**awt**[3]-h*uh*
de[4] **dan**[4]-*uh*n]
*tylwyth teg* [tel-**oh**-ith teyg]
Unseelie [**uhn**-see-lee]
Ylleuwyn [eel-**yoo**-win]

[1] "Gh" pronounced as "ch," but
more guttural.
[2] This sound falls between "ch"
and "k," as in the word "loch."

[3] This "t" is *almost* silent, and
is separate from the following
"h," rather than forming a single
sound as "th" normally does in
English.
[4] Strictly speaking, these "d"s fall
somewhere between the "d" and a
hard "th"—such as in "though"—
but a simple "d" represents the
closest sound in English.

# ABOUT THE AUTHOR

A RI MARMELL would love to tell you all about the various esoteric jobs he held and the wacky adventures he had on the way to becoming an author, since that's what other authors seem to do in these sections. Unfortunately, he doesn't actually have any. In point of fact, Ari decided while at the University of Houston that he wanted to be a writer, graduated with a Creative Writing degree, and—after holding down a couple of very mundane jobs—broke into freelance writing for roleplaying games. In addition to the Mick Oberon novels, with Titan Books, his published fiction includes *The Goblin Corps* and the Widdershins Adventure series (Pyr Books), *The Conqueror's Shadow* and *The Warlord's Legacy* (Del Rey/ Spectra), and *Agents of Artifice* (Wizards of the Coast), as well as several others and numerous short stories.

Ari currently lives in an apartment that's almost as cluttered as his subconscious, which he shares (the apartment, not the subconscious, though sometimes it seems like it) with his wife, George, and two cats who are nearly as crazy as their owners. He is trying to get used to speaking of himself in the third person, but still finds it awkward and strange.

You can find Ari online at www.mouseferatu.com and on Twitter @mouseferatu.

For more fantastic fiction, author events, exclusive excerpts,
competitions, limited editions and more

**VISIT OUR WEBSITE**
titanbooks.com

**LIKE US ON FACEBOOK**
facebook.com/titanbooks

**FOLLOW US ON TWITTER**
@TitanBooks

**EMAIL US**
readerfeedback@titanemail.com